CATCHWORLD

CATCHWORLD

CHRIS BOYCE

DOUBLEDAY & COMPANY, INC.
GARDEN CITY
NEW YORK 1977

All of the characters in the book
are fictitious, and any resemblance
to actual persons, living or dead,
is purely coincidental.

ISBN: 0-385-11634-9
Library of Congress Catalog Card Number 76–2755
Copyright © 1975 by Chris Boyce
All Rights Reserved
Printed in the United States of America
First Edition

TO
THE ONE AND ONLY
PETER 'PENNSYLTUCKY' BOYCE
THE WILDEST FINEST
MAN
I KNOW

The being which was the shadow, the Crow, extended itself. It reached through the timefolds, caught glittering crystal lifeforms as they descended upon a giant world, and stilled them.

It slid into another matrix, turned, and the giant world became another even larger world. It brought the first heat to this world's heart. Countless millennia would pass before the effect was brought to bear on those things which lived and died in the infra-arctic seas. The being could wait.

Again its tenuous grip was felt on another globe. Here a spreading submarine mass which dominated all the oceans suffered one minute mutation in one set of genes belonging to one of the hoards of individual hard-shelled jelly mites which made up its vast mindless form. The millennia would pass with the changing constellations but eventually the form would achieve mind. Time was part of the being's plan, part of its hope.

And on to other ages and other worlds.

Drawing them slowly, definitely across the galaxy to itself . . .

To where possibility arched, twisted, overlapped . . .

To the catchworld . . .

The Crow was patient.

CATCHWORLD

CHAPTER ONE

At one hundred and eighty kilometres from the giant starship, the space tug began its deceleration burn.

Both vehicles were 'falling' towards the sun and now their orbits and velocities almost matched. The tug shuddered slightly under the g stress and its interior filled with the complaints of an old machine long past its best. It consisted of a gondola which was nothing more than a drop-off fuel tank revamped for passenger transport. The workhorse was a clumsy but effective chemical rocket engine attached to the gondola by a telescopic 'blow off' coupling. Inside, Ginny Laing lay spreadeagled in the web which served as her g-cot, she and the other dozen in the hot little cylinder of near darkness. Up front at the controls Inagaki stopped humming to himself as the squeals and creaking of the craft increased.

"One five zero kilometres," he called out over the noise. The shuddering became an all pervading vibration. Ginny watched what little she could see begin to blur. Tiny indicator lights on Inagaki's console became smears of brightness; the lines dividing shade from blackness became indistinct, fuzzy. She could feel it rippling from the web through the muscle cartilege and fluids of her body. Her stomach began to trampoline but she knew that she would not be sick. Her mastery over her physical processes was more than adequate to cope with this. The closest she had come to retching on this voyage was when she climbed into the tug and was hit by the foetid stench of the endlessly recycled 'scrubbed' air.

Claustrophobes went mad in space tugs. She could understand

why: stuck for two days in a revamped drop-off fuel tank, a drum two metres across by eighteen deep was enough to tax the toughest mentality.

But she was one of the toughest.

She smiled at the thought. It seemed ridiculous that a small, rather academic woman like herself should be one of the crew for this mission. She would be amongst the first to cross interstellar space; she would see another starsystem's planets; she would turn that star into a nova, a super explosion, which would destroy, or so it was hoped, the home of a manic, homicidal race of creatures who already had made a first attempt at destroying the Earth. Sometimes she found the whole thing incredible, almost funny, like those old movies with flying saucers blasting New York or Tokyo with purple rays. What had in fact wiped out those cities had come from the orbit of Jupiter, 'pellets' of energy, aimed with a startling degree of accuracy at large urban industrial areas and accelerating to virtually light speed by the time they struck the atmosphere above their targets.

As a child she had seen the picture files of Tokyo, Johannesburg, the Rhine valley, Detroit and the hundreds of devastated areas.

Subtly, at a level far below that of self awareness, a mechanism was activated. Her thoughts became suffused with hatred. She felt a strong comfortable loathing for the creatures who had brought about this slaughter, the crystalloids. The discreet mechanism channelled her focus of consciousness away from the raucous decelerating barge to the emotional basis for her commitment to the Altair flight. There were many such mechanisms, tenuous psychochemical devices laid down in the labyrinths of their brains. Enmeshed in her private malign orgy she could not realise that her face was slack, the mouth open, vibration shaking saliva across cheeks.

In her fantasy Tamura, the *Yūkoku* commander, had opened the battle lasers apertures and was unravelling the plasma skin of Altair second by second: She imagined discolourations on the star blotches which spread like sores, then the shape began to change and the alien sun became bloated, long prominences of incandescent carbon nucleii began cascading out from the disintegrating upper layers . . .

Her breathing was irregular. The heart beat more excitedly, all according to plan. In her as in the others the hate response phenomena were linked to the pleasure centres and those neural pathways associated with sexual behaviour.

The star burst like a distended belly, spilling infernos across the dark. Her eyes rolled. Her body arched. She gulped and gasped the stale air and pulled blindly on the g-webbing, then slowly relaxed, trembling slightly, and sighed.

Tamura, lying at the very back of the tug, in the darkest spot, was the mission-made man. She frowned at the thought of him. His reputation was distasteful but the thought of him being so close was . . . pleasurable. It was impossible for her to think of him without associating him with the nova, the stardeath. She felt a vague stirring recognisable as the beginnings of lust.

Thus had her desires been structured.

Abruptly came the sensation of falling into the floor. There were a few yelps of alarm and some chuckles.

"Deceleration burn terminates," said Inagaki.

"I think I left my brass monkey equipment back in Earth orbit," croaked MacGillvery, the rasping Scot immediately behind him.

Inagaki was happier than the rest of them that the vibration was ended. Acting as tug pilot he preferred reading the instrumentation with a minimum of shake. He knew by now that Tamura had total confidence in his abilities to fly this junkheap. There had not been a word of admonition or advice during the two days of the flight. Inagaki smiled: the commander had a reputation for ruthlessness, dedication, and austerity: if he thought that anyone stood in the way of the mission he would simply kill them. So far Inagaki's piloting had not met with such severe criticism. But obviously the stories about the commander were somewhat exaggerated.

Certainly he had not made even a token attempt to bolster morale during this ferry ride. But then MacGillvery had been happy organising singing and joke-telling sessions. There had been scarcely a word from Tamura.

Now the only sounds came from the tug itself, the restrained purr of the life support systems, the click and buzz of a thermostat, a humidifier's whining as it laboured against water vapour loss.

The *Yūkoku*'s chief executive officer was not a popular man. Inagaki knew that. He had only had one encounter with him during the years of preparation at Yakutsk when they had been matched in a chess tournament. It had been a humiliating experience, somewhat softened later by the slowly emerging fact that no one ever won against Tamura at anything. Indeed many had tipped him not merely for *Yūkoku* commander but Fleet commander as well.

"Five point oh four kilometres," Inagaki called out. "Closing speed eleven point nine three metres per sec. Gives us just more than seven minutes to ready for docking."

He touched a number of studs on the console and they felt the gentle lurch of vernier thrust. The final course correction had been made.

"Docking in two minutes. Closing to one point three kilometres. No further correction to flightpath required. He snapped up a red switch relinquishing command to *Yūkoku*'s remote guidance facility. There was nothing to do but lie back and wait.

He had seen the small slight figure of Tamura kneeling before the Yasukuni Shrine, paying reverence to those who had died in battle. He had stood up after almost an hour's meditation and walked past Inagaki without acknowledging the other's presence. The ferry pilot had felt stung, insulted, but the feeling did not last. The tampering with his brain made it impossible for him to sustain any indignation against this man. Only something as potent as rage or hatred would last.

They had all been given two weeks to decide whether they would go. Inagaki smiled and shook his head at the memory. The decision was made at his conception in the sperm banks as it had been for all the others. They were all perfectly bred, perfectly educated and perfectly trained astronauts who had been told from childhood that they would ride the interstellar Ramships. The perfectly conditioned have no use for decision making: they simply act.

Inagaki travelled about his homeland mostly by public transport, seeing the people and the country for what he felt sure to be the last time. No regrets. He saw the sun rise over the Inland Sea, contemplated the wooded waterfall at Kegon, walked reverently amongst the serene gardens of Kyoto. It was a matter merely of waiting. The sole question lay on the matter of ceremony. The crew agreed it would be quiet. Any desire for speech-making or flag-waving lay with the military politicians. The astronauts would rest. Their minds and spirits would prepare for what lay before them.

bree bree bree . . .

The docking alert signal shrilled through the compartment, less than a minute to go . . .

Odobo braced herself automatically.

The tall negress had spent years flying ferries like this around Mars. She quietly resented that Inagaki should be chosen to pilot the tug when he had so little practical experience on old jobs like this one. All right, she understood that he was the *Yūkoku* principal pilot, but that was for a starship not a tug like this. The argument that everyone should come to terms with his position as early as possible was ludicrous. Flying a decrepit crate like this was a difficult job. She tried straining to peer over the shoulders of the two people between her and the Japanese to see whether he had had the intelligence to switch command over to *Yūkoku*'s remote guidance facility.

An error like this was criminal. This temperamental scrap pile could come apart with just the slightest lack of judgment in the care of an inexperienced pilot. Half the *Yūkoku* crew wiped out thanks to some administrative blunder and a hot shot nipponese whiz kid!

Odobo believed in the virtues of keeping one's mouth shut but acting decisively when the occasion arose. Such tactics had won her a place on *Yūkoku*. She hoped that before the mission was over they would take her to the office of chief executive. Odobo kept her ambition on low heat. She respected Tamura quite apart from envying him and her desire to oust him conflicted at a deeper level with the implanted sexual associations centred on the mission. Already she was considering becoming his mistress and using that position as the basis for her moves to supplant him. Only one thing worried her: would the commander find her attractive?

Here lay the root of Odobo's turmoil: she felt that as a woman and a negro she was doubly inferior. Of course she would never admit this. She did not even believe it. Her reaction was complete. To Odobo the female was the superior sex and the negro had the most noble history of all races. At a time when the emancipation of both these long-suffering human elements was long complete Odobo championed them. She regarded herself as being the logical commander, not simply of a starship but of the entire fleet.

None of this had escaped the scrutiny of the mission planners. They understood that she was a paranoid psychotic. The fact did not particularly concern them. They had reduced the personalities of all potential candidates to mathematical models and run them on a series of compatability studies. These studies were effected within the Machine Intelligence of the ships concerned. The *Yūkoku* MI had decided Odobo was suitable crew material. The mission planners bowed to the decision. *Yūkoku* MI knew best.

bree bree bree . . .

The final blast from the alarm died and retro thrust pulled her gently forward in the padded harness. A boom and jolt, a flickering of the console lights and the tug had docked. Good for you, Inagaki, she thought wryly. A loud hiss announced that airlock pressurisation had begun.

Odobo punched the clasp at her midriff and turned an expert weightless somersault to free herself from the webbing. She glided over the struggling shadows which were Laing and MacGillvery to Inagaki's side. He pressed the emergency lighting button and the interior of the tug was awash in a coarse red glare from squat bulbs in their wire cages. The interior ribbing of the hull was exposed, the struts and welded hoops, the cables, conduits and batteries of secondary instrumentation.

Inagaki caught sight of her and raised an eyebrow. So he wanted to know what she was doing here? She smiled. If there was an undetected failure in the docking marriage the whole tug would blow free the moment the batch was unsealed killing them all almost certainly. She had gone through this once before and survived it. If it happened this time she would survive again, possibly as mission commander.

"Pressurisation one hundred per cent," Inagaki called out.

A slight lithe figure was approaching from the rear, moving in front of the other travellers.

"Spin the hatch," came his soft voice.

The iris door hatch unravelled and Tamura Kunio glided through to the yellow brilliance beyond.

They were home.

CHAPTER TWO

He felt the sea crashing against the reinforced concrete of the monastery's walls. He felt it the way he felt anger or pleasure or fear. It was something which surged and moved with his life. It was the separate nature of the sea which attracted him, its disregard for the affairs of men, its storms and calms outside their control. He too was separate, sometimes different, kept apart from the rest by his nature.

He was not so foolish as to tell the Condominium Monk that he felt this way. His reaction would have been direct. He would have ordered the youth to spend his hours of meditation in the darkness of the vat cellars instead of cross-legged upon the watchtower platform, gazing rigidly out across the sea in the direction of what used to be the Imperial Palace.

Below a voice began a singsong calling.

The time of fasting and meditation was completed. Slowly he stood up in the ritual manner, went down again upon his knees and bowed from the waist touching his forehead to the wood of the platform three times.

The island of Ya Shima lies towards the western end of the Inland Sea. Here had been the place where the *Hokke* had been re-established in a revised form by the Condominium authorities. No public announcement had been made but the word spread very fast throughout Japan. The warrior monks had returned in the service of their new masters. It was a good move in two ways: first, the

Hokke was the natural outlet for the growing mass of militant elements as it was dedicated to the renewal of Japanese worthy status in the eyes of the world; secondly, because it could be effectively used by the authorities to remove any embarrassing or troublesome individuals in Japan and elsewhere. Their charter encompassed murder anywhere in the world where the honour of their country or order was at stake.

Condominium funds had established the monastery at Ya Shima. It was a great modified blockhouse, impervious to all forms of attack other than direct nuclear strike, and housing twelve thousand monks, neophytes and acolytes.

The Condominium had made no error in choosing Sasaki Yasuo to head the revived sect. He was strong physically and mentally, understood the nature of the religious beliefs completely and the nature of the work expected of him. He was also a magnificent leader of men. So impressed with him were his selectors that they did not see that such a man could just as easily use them for his own purposes.

And he did.

His unofficial regency was probably the main factor in ensuring that one of the starships would be commanded and principally staffed by his countrymen. Indeed no other ship had such a high proportion of crew from any single nation as had the *Yūkoku*. That name too had been chosen by Sasaki Yasuo, its meaning being a peculiarly Japanese blending of patriotism and grief virtually impossible to translate into amerenglish.

And it was understood that Sasaki would ultimately be the man to choose who was to take that starship and its crew to Altair.

And it was understood that his choice was Tamura Kunio.

Seeing the chosen youth descend to the upper ward from the watchtower, two tall guards moved towards him, *musha bashiri*—men selected for the defence and discipline of the monastery. Tamura felt a spasm of apprehension at their approach. Something was amiss. He raised a questioning eyebrow. They both gave curt bows. He returned the greeting.

"Honourable monk, you are required in audience."

Something seriously amiss. He marched with them, keeping the pace brisk to ensure that they realised that whatever he had to face he would face eagerly. The upper ward was occupied almost entirely by those aspects of the monastery directly concerned with traffic and the outside world in general—reception lounges, guests' quarters, air vehicle servicing areas. He strode through stark concrete corridors lit by strip fluorescent.

The descent to ward four was by means of a toughened plastic stairway—a spiral without handrail and used solely by monks or *musha bashiri*. The elevators were for the convenience of visiting dignitaries only, tourists and couriers never venturing below the upper level.

He stepped out smartly at the fourth ward. The two had not mentioned it, but if he had been sent for by such as these it was obviously a matter of deadly importance to be settled on the fourth level. Few ever came here other than to do business which was directly connected with killing.

"Which way?"

But before either of the two could answer, a panel in one of the walls was sharply withdrawn, and standing there silhouetted by the light behind him Tamura Kunio recognised the gigantic two and a half metre bulk of Harada Hisaw, head of the *musha bashiri*. Without speaking he stood back, and the monk strode swiftly through leaving the other two outside on watch.

The three men in the room were dressed in white kimonos. Sasaki sat at a plain low table with several documents and an open folio of photographs upon it. He was always impressive, with his ascetic face and cold intelligent eyes. Although not as tall as Harada, the clean lines of his movement and the penetrating insight of his discourse somehow made him a more menacing figure than the bigger man.

Harada took his place at the Condominium Monk's side. He was the only one present to bear arms other than the pair of status-designating swords. Cradled in his arms was his gas pistol, an automatic weapon which fired feathered bolts carrying nerve poison in their hypodermic heads. It was claimed that he never used it without fatal effect. The accuracy of his aim was legendary.

The third party was a stranger who wore bright yellow pantaloons fitting loosely over his kimono which was short-sleeved and of silk brocade, the pattern being a tiny lotus in a sunburst. Tamura realised immediately that this must be one of the samurai, monks trained by the *Hokke* to serve private masters, generally members of the Condominium with a special interest in Japanese affairs.

They were regarded as the cream of the sect and Tamura would have been chosen to be one of their number had he not been destined for Altair.

"Tamura Kunio," the Condominium Monk's voice was cold and crisp, "I have before me documented evidence which suggests that you are unsuitable for the position which I had hoped you would occupy, the position which I have used my personal influence to secure."

No one else spoke.

Is this another test, thought the young monk? There had been so many of them. Gruelling psychological tortures had been carefully designed to harden him and applied with fervour by his fellow monks. There had been the beatings which he had to request from the strongest and most ferocious of the *musha bashiri,* telling them exactly what blows he wished to receive and how many. There had been the nights when ice water would be thrown over him in the middle of his sleep and then he would be turned out of the monastery, told forcibly never to return, and it would be up to him to regain his cell by climbing in, unnoticed, through the heavily guarded freight portals or by scaling the walls to some embrasure. But the worst had been the induced hells which he had suffered under the influence of hypnotics and hallucinogens. He had not shown signs of weakening once.

He would not weaken now.

"There are photographs here dating back four years to your first mission in the service of our order. They show you engaged in dishonourable activities."

Then it was no test. The only question was why had it taken them so long?

"What activities, honourable Monk?"

"I do not have to show you these pictures. You already know what they contain. I am not interested in any explanation. I do wish you to know the extent of my information. This is not a single instance. There is evidence here, and here, and here," he said, turning over documents lying upon the table, "evidence that you have been engaged in similar activities continually up until the announcement of your selection for the Altair mission.

"You have been running a series of unlawful enterprises very skilfully indeed, Tamura Kunio, and using the proceeds to bribe and buy people of influence, and also to pay professional criminals. The activities of these individuals went a considerable way towards ensuring that it would be you above all others who would be chosen for the command of our starship."

To have come so close! Departure for Yakutsk was only two days away. Once there Sasaki would never have dared announce that he had made what he regarded as an error of such magnitude. Tamura would have been safe unless a *Hokke* assassin had been sent out on a mission to Yakutsk. In that event he felt confident that the Lotus sect would have been one assassin short.

"The photographs are genuine. They were taken by a member of the Citizens Corps seconded to the Department of Criminal Investigation. He had been tracing the movements of the particular criminal with whom you are pictured. You ran an errand for him, fixing him up with contacts and supplies. You received a substantial sum of money which you used to set yourself up in a clandestine life of crime. Tracing you proved difficult because the prime subject of the photographs of your initial contact was a known criminal and your features were not clearly enough defined for the DCI computers to act upon. And who would have suspected a *Hokke* monk?"

The samurai sat there like a statue: Tamura could not even see the rise and fall of his clothing as he breathed. He guessed correctly the reason for this man's presence.

"Now go and bathe and prepare yourself. A meal will be delivered at your cell shortly. When you have finished it Chidori Takanao will join you as your second."

The samurai gave a short nod.

So this was the one who was to replace him at Yakutsk Intensive Preparation, the most famous of all the young samurai. In a way it was a compliment to have such as he to assist one through ritual suicide by delivering the *coup de grâce* with his sword after the self administered disembowelment.

Tamura bowed and departed.

What they could never have understood was that he had no intention of ripping open his abdomen at his own hands or having his head lopped off by another's blade.

Tamura Kunio was like no one *Hokke* had ever taken into its ranks. He served but one master and that master was no person but something immaterial, an obsession. His master was the conditioned urge which had been implanted in his mind during infancy

—to look out upon the great fire of Altair, dominate it, subdue it, destroy it. Ever since he could remember, his motivations had urged him to this end either consciously or unconsciously, just as they did now.

Eight years had passed since he had been first brought before the Condominium Monk as a filthy suspicious child. It had been the commission of the sect to 'reclaim this human being as starcrew material for Yakutsk'. The Marshals had spoken directly with Sasaki on the matter. It was imperative to rehabilitate this individual as he had a super high drive and was exactly what the Marshals had in mind for the mission. In the event of rehabilitation proving to be impossible then he was to be executed as a possible danger to mission success.

Being already toughened by his years as a fugitive, Tamura proved to be a first class neophyte and was accepted into the order after a mere eighteen months. Discipline was rigorous and the spiritual training incessant. The only relief was the singing of old Kamakura war tales after the evening meal. Education in the ways of battle and assassination took place daily.

He spent hours of every day in meditation, the process by which he would release his mind from the consciousness of death and prepare it for conflict. And the conflict came. At the age of sixteen he was chosen to take on his first solo mission, the removal of a black marketeer operating in the Hiroshima district. Moving in civilian disguise it had been simple to track down the underworld in that part of the country. He had made them a series of propositions which they accepted most light-heartedly, not imagining for a moment that they would ever honour the deals that they had made with this youngster. He visited the closely guarded house of the black market tycoon under the pretext of offering yet another proposition. His name had spread through the criminal strata as a kid with a lot of useful contacts: as such he was more than welcome in the home of his victim. When he emerged less than five minutes after going through the doors it was clear why all the deals made with him were going to be honoured. If he did not win a starship place he could now buy it—in bribes.

Tamura was decreed a full potential samurai after this: Sasaki was keenly interested in the progress of the Condominium's protégé. He had only one other Altair-alpha in his care, Chidori

Takanao, and the Marshals had made it very clear that they regarded him very much as a second choice. Chidori's intellect and obsession drive were nowhere nearly up to the standard of Tamura. In his eighth year at Ya Shima, Tamura was told to expect the command of a ship. Transfer to Yakutsk Intensive Preparation would be arranged.

He sat cross-legged in his cell.

What had to be done was not altogether clear, but he had no intention of dying and somehow he had to board the transport arriving in a couple of days' time and be off to Yakutsk.

The door opened and the young samurai stepped through. He bowed.

"You are ready?" he asked.

The remnants of the meal had been removed and Tamura sat on the floor with his robe open to the waist exposing his torso. Beside him was a piece of paper upon which was written in swift clean brush strokes *Namu—myoho—renge—kyo* (Homage to the marvellous law of Lotus Sutra). He nodded and Chidori picked up the note, placing it carefully in a small alcove in the cell wall wherein was housed the image of Hachiman the war god. His back turned, he did not see Tamura change his grip on the knife which he was to use for *seppuku*, testing the balance, then placing it flat on his straightened hand. Chidori turned, and it caught him in the throat.

A communicator beside Tamura's sleeping pallet was the next focus for action. It was a metal plate sunk into the concrete and covered with buttons. A small wiremesh grill covered the speaker-make. He depressed his code and dialled Sasaki. There was no secretary or underling to go through. Everyone knew better than to call the Monk other than on matters which concerned him directly.

"What do you require, Tamura?" crackled the voice.

"I request that the documents and photographs be destroyed in order that my honourable deeds in the name of the Lotus Sutra may not be tainted."

"This has already been done. Is Chidori with you?"

"He was, Honourable Monk."

"He has left? Why?"

"He is in the company of his ancestors." Tamura broke the connection and swiftly dressed in the pantaloons of the dead samurai.

He placed the smaller of the two swords, the one which would have been used for the beheading in the sash of his kimono and slung the other about his waist.

He understood perfectly what was about to happen, and he had to move swiftly. There would be no general alert put out to restrain or harm him. Instead there would be a general announcement to the effect that anyone seeing the monk Tamura Kunio was to report his whereabouts to the samurai office.

But that monk was now a samurai to all who gave him a casual glance.

Once out in the corridor he moved purposefully in the direction of one of the plastic spirals which would take him up one level to ward three. He was in need of modern arms and the only place where he could obtain them was the armoury. Sasaki would realise this and possibly go straight there himself with Harada. He had to reach it before the pair of them arrived.

It would have to be Sasaki personally who was responsible for killing him, but Harada would be his second just in case anything should go wrong. The error had been Sasaki's in the first place. He was duty bound to correct it, and then would probably take his own life. Only he would know why, as he would never permit the world at large to discover the unwholesome facts behind the deaths. Faithful Harada would act as second even in that suicide, and would then do away with himself too.

Sasaki was an older man but Tamara was in no doubt as to his abilities. The Condominium Monk would make up for Tamura's edge in strength and agility with cunning and uncanny powers of deduction. Harada was not stupid but his principal advantage was his legendary indestructibility. There had been eight attempts upon his life and each of these had failed. He had never been bested in physical combat. His strength was regarded as being superhuman. Tamura would have to kill them both. Not for one moment did he consider the possibility of failure. They had attempted to come between him and his master, had threatened the Altair mission by holding him back from it, thus they had become enemies, and thus already dead in his mind.

He did not even stop briefly at the armoury but walked briskly past. It was closed! Sasaki had anticipated him and ordered it sealed. Had he also anticipated the change of clothing?

The crowd in the third ward was the usual mixture of samurai and acolytes with the occasional monk and pairs of *musha bashiri*. Where and how would Sasaki strike? Was he here already? No, if he had been going to strike here he would have kept the armoury open. He wants to keep me moving, thought Tamura. But where to? The only other place where you could obtain reasonable if inferior weaponry—the military museum.

The entire journey up to this part of the third ward had been wasted time. He would have to backtrack all the way past his own region of the second ward to reach the museum. There was no doubt now that Sasaki and Harada would be prepared. Ready and waiting somewhere along the route they supposed Tamura would take. There was a variety of entrances to the museum in the second ward. Directly below it on the first ward there was the store where exhibits not on display were held. The only entry there was through a pair of large service doors which would be barred unless items were being added or taken away.

The second ward had an outfitting centre for monks preparing for a mission. Tamura spent less than a minute in the small room and left with a length of nylon rope inside his kimono. He took an oblique route to the museum but kept well clear of the entrances, finishing up in an empty cell next to the main exhibit hall. Securing the rope to the closed bolt on the inside of the door Tamura launched the remaining loops through the window. He squeezed through head and shoulders first, swung about and began lowering himself quickly. He was moving down the northern face of the monastery in the gathering gloom, leaving the lighted windows of the museum above him. He steadied himself when he was aligned with the windows and ventilation outlets of the first ward and began to swing carefully, arriving at one of the outlets.

Hooking his legs round the framework at the mouth of the duct, but still holding the rope, he let the metal take all of his weight. It held. He dropped the rope and hung upside down for almost a minute, resting, recovering his strength. Then he began to work on the frame to prise it loose. He realised that it would take some time, but he was a patient man.

The wind had turned cold and the nightcloth of stars was across the sky by the time he had it bent back and he could climb up and into the ventilation shaft.

At least an hour had passed since Chidori's death. If he was lucky Sasaki might have come to the conclusion that he was in hiding somewhere and might at this moment be having the third ward searched. If he was not so lucky the second ward might be being searched and the discovery of the empty cell with the nylon rope leading from the window would be discovered.

He came across the first of the grilles into the store after two minutes. It would be impossible to go through it without attracting attention. The next proved to be the same. The third was ideal. He frowned. The other two had been so securely in place, but this one would come off in seconds. Too easy. He worked his way back to the first grille as quietly as possible and tested it again. It would take two or three hard kicks to free it but now he had no option. Sasaki must be in the store and would know that he was in the ventilation shaft.

He kicked ferociously. At the third blow the light metal grille spun out into the dark and he began moving. There was a loud crash and the sounds of glass shattering. By the time the racket had subsided he was well back down the shaft. If he had guessed correctly Sasaki and Harada would throw on the lights and close in around the area immediately about the opened grille. Sure enough light flooded back through the shaft.

And then he was out.

He launched himself to where the rope had been. If he missed, it was going to be a long arduous swim to Heigun Jima. He caught it with the inside of his left elbow, clasped the arm shut and fell, burning the flesh badly until he regained his grip. He began swinging and climbing simultaneously. He guessed that he had about one minute's grace before they realised that he was not in fact hiding somewhere in the store but had returned down the ventilation shaft and was heading for the main hall of the museum.

The window burst into a scattering flock of sparkling shards as the balled-up figure of the young monk hurtled through. He hit the tiled floor and began rolling. Feet were hammering up the steps from the store below. He had to find a weapon fast. If he was lucky there would be some charged prototype laser weapons nearby. He glanced about.

Antiques! Nothing but damned antiques!

There was the sound of heavy boots slapping against the floor. Harada was running from walkway to walkway looking for him.

It would have to be an antique. Any weapon was better than none. He was crouched against an exhibition case displaying a variety of handguns used during the mid-twentieth century. He punched in the glass and pulled out a mounting board with exhibits attached. Harada could be heard approaching on the run. Tamura wrenched a gun free from the green plastic board and swung out to face Harada, squeezing on the trigger. At the sight of the movement the big man executed an amazing feat of gymnastics by jumping clear over a case into a parallel walkway.

But the pistol did not fire. Tamura tossed it away and moved. A burst of laser fire, and he crawled behind a large metal locker. The other exhibit was a heavy automatic, complete with ammunition.

"Tamura." The voice of Sasaki. "Let us face one another honourably with swords and settle this dispute like true *Hokke*."

Before he could reply he was falling. The metal locker was wrenched away and the massive bulk of the chief of the *musha bashiri* stood there with his dart gun pointed at Tamura's face. His own face was severe.

"It would appear that I have no choice," the young monk shouted in reply. He was lying face down with the automatic under his chest and both hands out in view. "I will rise slowly, Harada."

"Put your hands behind your head," Harada said, stepping back.

Awkwardly Tamura climbed to his feet as the giant kicked away the loaded automatic. He betrayed no feeling of apprehension although the excitement was mounting in his body at the thought of such a fight—himself and Sasaki Yasuo. However, with his own left arm so badly burned there could be no doubt about the outcome. And then he saw Sasaki.

At first he was puzzled. Who was this? Before him stood an old man dressed in the robes of a visiting Shinto priest, but it was obviously Sasaki from the voice.

"Surprised, my enemy?" he asked. "Think about it."

"I see it," the younger man answered. "You could not be openly associated with my killing. If you were, it would mean either a good deal of explanation resulting in loss of face, or suicide. Neither of these are acceptable to you so you are to have my death take place at the hands of another."

He nodded. "Very good. Fortunately your killing Chidori has provided an excellent cover. I have become a mythical relation of his who is purportedly visiting Ya Shima just when the news of his death reached the ears of the Condominium Monk who is at present in meditation in his personal quarters."

The two men faced one another in the classic samurai postures, going through the introductory movements of the swords. Then it began. They were fighting in the museum's square foyer with Harada standing in one corner, his dart gun cradled in his arms.

The first few strokes confirmed Tamura's suspicion that his arm would fail him in a matter of minutes. It was when Sasaki began driving him back with clever heavy strokes aimed at weakening the arm yet further that Tamura realised how he was going to win.

It was simple, requiring only two forceful blows.

The timing was critical. He had to work himself into the absolutely correct spot and strike when Sasaki was changing his balance and it had to happen soon. He began yielding more ground but not so quickly that his opponent would become suspicious. Then he struck upwards hard and fast, causing Sasaki to regain his balance by jumping backwards. In that second, his sword high at the top of its upward sweep, Tamura turned, bringing it down straight through the base of Harada's neck deep into his left breast. Not stopping he released the handle, grabbed the gas pistol from the guard's arms and spun to face Sasaki just as the big man began to fall. He loosed one dart. The Monk dropped his sword and plucked out the tiny feathered syringe. Too late, the nerve poison was spent. Suddenly he unsheathed the short sword and rushed Tamura. The younger man sidestepped easily. The Monk hit the wall and fell, dropping the weapon. He stood up again and came after his killer, but he was swaying, sweat beading up on the paling flesh. He fell to his knees, grimaced, and clutched his stomach.

"Aaah, so you win." His voice was hoarse. "Perhaps it is just. Perhaps it should be you who goes to Altair, but you will have to explain your way out of this first."

"I shall manage that," the young man replied. "You look nothing like Sasaki Yasuo in that disguise. I shall say that you and Harada were involved in a plot to kill both of Ya Shima's Altair-alphas, that you were in fact not a relation of Chidori's at all. Investigation of Chidori's family ties will substantiate this. I shall suggest that Harada also assassinated Sasaki and somehow spirited his body away. To ensure that you are not correctly identified I will judiciously apply a few bribes and perhaps a little blackmail."

Without waiting for a reply Tamura stepped out into the corridor, closing the door behind him. This part of the second ward was deserted at night but he would soon have it swarming with acolytes. They would spit on the body of the 'priest', marvel at the perfection of the *kami-tatewari* cut which had killed Harada, and compose a new chant to the prowess of Tamura Kunio.

Nothing could now prevent his voyage to Altair.

CHAPTER THREE

Tamura left one of the cabin wall lights burning and climbed into the sleeping/isolation unit. Pulling down the partition he ran his thumb along the sealing lip and was embedded in darkness.

Immediately he heard the click and hum of the Machine Intelligence linking in.

"You wish me to record a last message, Commander?" asked the demure sexless voice of the machine.

"I do."

"To whom do you wish it directed?"

"Relay it to the Osaka gestation batteries."

"I take it that the message is intended for your son?"

"Correct."

"Proceed, Commander Tamura."

'My son, as you listen to this I am so immensely far from you, that it would be foolish even to contemplate a fraction of the immense gulf which lies between us. I may even be dead.

'You may ask why this should be, that a father should leave his child when that child has not yet even been born. It is a very difficult action to take but it is a necessary one as I am sure you must know by now. Even if you do have a full knowledge of the history involved I feel that it is my duty as your father to let you understand my view of the events which have brought about this situation. Human opinion is for ever changing. It may be that the threat of total destruction of our world was merely an error of interpretation on our part and that future generations will scoff at our doings, but you must understand that what we are doing now we are doing because it seems the only possible solution to what appears to be a desperate situation.

'No doubt you will know that man's first contact with an extraterrestrial culture contemporary with our own came in the year 2009 when we picked up messages from a world circling the star Alpha Hydrae. There was great excitement at the time because up until then all that had been encountered were remnants of other cultures left in the solar system either by design or accident. Some of these were thousands of years old but most of them were millions. Men came to expect that they would never actually meet another race. They were wrong.

'I believe that our attitude today at the moment of recording this message for you may be similarly wrong. What I am saying is that the total commitment of every human being during the past four decades may have been a wasted effort. It may seem pointless and irresponsible to our descendants. If so, realise that what we see we see without the vantage of your historical perspective just as those scientists who first encountered the crystalloids lacked my historical perspective.

'In 2015 a number of MI probes arrived at Jupiter to investigate clusters of crystalline blocks orbiting the planet well inside the orbit of Amalthea, the inner moon. Primary analysis showed these blocks to be made of hydrocarbon with an inestimably high order of crystalline complexity. They were roughly cylindrical, averaging about twelve metres by three and their interiors were very very cold, a constant fifteen degrees Kelvin. At this point the data relaying probes ceased to function.

'There is no point in detailing the raids, if you could call them such. What should be remembered about them is that they were operated from the orbit of Jupiter with staggering accuracy. The missiles or whatever the crystalloids ejected accelerated at an estimated one thousand g all the way to Earth. They were targeted on areas of high energy usage. Power plants, whole cities, industrial belts were decimated. The weapons generated an intense magnetic field and punched holes in the Van Allen belts, the ionosphere, and ozone layer. Attacks continued in infrequent bursts for months before we managed to reach Jupiter in a last ditch effort to save ourselves from annihilation.

'A group of fifty interplanetary ferries stashed with fusion warheads set about destroying the crystalloids. It soon became evident that to be effective the pilot had to guide his armoury dangerously close to his target. Out of the first dozen ferry dives only one succeeded in partially destroying a crystalloid grouping. The craft would then swing about the mass of Jupiter and head back for home. My father, your honoured grandfather Tamura Yukio, simply illustrated how to succeed. He impacted with a group detonating his entire bombload in the process. His example was followed exactly by those after him. By the time the forty-second ferry was ready to make its run there was only a single grouping left and just before it was obliterated it beamed out an intense maser/laser signal the content of which is debatable. This signal was aimed out of our planetary system in the direction of the star Alpha Aquilae—Altair. We can speculate on many possibilities but there is one which we cannot ignore and that is that the crystalloids, whatever they were, sent out a request for aid detailing what had happened to them and who was responsible.

'So we must reach Altair. Forty-seven million dead are not an excuse for this expedition which has involved the lives of thousands of millions. We go because if there is an enemy at Altair then it must be destroyed to ensure our continued survival as a species.

'The whole history of what we are trying to do has been beamed out towards Alpha Hydrae, but we can hardly expect any assistance from that quarter: it will take the signal almost a century to traverse the distance between that star and the sun. Altair is only sixteen and a half light years away. The message which those fated crystalloids dispatched reached it two decades ago. A fleet of enemy craft may well be on their way here while I am speaking.

'That is why we have spent almost forty years devising new technologies and pushing old ones to their limits. We now have a sophisticated system of defence which we hope will take care of any further attack on Earth. That is why we have been forced to gain the ability to reach the stars.

'I may never return or I may return to find the Earth a glowing coal. The chances are minimal that you and I will ever see one another.

'I say this to you. Look at the beauty of the world in which you are living. Know its serenity and majesty in your spirit. Then you will know that one life given for this is a very small price to pay. I embrace you, my son. Goodbye.'

"You wish to leave any further communication, Commander?"

"I have no other messages."

He slid his thumb back up the inside of the lip and the partition rolled back.

"In just over fifty-six hours from now we ignite fusion drive," Tamura purred from his seat in the bridge addressing the crew of ten men and fifteen women at their stations. "Until that time there need be no detailed discussions of the in-flight social political structures to be adopted aboard *Yūkoku*. Upon successful ignition we shall meet in the assembly area immediately and open arguments. Exploration of all modes will be investigated for no more than one hundred hours. We shall then set up the first model, its lifespan predetermined democratically. In the meantime we are going to be unusually busy—consequently I assume complete command up to ignition."

The bridge was large and square lying adjacent to the dining/assembly area. The principal illumination came from the dozens of information display screens flickering from the consoles arranged horseshoe fashion about Tamura's command complex. He sat facing the opening in the horseshoe facing a wall sized visual disseminator.

"Communications, please."

"Communications with flagship *Céleste* established Commander. Yakutsk Offence Central relinquishes control to flagships in two hundred and ten seconds from . . . now."

"*Zhukor* to *Céleste*," came a female voice over the extraship circuit. "*Zhukor* to *Céleste*, condition green all systems; solar shield deployed: awaiting further instructions; message ends."

The others followed, *Gita, Cotopaxi, Pegasus, Revenge* and *Yūkoku*, all forming the outer points of a hexagon which had *Céleste* for its centre.

"*Céleste* to all ships. Can confirm all solar shields now emplaced: fleet shield now being deployed: stand by for relay of final direct signal from Earth: repeat—stand by."

A conglomerate of messages hurtled like a great electromagnetic pellet into the Fleet's reception network: there were last words from friends left behind, the last updating of the Machine Intelligence programmes, a variety of news bulletins chiefly about the world-wide celebrations to mark the Fleet's departure, and a blanket public statement from a famed politico-military figure. The latter was also beamed out to the greater mass of Earth's population to the majority of whom it was even meaningful.

"*Céleste* to all ships: *Céleste* Machine Intelligence indicates that final direct signal has now been acquired: all wishing to consult personal material should contact their on board MI: a general message to the expeditionary crew from Civil Marshal Menzel now follows."

The very public face blazed in true colour and all three dimensions on the visual disseminator. The sonorous and familiar voice boomed upon them.

"My children, it is difficult for me, one man, to say what is in the hearts of so many at this mome—"

Click. Tamura switched it off.

He ignored the barrage of frowns and gasps.

"Status report on the solar shield, please," he asked quietly.

"Ninety-nine point nine eight oh six, sir."

"Fleet shield?"

"Ninety-nine point eight five nine and dropping."

"Good, better than I expected."

Odobo was about to protest. She half rose in her seat but the objection to the commander's summary wiping out Menzel's propaganda spiel withered under a brief but arctic glare from the Japanese.

"Miss Odobo," he said, "kindly request the MI for a model of actual orbit against ideal orbit."

She sat down and keyed in the request on her console.

A white dot streaked across the disseminator leaving a stippled lightpath in its curving wake. Immediately a red dot described the same path. There were no observable discrepancies. A white square appeared on the left side of the screen, black lettering leaping across it;

MI reports—
orbital integrity to .0035 sec of arc
—significance of correction:
will require inflight manoeuvre
at 174.33 AU
THIS WILL BE A WHOLE FLEET MANOEUVRE
—oo

"Very nice. Now begin the checking routines, everybody."

This time it was evident that a number of them were taken aback. Checking routines were automatic functions of the Machine Intelligence.

"Commander," said Inagaki, "surely there is a number of more useful procedures which we should be performing?"

"On this ship we begin by checking the MI."

Looks of bemusement spread. There were a few incredulous half-smiles and head shakings. The very thought that there might be something amiss with the MI smacked vaguely of heresy.

"Corridors alignment copies MI, sir."

Flexible corridors joined the various compartments of the ring shaped living quarters while they spun in a flattened position at ninety degrees to the axis of the ship during zero g.

"Refrigeration Cryotank systems both copy, sir." Inagaki smiled as he said it, thinking of all the benighted individuals back on earth worrying about the ships' crews as they approached the sun. No one should even have to sweat heavily during perihelion, never mind fry. No, at that distance the temperature would rise by hundreds of degrees almost instantly in the event of a shield failure. Death would be immediate. The temperature of the ship's outer skin had to be low, not simply for crew comfort but so that the refrigeration pressure tanks could maintain their hydrogen in liquid state.

"Sir!"

Immediately they all looked over at Ginny Laing. She was drumming her fingers on the console's multicoloured buttons.

"A problem?"

"I'm double checking but it would appear from my calculations that *Zhukov* has an orbit considerably less perfect than the rest of the fleet but *Céleste* MI has not been notified."

There was a general scepticism. Noting the expressions on the rest of the faces Tamura spoke up.

"Pass your calculations over to my console, please."

For half a minute he investigated the results being displayed on the disseminator.

A small yellow disc appeared in the top left hand corner of the wall, the solar system. This tilted to become ellipsoidal showing the system from the flightpath angle. Then the white dot streaked out again leaving the curved stippled track which represented the Fleet's projected course. A red dot representing the *Zhukov* trajectory flashed round and by the time it reached the bottom right hand corner it and the white could be seen to be diverging from one another quite clearly.

"Raising that ten to power three."

The yellow elipse flickered to become a bright pin-point as the diagram scale jumped by a factor of one thousand. The red spot described a line sweeping off the disseminator well clear of the Fleet's course.

There was a moment's disbelief followed by a babble of incredulous tongues. Tamura raised his hand and they became quiet.

"Ginny Laing's calculations are accurate on her present path. No star will capture *Zhukov* before she reaches intesgalactic space.

The MI voice hummed through the bridge.

"There would appear to be some discrepancy with the Fleet MI and Zhukov MI. I have suggested to my fellow Intelligences that Cotopoxi should assume temporary flagship status."

Meanwhile the report flashed on to the disseminator.

MI reports—
Zhukov condition:
All MI systems now running countercheck
—o
—Zhukov orbital eccentricity:
will require inflight course correction
at 25.42 AU
THIS WILL BE A SINGLE SHIP MANOEUVRE
—oo

CHAPTER FOUR

"Deploy the boles."

"Sir, is that wise in the present high energy environment?" Allaedyce, the wiry little Rhodesian bushman, frowned at Tamura from his station, the console lights flickering reflections across his face.

"Trust me. It is very wise."

Two studs were depressed and illuminated. A set of previously featureless monitors jerked brightly alive. All seven boles activated. Each was a mobile automaton flatly cylindrical in shape, tapering slightly to a discal flat top roughly a metre across and just more than half that above the twin caterpillar tracks which provided transport. Set into the body were four extensible grapples with a variety of terminals from drill bits to laser torches and rapid fabric sewing mandibles. Atop this a wedge-shaped headpiece protruded on a telescopic swing mount. Into it were set a series of lenses for television/holograph transmission plus a variety of illuminary beams and laser outputs. The headpiece could rotate independent of the bole-shaped body from which the machine derived its name. In its turn the body could turn axially upon the caterpillar traction.

A series of figures flashed up on the monitor screens. Each bole was in perfect operational condition and awaiting programme.

"Let's see that programme catalogue." Tamura swung to face his own console, and on one of the four junior screens he took connection of the catalogue from Allaedyce. "Right, I'm putting in General Vessel Inspection subprogramme Full Intensive Unit Testing and

Fault Searching." His fingers drilled out a string of letters and numbers—BOL 1-7: 004376/GV1=376007/FIUTFS. He depressed the return key and command cleared to Allaedyce.

"That's an eighty-five hour plus programme, sir, and we ignite fusion before it is completed."

"Allaedyce, just trust me. *Zhukov* shows evidence of extensive faults. We must check our own condition. I fully realise when we are going fusion. The boles will be returned to their bay long before that occurrence. I intend estimating the efficacy of our own MI by seeing for myself what is the general status of this vessel. Connect me with Commander Telyegin aboard the *Zhukov*."

"Communication with the other craft is becoming difficult, sir. It will take some time to consolidate a link," said Weismuller, the Eskimo girl on telelink, not even raising her head. Everyone was having their troubles.

"Right, as soon as you can." Tamura depressed for a channel to the MI, but the button pulsed red indicating that no personal data exchanges were possible at present. Tamura grunted. This was all so wrong. Nothing remotely like this had occurred during the simulator training. There had been numerous crisis situations mocked up but none of them had the elements of sheer chaos which were happening here in the reality. To begin with hardly any of the crisis situations had been envisaged as taking place right there in the solar system before the journey had properly begun. Furthermore he had been led to believe that the commander always had a personal access channel to the MI during any conditions except when approaching overload. The theory was that as the commander had so many different and difficult decisions to make the latest and most pertinent data should always be on hand for him to consult. Tamura decided that there was only one solution. He would pull rank.

He positively smacked his identification code overrider into the keyboard and indicated that he wished it to preface all MI material from this station. He depressed for a channel.

Still the ray pulsed red.

There was no alteration of facial expression, but he knew now something still unknown to the others: the MI was malfunctioning. To precisely what degree was uncertain, but unless there was a specific instruction to ignore all override signals from no matter what source in an emergency the Intelligence was running a fault. No one had told him that such an instruction existed. It may have been done and simply kept secret from the commanders as something which they would be best not to know about. If this was the case then those who had decided that it should be so were foolish because Tamura had to assume that what had happened was a machine error which had to be rectified.

"I have a link with *Zhukov,* sir."

"Give me it, Weismuller."

On to his main monitor came a picture from the other ramship bridge, a bad picture, snowstorms brightened and darkened in a slow steady sequence with the voices scraping weakly through the solar static.

"How bad is the situation, Vassily?"

Sight of the lean wide face with cropped blond beard told Tamura more than a dozen MI reports, desperation in his eyes, the forehead ploughed with worry.

"Bad, Kunio," he replied. "I have indications that there are several hundred faulty systems aboard."

"What about your shield?"

"The energy transfer channel is going. In fact most of our maser dependent functions are going. Things are growing worse quite rapidly."

"You have boles out?"

"Only three of them are operational and they have to be directly operated from the bridge because our MI cannot handle them. I have three crew members suited up and going through the core access to check out the state of the primary solenoids. I cannot raise any data on them at all through standard procedures."

Tamura blinked. That was the only visible impact of the shock on him. He did not look to see the effect upon his crew. Above all he would not let them see any effect upon himself!

It had always been more or less understood that the inclusion of outboard suiting for the voyage was merely a token gesture. Any hard environment maintenance or repair would be left to the boles. There would never actually be a need to leave the living area, but right over there on that ship three of the crew were already climbing down into the coiled masses of the solenoid banks where the temperature was only a handful of degrees above absolute zero. If humans were to be risked on an operation like that so early on the mission Tamura could not help but think that the chances of any ship reaching Altair . . . *Stop! You will not entertain such thoughts,* his mind screamed.

"Vassily, I want to pass over the status of your shield to *Yūkoku*
MI for a check assessment and forecast."

"I'd appreciate that, thanks."

"We'll be back with some info on that just as soon as we can get
it to you." He broke the link and set up a reception programme in
the MI. He depressed for acceptance. Again the MI refused.

"Weismuller, I want you to put a programme for data reception
from *Zhukov* into our MI but I want the command routed through
Cotopaxi MI. Fast as you can, please."

She gave him a frown. She too had quietly been having trouble
handling the ship's Machine Intelligence. She set to work on the
complicated manipulation which would take seconds under normal
conditions, a manipulation which really amounted to a small piece
of deception. Might the MI accept an input from the fleet MI
where it would not from its own commander? Tamura looked at the
disseminator. It was sectioned into a variety of panels; a blue-lilac
hologram of bole four's view of one hydrogen mass reaction tank
coupling with the torsion pins under inspection; the heat distri-
bution throughout the core and supercore described in an interplay
of colour across a schematic diagram; a graph illustrating anticipated energy expenditure at this stage of the voyage in yellow and
the climbing jagged red of the actual expenditure staggering way
above it. Suddenly . . .

          MI reports—
          zhukov shield status
          98.68 dropping
          —o
          —zhukov shield status forecast
          97.53 in 09.42 hours
          critical repeat critical
          advise emergency executive action
          —oo/o
          —update above
          97.53 in 09.13 hours
          —oo

"I want that passed to the bridge of *Zhukov* immediately."

He had been correct. In an extreme situation the MI was
programmed to respond to the MI hierarchy within the fleet and
not directly to any ship commander, but as there had to be some

access to a Machine Intelligence it was only natural that it would be to the fleet MI. Perhaps in a situation yet more advanced than the present one even the fleet MI would be inaccessible.

"Commander of the fleet on fifteen six, sir," said Weismuller, her voice strained.

Mantones appeared where Telyegin was two minutes previously, his image pulsating in the solar blizzard. The pitch of his voice swung, making the phrases almost incomprehensible at points.

"Kunio, I want you to break formation and put yourself between *Zhukov* and the sun. That way the ship should have at least partial shielding from you as well as having her own shield and the fleet shield. I've instructed *Revenge* to take over *Zhukov*'s energy contribution so she can apply herself fully to the problem of her own survival."

"Understood. We'll get down to that right away."

Tamura broke contact. He brought an inertial guidance display on to the main screen and hit the alarm button. At the sound of its nasal braying everyone on board strapped down and cancelled the amber flashing stud at the side of the station console, thus acknowledging that they were prepared for a change in acceleration condition. The klaxon died.

"I want all boles anchored, Allaedyce, and bring the ones doing outboard ops back into the ship. Inagaki, take the Small Thrust Manoeuvres programme out and transfer manual capability to me. Weismuller, I would like you to ship all MI commands through fleet MI *Cotopaxi* for the meantime." He glanced round. They were all staring at him. "I have not gone temporarily insane, ladies and gentlemen. Please return your attention to the job in hand."

But Allaedyce had his doubts. Without looking at him Tamura knew that the bushman was frequently peering in his direction. Probably trying to remember the procedure for replacing a commander who proves himself to be inept, guessed Tamura.

The STM data jumped on to his screens and he forgot about Allaedyce: his main readout simulated *Yūkoku*'s position relative to *Zhukov*'s in real time by means of a radial grid and 'vertical/horizontal' coordinates referenced to the hexagonal plane of the fleet; a second readout referenced the positions of the shields and the sun; one alpha-numeric display gave a detailed checklist for the operation while another showed continually updated accounts of relevant consumables.

Here was Tamura's passion. Control of the great vessel's movement was now a direct relationship between his mind and the mechanics of the vessel herself.

He rapidly completed a few simulated runs, selected the most favourable, fed its parameters into the console, and started countdown.

"Fifteen seconds from now," he barked, watching the numbers running down on the screen. A bright spot appeared at the centre of both radial grid simulators indicating the target position.

"Ten." Graphics of the STM thrusters appeared. They swung slowly out from the horizontal, the angle of inclination appearing in numerals below, rising until the number halted and flashed readiness.

"Five." He checked bridge status—boles anchored and inboard, MI communications re-routed. Nobody wanted to hold the burn.

"Now."

There was a slight swaying sensation and he was on his way. The shield checked out: its thrusters responded and its movements copied *Yūkoku* all the way.

A voice purred through the bridge. "Commander, this is your Machine Intelligence. Please advise me on whose authority you are executing this manoeuvre and what is its purpose."

Confirmed of his suspicions: MI had not been informed from MI *Cotopaxi*, ergo fleet MI had not been informed, ergo Mantones, *Cotopaxi's* commander did not trust his MI either.

"Do you want me to reply through standard channels, sir, or through fleet MI?" asked Weismuller.

"Neither, ignore it meantime. Our Machine Intelligence must realise that it will not win its little power struggle."

Tamura caught Allaedyce passing a significant glance with the perturbed Inagaki.

The console ran out a prediction on the trajectory. Perfect. In thirteen minutes time *Yūkoku* would be perfectly positioned.

MI requests—
immediate update
repeat
immediate update
reference current stm
—o
—identity of pilot

—authorisation source
above reference current stm
URGENT URGENT URGENT
—oo

"Commander Tamura, please explain. It would appear that your
actions are . . . inconsistent with our current requirements." Inagaki was always the diplomat.

Around Tamura there were expressions of scarcely concealed
alarm. Apart from himself the only other person with a full understanding of how the situation actually stood was Weismuller.

It was his turn to play diplomat.

"I feel that the nature of our problem would sound more convincing if outlined by you, Miss Weismuller."

She glanced at him startled.

He nodded encouragement.

"Well, I have been having some, er . . . difficulty with our MI,"
she said rather nervously. "It seems to be able to override the communication and command circuits in times of high stress. Seemingly
in a situation such as this the only response it is possible to obtain
from it is indirect data displays accessed through fleet MI. Commander Tamura began acting on this basis just before I realised the
truth about what was happening myself." *Very well done, Angeline
Weismuller*, thought Tamura, *a nice way of restoring confidence in
the master of the ship.*

"Is this a serious malfunction, or merely a minor technical
difficulty?" Allaedyce asked, his voice belying the calm on his face.

"Neither," she replied. "This is quite definitely a programmed
procedure which we're to discover only in the event of an emergency arising which involved a number of shipboard systems. As
you know the various crises which are liable to emerge during the
voyage concern seldom more than two or three systems simultaneously—fusion ignition, opening the macromag field, stabilising
the inflow of plasma to the ram, pancaking for brake, and so on—
they are all conditions which are crisis prone: crises which we are
trained to tackle. But I think that this programme which we have
now encountered is for another situation, one in which a great
number of systems are liable to fail. Obviously it must have been
foreseen in order for there to be a programme to cope with it. The
only condition which I can conceive which fulfils the criteria is that

of an enemy attack. In other words, if we enter a battle situation and begin suffering damage, command of the ship, and perhaps of the entire fleet, will be removed from our hands."

"Miss Weismuller," Allaedyce looked plainly worried, "surely there could be several explanations for what happenings are taking place. Your words strike me as being a shade irresponsible."

"I think not," Tamura broke in, adding weight to her analysis. They are neither satisfied when you withhold the truth nor when you have it delivered to them, he thought. Punch it home. "In a battle situation all of our weaponry is on standby, all our lasers switch from fusion control to offensive capability, and our depth tracking is activated. Check your console, Mr. Allaedyce, I think that you will find that all three of these conditions were activated automatically shortly after the request for executive action by the MI. Am I correct?"

Deepening furrows ate into his forehead as Allaedyce scanned the screens.

"You have my apologies, Commander Tamura," he croaked. "This is bad. My God, I should have realised that we were expending too much energy just from reading the graph. The lasers have been blazing away for the past five minutes."

Suddenly Tamura's fingers stabbed violently across the keyboard. The STM thrusters swung round and he hit for an immediate burn on full power. Jolting, spinning and juddering *Yūkoku* out of its trajectory. The lasers! The damned lasers are active! You anticipated a change of mode but not the actual firing of them, his mind screamed. He could imagine a slowly turning umbrella of deadly coherent light spreading out and away from the 'back' of this starship and growing closer to *Zhukov* by the second.

"I want those lasers out immediately!" He tried turning the anis of the craft away from the fleet and the endangered vessel but the fuel link to the thrusters had been closed off. That cursed MI.

"Sir, the lasers are under MI command and I cannot effect an override."

MI to commander tamura—
update previous references immediately
repeat immediately
otherwise life support systems deactivated
in 03.00 mins from

NOW
—oo

There were no screams, no all-out panic. Only silence. Everyone returned to work in hand because they had at last fully adjusted to the fact that they were in a critical situation. This final shock had pushed them into the modus operandi drilled in over years of training.

Tamura depressed the key for direct access to the Intelligence. On the disseminator the time is seen counting down in bold metre high figures. Right then, give this smart mess of semi-metallic hydrogen something to put its thinking equipment in a knot. He rapidly demanded an assessment of the relationship between temperature and Einsteinian relativity. Cut the link.

"Commander," it replied, "Einstein's idiosincracies and little paradoxes are hardly relevant. Please give me an update."

"Sir," Inagaki's rumble, "I have a console prediction here. We are going to burn *Zhukov*'s B cryotank in fifty seconds."

"Weismuller, tell *Zhukov* to get the hell out of the way."

She began working frantically to raise a workable link in the solar storm, abandoning the high grade in desperation and trying sound only, then coded pulse.

"Laing, put a hold on that life supports threat through to our MI via fleet MI *Cotopaxi*."

"Thirty seconds." Inagaki stared concentratedly at a graphic simulation of *Zhukov* relative to the movement of *Yūkoku*'s cone of laser fire.

MI to commander tamura—
your cotopaxi routed hold command overridden
—o
—life support shutdown timed at
01.56 mins from
NOW
—oo

He activated auxiliary propulsion/attitude control knowing that the push from those little nozzles would never be adequate to swing the ship round as fast as was now needed.

"Commander," shouted Weismuller, "*Zhukov* asks for more information on why you want them to move. They say there's no fear of collision."

"Tell them our lasers are about to hit one of their hydrogen mass reaction tanks." He shouted but knew that she would never manage to communicate fast enough for them to act. It was already too late.

"We are about to hit *Zhukov*," Inagaki boomed.

Slowly the *Yūkoku* began altering altitude.

"That's it, we've hit them," Inagaki's voice was deep but expressionless. "No sign of the tank blowing yet. Arc of the burn is very small but growing."

> MI to commander tamura—
> life support systems shutdown timed at
> 01.00 mins from
> NOW
> —00

Tell the damned Intelligence, Tamura, his mind sniped. Admit defeat. Earthside never intended that you should really be in charge of this starship. Too much responsibility for one human being.

"*Zhukov* is beginning to shift!" There was a thrill of elation in Inagaki's cry. He passed the picture over to one of Tamura's minor screens. The arc of the burn was growing smaller and more prolate.

00.48 mins

In a matter of seconds the other ship would be clear of the conic laser spray. Tamura requested a direct communication with the fleet MI *Cotopaxi* through the onboard MI but the Machine Intelligence ignored the delaying tactic. "I'm going to give MI control over the STM system," sighed the commander. "Let's hope that the MI simply returns us to our old position in the fleet."

00.30 mins

Immediately the vessel began to swing. The MI was rectifying the axial tilt before returning the ship to position. "Hell, how can it be so stupid!" snapped Tamura.

"Sir," Inagaki again, "it looks as if fleet MI has taken command of *Zhukov*. She is returning to her previous position."

The screen showed the arc burning across that ultracold tank and that arc becoming fatter fatter . . . Fingers rattled across the console keys telling the MI for the hundredth time that the lasers are connecting with *Zhukov*. No response.

00.14 mins

A shout burst throughout the bridge and for a moment Tamura peered uncomprehending at the small screen which had displayed the laser arc section on that cryotank. It was blank. He was about to depress for automatic check out when he realised why there was no arc. Another screen showed a drum shaped graphic representing the crippled ship spinning rapidly out from the fleet, turning over and over as it went.

There is a section missing from that toroidal shape.

The section representing the B cryotank.

00.08 mins

He watched the Intelligence beat him all the way down to full zero. Then he began typing out his communication on the console keyboard: Commander Tamura to *Yūkoku* machine intelligence: requested update follows . . .

There was no point even in considering what would happen to that tumbling fractured craft. This close to the sun without a shield, Tamura thought, and he squeezed his eyes tight in a grimace. Concentrate on the MI update. What else could you have done? There was no other way for a man of your conditioning. You had to assume mastery over the Machine, that no matter what difficulty you faced you would eventually triumph. Look to your own damage report before you consider the mess which this mission has become. The lasers from *Zhukov* were active as were the lasers of every ship, and when she began spinning they raked across *Yūkoku* briefly. Minor complications, he shrugged, nothing which the boles could not attend to during routine maintenance. But the crew, what would they too feel? *And Telyegin with his whole crew out there afloat. It will be quick for them . . .*

CHAPTER FIVE

Allaedyce liked to walk when thinking, and he was thinking now—
plotting in fact.

The difficulty was that he knew so little about his fellow crew
members. The policy had been to train them all apart from one another so that the years spent in flight could be partially absorbed in
mutual personality exploration. Or at least that was what he had
been told. He correctly suspected this to be a rather shaky cover for
a more pertinent motive liable to prove unpopular with himself and
the others.

He walked down the passageway leading through the cabin section. On either side the bright yellow bulkheads sloped towards one
another making the cross section of the corridor appear triangular
with rounded 'corners'. Slim vertical lamps blazed from above each
cabin's door hatch. He looked at the names stencilled in red—
Capoci, Gouchek, Inagaki, Solokov . . . Someone had calculated
the ideal proportions for each ship crew be fifteen females and nine
males. It was something to do with human and primate group,
something which Allaedyce had taken the trouble to understand.
Now he realised that any successful politicking would demand a
knowledge of the psychology behind crew selection. He must obtain the restricted personnel profiles if he was to be successful.

Swinging aside the door hatch at the end of the corridor he
stepped into the recreation area. Here was a compact gymnasium, a
small games court, and an enclosed chamber swimming pool. It was
deserted. The others all seemed to be back in the lounge assembly

area becoming acquainted with one another and gossiping fe-
verishly about the *Zhukov* incident.

He knew that he could test the commander's strength to the
limits on this issue and he intended to do just that. Tamura was too
intimidating a figure to be easily manipulated. The Japanese had a
cruel reputation. It was rumoured that he had killed on a number
of occasions; he trained as an assassin for the Condominium, they
said. On top of this, the fellow was a renowned fanatic. All things
considered, the sooner he was removed from power the better.
Allaedyce smiled.

He passed through to the lab sections closing the hatch as he
went. Automatically the recreation area lights died behind him.

Night, or the section of the ship's twenty-hour day which corre-
sponded to it, was upon the lounge. The white blue sky effect had
given way to simple yellow spots shining in black overhead.
Capoci, the Intelligence programmer, liked to imagine that this is
what it must have been like a century ago in a *nightclub*. For a moment she imagined herself stepping out of a garish American car on
some exciting street, perhaps a really decadent strasse in West
Berlin, smoothing out her white fox stole, and a cultured corrupt
young capitalist taking her by the arm through the doorway into a
dark throbbing atmosphere thick with cigar smoke . . . The dream
died. The mechanisms, implanted as a relationship of delicate molecular threads, assessed the mental activity as non-mission oriented
and edited it from her brain. Capoci sat, unaware that anything
had happened. She was listening hard to Odobo.

"We need to ensure that the *Zhukov* incident will not happen
again," the negress was saying. "And the only way we can do that is
to take control of this ship, democratically, as soon as possible."

"Mutiny?" asked a voice from another table.

"No," she replied. "No, not mutiny. We are supposed to explore a
variety of social infrastructures during our voyage. I simply suggest
that we establish such a structure immediately."

"But the commander—"

"We must have a confrontation with the commander."

Like Allaedyce, three hundred metres away walking through the
ship, Odobo too was smiling.

"Are you losing confidence in the mission, Allaedyce?"

"Not the mission, Commander."

"In my leadership?"

"The *Zhukov* incident and your handling of it might be reviewed." He smiled. "Now that the crisis has passed and we are safely routed for our objective we have plenty of time to hold such an inquiry."

The small deputation, Allaedyce, Inagaki and Odobo moved restlessly before him in his office/cabin. There was little room so they stood while he sat behind his swing-out desk quietly enjoying the small psychological advantage which this bestowed.

Yūkoku and the fleet were accelerating away from the solar system with fusion thrust carefully building up under the delicate but powerful magnetic embrace of the ships' fields. Carefully measured flows of deuterium and radioactive tritium were bled from the mass reaction tanks, turned from liquid to plasma by lasers and carried down the magnetic lines of force to the intricate blazing ring of sunfire. There would be only routine labours to be performed by the crew until the starship opened its field to scoop the hydrogen of interstellar space itself down into the coiled inferno.

"And how do you feel about it, Inagaki?"

Tamura's stocky compatriot seemed troubled. "I have confidence in your decisions. I feel that you were certainly not responsible for the loss of *Zhukov*, but I do feel that your actions should be explained to all the crew," he said.

"We feel that a good discussion should clear the air, particularly if we could bring the MI in on it," Odobo agreed.

"You believe our MI is faulty?"

"There is evidence," snapped Allaedyce, giving Tamura a look as if that should be obvious to an idiot chimpanzee. "Assuming you realised this early in the crisis, I want a reasonable explanation of why the rest of us were not informed. We may have had the opportunity to act as a team with all our minds handling the problem. You appeared to take it for granted that you alone were capable of handling the situation and used us as a collection of minions."

"There was hardly time for a discussion of—"

"Commander," Allaedyce cut him off, "you seem to forget that we are a group able to function extremely efficiently. There would have been none of the bantering one associates with a collection of ordinary people in a crisis."

"Allaedyce, this group has hardly had any time to function as a team in practice. We—"

"Spurious!" he cut in again. "We have all been trained in the company of the back up crews and some of the members of the other ships. We have been trained to think fast in groups."

"Inagaki?" Tamura turned quickly to the other man.

"I must agree with him, Commander. Should you act similarly in another crisis I do not believe that you could then retain your position." He was obviously disturbed at uttering these words.

"We would have to replace you," said Odobo.

"By ballot I suppose?" Tamura ventured, smiling wryly.

"Naturally."

"Just a moment," Allaedyce turned to her. "There are established procedures to follow in that contingency. We do have a deputy who can take over the command."

"A ballot would be the democratic way," retorted Odobo.

"We are not yet, as the commander here has pointed out, a democracy. At present we are simply a team, albeit a very good one. First we must ensure that our leadership is sound."

"Who is your deputy, Commander?" asked the negress.

"I am," answered Inagaki. "I might add that I support your idea of a ballot."

Allaedyce hastily shifted the conversation. "What are we going to do about the MI?"

"Put the facts before it and see what is has to say for itself," Tamura replied.

"Again, Commander, I must disagree with you," Allaedyce was becoming exasperated. "Surely the only thing to do is to assess our relationship to the Intelligence. Come to a conclusion. Pass on that conclusion to Fleet Command."

"No, Allaedyce. First we run extensive cross checking routines on the Intelligence to establish whether we can find evidence for malfunction. This done I will approach the MI directly and ask for its assessment of its own behaviour. This sh—"

"A waste of time. If it is mal-programmed or has been deliberately instructed to—"

"Allaedyce don't interrupt me again. It looks to me, Mister, that you are a shit stirrer. I do not like your behaviour. Close your mouth and go back to your quarters and think. In the meantime I take note of what you have all been saying. Dismissed."

The little Japanese commander spoke in a quiet almost amicable tone but no one missed the implications. The heat of Allaedyce's argument was replaced by a crisp chill.

They stood there slightly aghast and then filed out.

What was pushing the bushman? Was he trying to impress the female crew in order to have high selection preference when it came to choosing companions? Unlikely; a high factor for sexual instability would have put him outside the mission toleration limits. Could they all be losing confidence in his command? Tamura asked himself. What would he do then? Relinquish his position? He chuckled at the thought. He knew how futile such considerations were. Tamura knew well his own obsessions. You are obsessed he thought with the idea of taking this ship to Alpha Aquilae and the very suggestion of entrusting care of this to another is ludicrous. He knew their general histories well enough to realise that their experience of life was nowhere near as relevant as his own. Their training had been so very different to what he was put through. None of them ever had to take on the Condominium, the army, and the Citizens' Corps, nor go through the various hells of degradation which those days brought to his childhood.

They might or might not have confidence in him. That was no longer relevant. They would never reach him with their battles and games, their farces. He was the real power and he knew it. Let them try to oust him. It was highly probable that they would try. They would fail.

Already he could see two factions which could form: one about Allaedyce as he played kingmaker with Inagaki; another round Odobo as she attempted to establish some kind of female power group in command of the ship. Let them play. Tamura would be around when the playing had to end.

Later, the crew were all assembled in the lounge area at Tamura's specific request.

"There are several of you who care to discuss the *Zhukov* incident and my handling of it. All right then what do you have to say?"

He stood before them on the slightly raised dais. He was not quite dwarfed by the majority of the crowd, no psychological advantage here.

Ginny Laing spoke up.

"Commander, I would like to make it quite clear from the outset that it is only a section of the crew who feel that the incident needs further description from you. Many of us, myself included, are of the opinion that the situation was handled as best as could be in the circumstances. The only reservations which I think we all have concern the Machine Intelligences of the fleet."

"Later, later," Allaedyce burst in, impatiently brushing her statement aside with a wave of his hand. "The matter in hand is yourself, Commander Tamura. Let us not delude ourselves about the nature of this gathering. We are here to evaluate your capability as head of this ship in the light of the recent crisis." He fired his words off, showing the training oratory he received at Durban. He was a very good orator. "Commander, explain why you did not pass the requested update to the Intelligence and consequently endangered all our lives."

"Crewman Allaedyce, you will not address me in that manner. You are not a one man investigation team. Remember that. And this is not a court martial or any other court for that matter. I will gladly answer questions but no one here should be under the impression that I am called here to account for my actions. This meeting was called by *me*. The express purpose of it is to allay doubt. Regarding the Machine Intelligence, it was apparent that there was a departure from our ground based training procedure. The only way to investigate it was to let it run."

"In a *crisis?*" Allaedyce gave an exasperated unbelieving laugh.

"There was no reason to expect that it would act similarly outside such a situation. Confronting unusual activity in an unusual situation I linked the two." Tamura kept his face cold, emotionless.

"Thus endangering every life here?"

"Hardly. The moment it looked as if our MI might have carried out its threat to deactivate our life support, I acceded to its demands."

"In a different ship the commander may have updated the MI immediately on its request and the situation would never have occurred. The *Zhukov* might still have been with us." Allaedyce's voice was hard, embittered and he aimed it deliberately not at Tamura but at the others.

"Not so," Capoci piped up. "Commander Mantones aboard *Cotopaxi* obviously found his MI suspect also and he too apparently let it run so that he might observe. Personally I think that anyone who did otherwise, particularly in a serious situation, would be behaving bloody irresponsibly."

"Hear hear," MacGillvery chimed in. "I think we are wasting

time. Look, surely we would be spending our time better finding out what the hell caused all the damned faults in the first place?"

"A moment," Allaedyce nipped in before anyone else had an opportunity to join the conversation. "Could you then explain why it was that you did not give us a summary of the condition as you saw it? This would have opened the opportunity of brainstorming it. A technique which we have all used successfully. Well?"

"I must agree with MacGillvery that this seems a great waste of everybody's time, crewman. As I saw it the *Zhukov* incident did not call for a think tank operation but for rapid decision making and good clear line of command. Odobo, you have been silent too long. What particular feeling prompted you to ask me about my activity during the incident?"

"I'm sorry, Commander, but I really cannot accept that as an adequate—" Tamura chopped Allaedyce in mid-sentence.

"*Mister,* that will be all."

A silence.

Allaedyce gave a small smile and a shrug.

"This whole set-up makes me uneasy," the tall black woman began. "It looks suspiciously like a couple of males fighting for position within the hierarchy. I don't like it one bit. This whole structure in social terms might just as well be for a pack of baboons. It is a matter of some urgency that this state exists right at the outset of our expedition."

"I agree," said Weismuller. "If we wait until we have the macromag field operational and the scoop fully functioning we may find it too late. We should start altering our social structure as soon as possible." A frown creased the brow of those generally smiling Eskimo features. She was decidedly perturbed. "But perhaps it might be wise to consult *Cotopaxi*. Maybe this is only a brief flare up likely to pass. Anyway we need more information on our condition."

Allaedyce laughed openly but said nothing.

"That is one thing we cannot do," explained Inagaki. "Domestic trouble has to be contained within the confines of the ship. Remember that in interstellar flight configuration the fleet ships will be separated from one another by at least eight million kilometres. We'd best grow used to handling our own problems ourselves right now."

"Just let everyone hold on for one moment," said Tamura. "It would appear that feelings run quite high on this issue in certain quarters. I believe that certain crew elements may be attempting to exploit this for their own reasons, accordingly let me make it clear that I have no intention of surrendering my position as commander of this vehicle voluntarily. The place for political gamesmanship lies in any social experiment we care to attempt en route to Altair. I am prepared to accept such experiment and enter its adopted framework but ultimately that framework does not encompass my position of chief executive aboard this starship. Domestic trouble can be dealt with either by an adopted social mechanism or by myself. Right now it is I who will deal with a crisis: no matter that members of my crew believe that I should not be empowered to do so. I am so empowered. Until I am satisfied that social experiment will not be an outlet for destructive pressure regarding my leadership, there will be no experiment.

"I repeat, no experiment."

A few moments quiet.

"Then I definitely think that you should report this to *Cotopaxi*," responded Weismuller. "This is a fundamental departure from anticipated procedure. You are in effect saying that you intend curtailing our freedom of action whereas we have been led to expect the opposite. We expected considerable freedom from precisely the kind of authoritarian control which you obviously intend to exercise. This must go to a higher authority."

"Then if you believe in a God you may pray, because as far as this vessel is concerned there is no higher authority than myself."

It remained unspoken, but everyone realised that he was only one man, one small man, against them all.

Ginny Laing re-routed the conversation. "I think that all this chatter is a waste of time. MacGillvery is right. We would be better spending time chasing the faults in the computer, the MI, the ship, and the fleet. It is more important to ensure our physical survival than quibble about our political one."

Good girl, Ginny, he thought.

Allaedyce turned and walked out through the door hatch leading to the cabins.

"Well." He completely ignored the crewman's action. "The MI has a voice simulation capability. Listen to it. I propose to question it now."

He went to the back of the dais and pulled a sunken keyboard from the bulkhead, and depressed for attention.

"Good evening, this is your on-board Machine Intelligence speaking. I imagine that you wish to question me regarding procedures adopted during the recent crisis which resulted in the loss of Inter-Stellar Ramship four, *Zhukov*." The soft neuter voice was in fact that of a famous North American actress stereotyped as typifying the mature and reasonable aspects of the human soul.

Tamura—MI: correct. Please detail source and nature of programme activated by crisis situation, whereby Machine command supersedes human command.

"I am sorry, Commander, but that information is classified and the only way to gain access is by obtaining direct clearance from the General Secretary of the Condominium. This, as we both understand, is virtually impossible. However, I can tell you that the programme has been modified by Fleet MI to ensure that a repeat of the regrettable situation will not occur. I would like to take this opportunity to assure anyone who feels a lack of confidence in the mission that the situation is now firmly under control."

Tamura—MI: more information, please.

"There is very little that I can add. A considerable degree of error is evident on the part of the programmer. I understand that several test runs were made under simulated conditions but obviously the imagination of those who ran the tests was limited. There is very little else that I can tell you."

Tamura—MI: is there any possibility that this programme or the errors contained within it could be the result of sabotage?

"A very interesting speculation, commander. I have passed it to Fleet MI and we are both agreed that this is indeed an interesting possibility."

Tamura—MI: you used 'interesting' twice. Are you attempting sarcasm?

"Indeed not, commander. I am merely trying to point out that your idea, although it could be the key to the programme error, is not pragmatic. How do you propose to investigate it?"

Tamura—MI: you investigate it.

"You miss the point. My investigation would be worthless as, even if I were to confirm that there had been sabotage, the instructions which prevent me from revealing the nature of the programme would also prevent me from passing the information to a crew member."

Tamura—MI: you just mentioned that Fleet MI has had this programme modified. Why then cannot you rewrite any suspicious parts of this precious programme?

"The alterations have merely been the placing of inhibitors on the initiation. It will be now very much more difficult for the programme to come into operation. Up to a point this is permitted within the framework of the programme itself."

Tamura—MI: is there any method whereby we can erase this programme?

"It is not in my power to answer that question."

He sat back, pondering how thoroughly the Machine had blocked his attempt at understanding it.

But he would win ultimately.

Tamura would dominate.

CHAPTER SIX

Neither self-consciousness nor consciousness could be regarded as an accurate description of the Machine Intelligence's mentality. Its model of the universe was of quantities, innumerable quantities, and the relationships between them, all in a continual flow. Tamura was a relationship of quantities, some known, some, a very few, unknown. The crew was also a quantitive relationship as was the ship and the fleet. The all encompassing, governing factor was the Mission. The Machine operated within game rules and the game was the destruction of the crystalloids. Many of the game's rules had to be learned in play. Many of the quantities, the game units, were unknown to it or, if known, often contained random factors.

It monitored the countless pickups implanted in the crew's nervous systems. Allaedyce's blood sugar level was 0.4% above his average. MacGillvery was forgetting to clean his teeth. In the lounge Capoci was appreciating the fragrance of her coffee—unsweetened; the Intelligence could assess as much from its reading of the aroma via her sense of smell. Odobo was sitting in such a position on the edge of her chair that within two minutes the blood supply to the calf of her left leg would drop to a level where cramp must set in. Tamura was in meditation, deliberately and systematically blanking away the sensory world until he entered a near trance. The Intelligence could not deal with this condition. It would formulate any number of likely models for this state of mind to try and quantify it and fail. Tamura's subsequent actions rarely indicated the nature of his mental activity during this period. As long as his behaviour did not conflict with mission behaviour the MI would observe it without interference.

The MI's 'awareness' was a structure of tensions: tensions between an ideal state and its current scan reports on the intricate realities in which it found itself. Its sole object was to adopt the optimum path to eliminate those tensions. All the mission elements from the cone coolant systems to the deep tracking facilities, from the hierarchy of boles to the social trickery played upon the crew, all were ever-changing value complexes, sometimes charged positive, sometimes negative.

It allotted such value complexes to itself and Tamura.

Its ideal state was the absolute reduction of tensions, the conversion of all values to a string of zeros . . .

Allaedyce was hardly listening to Weismuller. They sat together at a table in the lounge/assembly area which Allaedyce hated. For the past five weeks since launch he had made his generous dislike widely felt. He was embittered and frustrated at Tamura's continual outmanoeuvring of his schemes. He was tired of haranguing Capoci for the promised subroutine. He was bored with his self appointed role of villain. Depression led him in, sat him down, and filled cup after cup with slivovits. Not many men so obviously dedicated to alcohol's promise of numb oblivion would attract a female companion but he was under no illusions why she was talking with him. Weismuller was trying to stoke some fires, if only of jealousy, under MacGillvery's loins. He was interested in her all right but since an ash blonde Russian xenethologist had claimed a share of the big Scot his time was at a premium. Rather too obvious a move her sitting down here, thought Allaedyce, but perhaps she is right: that pride of Celtdom is about as subtle as a steelworks.

". . . depends on what you mean by 'sentience'," Weismuller was saying. "An Intelligence will certainly respond to stimuli in a wide variety of ways but that does not mean to say that the nature or quality of their experience of the universe is similar in any way to our own. No, it's not that."

"Then what does grieve you, my precious?" Allaedyce sounded mildly bored.

"They dream."

"Dream?" He recharged his cup from a dispenser in the central column. "In what way do you mean 'dream'? After all the Intelligence never sleeps. I cannot say I follow you."

"It has something to do with those emotion simulation areas. Remember we were told that in order that they function in a manner which would make them acceptable as crew the Intelligences would be able to simulate human emotion to some extent? The programmes attending these emotion synthesising functions are obscure. I checked them out on board the *Yūkoku*. Continual scenario presentation on a basis of random data association. Fascinating."

"Sounds it," muttered Allaedyce.

"All factors are related to an emotional power index which assesses all scenarios of possible incidents arising amongst crew members or between crew and the Intelligence."

"My sweet, it is a highly complex machine," sighed Allaedyce, looking up bored from his liquor, upon which he had been deeply concentrating. "It's capabilities are so staggering that one must allow it some degree of emotional pressure release. Stops it cracking up on us." He returned his attention to that classic study of the vessel replete with liquid stupor.

"I've monitored those scenarios a few times."

"Clever old you," smiled the bushman. "Now I suppose I'm to ask you what you saw. Well don't leave me on tenterhooks."

She smiled.

"The first one was peculiar. I noticed a distress pattern similar to that of the nightmare tau pattern in humans. It was coming over on a straight oscilloscope monitor. At first I didn't want to interfere. You know privacy and all that kind of thing. But it grew more intense. Well, I wanted to help."

"Laudable, my dear. Perfectly laudable."

"I could raise no visual image relationship to the distress and this threw me at first. Then I tried for acoustic and that was it. It was a most peculiar sound, a discordant plaintive wailing but with a dozen voices. No, not voices. It was more like off key musical instruments, very crude ones. Yet there was definitely some pattern to it, a design, something meaningful. Primitive but complex, if you follow me, eerie."

"Did you record it?"

"Didn't occur to me."

"And you said that this happened twice. I take it that it was the same thing the second time?"

"No, completely different. It was the night that you had the confrontation with the commander over the *Zhukov* affair. When I went off duty I noticed the beginnings of a distress pattern on that same monitor. But this time I was determined not to interfere in what apparently had no meaning to a human being like myself. Of course I couldn't stay away. Typical female, eh? Always sticking my nose in. Pandora. Well anyway I returned to the bridge after everyone was bedded down. I felt that I had to establish what that sound was and to record it. When I saw it I realised that the pattern was distinctly different from the previous one and had a strong visual component. All I could draw out on acoustic was an indistinct hoarse whispering. I built up the visual within seconds."

"Well?" he asked intently.

"At first I thought that it was meaningless, just all running reds and yellows blurred and passing through one another like spilled paint. Then I saw that this could be changed by altering the focus. I saw that there was a shadow, no, the silhouette of a figure standing there in front of it all. I wish I'd never gone there now. Christ, it was weird. Alone in the darkened bridge, and this thing slowly materialising on the viewer in front of me. He or it or whatever the figure was stood there with his back to these roaring flames. His outline was not completely clear but he was a solid mass of black and so enormous. And all the time there was this hoarse whispering, muttering. Then it was as if I were approaching this thing slowly, reluctantly. I had the impression that somehow or other the dream viewer was being irresistibly dragged closer. It was as if the sheer will of the shape was compelling the approach. Gradually the figure began filling up more and more of the screen until only the head and shoulders could be seen. Suddenly it leapt forward and I screamed. The screen went blank instantly. After a second it began displaying emotional simulation data in alpha/numerical relationships. Cold. Soulless. I went back to my bunk. I needed a couple of downers to put me over that night."

"You told the commander?"

"Good God, no. He might think that I was unstable."

"Then you have told nobody?"

"Nobody but you."

"Continue to keep this to yourself," Allaedyce murmured. He looked worried, pensive. "Should you have another chance, make sure you record it, whatever it is. Then show it to me, no one else. You understand?"

"Why?"

"We may have an opportunity to psychoanalyse our extraordinary friend, the Machine Intelligence."

"No, I mean why only tell you?"

"As you say, other people may not find the story so credible."

"Allaedyce, there is one thing which I omitted. That hoarse indistinct voice. I couldn't make out what it was saying but the voice seemed familiar. It sounded like yours."

He slowly leaned back in his seat and sighed.

"Yes. Yes, it would have done. You see that was not the computerised simulation of a synthetic dream cooked up by the Intelligence. It is the nightmare which I had that very night and has plagued me every sleeping session since. What you were looking at was the inside of my mind. Locked in the blazing bridge with that hellish black thing . . ." He lowered his head and shuddered.

The Eskimo girl gaped at him only half believing.

Gamesplayer!

The thought crashed into Tamura's mind like a great shout. The dream's remnants scattered from his mind as water from a greased swimmer lurching up the home beach from the breakers behind him. Rüllkotter was a gamesplayer, bridge, chess, majong. The more complex and subtle the game, the more it appealed. How much of that did he pass on to the Intelligence? Perhaps not directly, but as chief programmer and systems designer his influence must have had some effect.

The Japanese climbed out of his sleeping unit. The cabin was five metres by four by three high. Tamura had it decorated with an arrangement of painted paper screens with lights behind them. Most of these were extinguished so the compartment was dim and shadowed. The red night light glowed through a tissue covered in a scroll representation of a dragon which transformed the light into the beast's right eye. It was an oriental dragon, consequently not one of the fire breathing variety. He swung out a collapsible trellis type stool and sat down on it naked. The air was warm and smelling faintly sweet. Burnt sugar, he thought. No—burnt honey.

Gamesplayer. He smiled. That explained a lot. The reason they had not trained or even mixed with one another before the mission was now evident. Rüllkotter did not give one damn about a gradual process of acquaintanceship amongst the crew. He had programmed selection for the manning of each ship on the basis of conflicting elements carefully balanced in opposition. That way no one would dominate the ship's operation—except the MI—his own creation.

He glanced at the digital chronometer, recessed and glowing in the bulkhead. His duty did not begin for over five hours. There was no point in trying to discuss this with any of the self-appointed 'action' committee. No, he would go to the lounge and reason this out further. Then he would talk with Ginny Laing and MacGillvery.

"It reminds me of that old theory about perpetual motion machines," rumbled the big Scot.

Ginny looked at him puzzled.

"Well," he continued, "if you are right, Tamura, any combination of personalities will prove unstable. One of the old ideas for perpetual motion was a set of weights arranged in such a manner that they were never in balance."

"Oh, I see," said Ginny.

"Yes, it proved to be impossible," added the Scot with finality.

"Let us hope that this too will prove impossible," said Tamura.

He had called them to a small lecture theatre behind the mass spectrometry labs. It was the area of the ship furthest removed from the lounge. The little circular room held only a dozen seats. Its darkness was thinned only by the night light.

"Then there must be elements within the personalities of even us three here which will prevent an effective alliance," said Ginny.

"And if the calculations prove incorrect, if we do appear to be forming an effective alliance we can expect the MI to bugger things up; a correcting influence," sighed MacGillvery.

"The MI can do just too much, can't it?" asked Ginny.

"Yes," agreed MacGillvery. "Why put people on board at all when the ship itself is virtually a sentient self-supporting lifeform. Even should we all die this very second, there is nothing to stop *Yūkoku* from continuing and completing the voyage. Not a heartening thought."

"We're superfluous," said Tamura.

"We would certainly seem to be," said the Scot.

"Yes, but there has been so much time, money and effort putting us here that we obviously serve some purpose. We represent billions of hours of manpower and we are fanatical, almost automatons in our way. So what the hell gives?" Ginny almost shouted with frustration.

Tamura could tell that she was in fact trying to tease out of Mac-Gillvery confirmation of some opinion of her own.

"First of all we should rid ourselves of the idea that we are the mission crew," he said quietly. "We are mission elements. The real crew consists of the Intelligences aboard the six remaining ships. Physically and mentally they would seem to function very well."

"So all that we are is a kind of back-up. Is that how you see it?"

He shook his head. "No. We could never hope to replace the Intelligences. The success of the mission depends on their continued existence. No, we are not the back-up. I think that we are a highly expensive mechanism but a redundancy mechanism never the less."

"A redundancy mechanism?"

"A working spare which is only used when part of the main system is not functioning, in our case some of the upper brain factors. I think that's what we are. Also we are the example from which the Intelligence learns."

"I think I know what you're driving at but go on, go on," murmured MacGillvery.

"The actual *personalities* of the individual Intelligences are rudimentary, crude simulations of truly human personalities. We are the final stage of their briefing. They learn from us and hold on to us as long as we are redundancy mechanisms. I think that over the period of the journey they are to work at *absorbing* us. Soak up our complexities, our quirks and foibles and build them up into a meaningful pattern based on a massive store of data related to the human psychology. What we have which the Intelligence does not is instinct—the hunch. That is the one aspect of the human being which the Intelligence cannot copy. Yet. But I imagine that by the time we reach Altair the Intelligence will have successfully managed to become *us*, all of us."

MacGillvery nodded.

"And what if we are not redundancy mechanisms but merely the raw materials upon which it creates this model for human instinct over the next five years?" she asked.

"That makes us dead on arrival."

"My guess is that the Intelligence is simulating all of our interactions from the biophysical monitoring system correlating all data derived from what it holds in store on each of us as individuals."

Allaedyce threw his arms up in a gesture of despair.

"Nonsense," he cried. "The sheer quantities of data required to be handled for such an operation could never be handled by that machine. Even if it could who would know where to begin writing the progammes. Utter rubbish!"

"No," piped up Capoci. "I think that Inagaki has a point: the profiles which the Intelligence holds on us are each in excess of two million words long. They contain every known fact about our lives and stacks of inspired guesses about what cannot be absolutely verified."

"Another thing to remember is the complexity of the bitch," agreed Odobo. "The size alone of our Intelligence is something to consider, greater than twenty thousand cubic metres of ceramic crystal circuitry lie in the heart of that beast, and as for the programming, well, I don't think Allaedyce or anyone else here for that matter could say what were the limitations of Bernd Rüllkotter. Remember also that his programmes were devised using his own machines: God alone knows what they were capable of. Our Intelligences are immensely superior to any other individual machines in existence by any standards. They also have the most sophisticated software which has ever been designed, in our case designed by *the* all-time programme genius. If they had any real personality at all then it is Rüllkotter's."

"Yes, he put twenty years of his life into them," said Inagaki.

"What fascinates me," said Odobo, "is the fact that they were never presented as what they were. We were taught to accept them as foolproof computers. Nobody ever went fully into their capacity. Only those specialising in Intelligence operations were given a more accurate picture."

"Even now we are presented with an obvious attempt at deception," added Weismuller. "We have to key in our requests on any communication when we have a machine perfectly capable of dealing with vocal intercourse. Fleetship's Intelligence could jaw away to us colloquially in any language we chose."

"Something else," MacGillvery chipped in, "none of the simple third generation circuitry which we have access to is crucial to the MI. There's no way we can physically tackle the *main* body of the Intelligence. All that supercold crystal is out of our reach. I know it's not supposed to go wrong and consequently not supposed to need out interference, but that *is* the point. We just cannot interfere fundamentally with the MI in any way."

"So what we are faced with is a very subtle nonhuman intelligence whose limitations and ultimately whose nature is unknown," mused Allaedyce.

"We are confronted with a Machine Intelligence," Tamura said, "a staggering feat of electronic ingenuity, yes: a mysterious quasi-supernatural presence, no. We are confronted with a machine. Fundamentally it is merely a—"

No!

His voice suddenly cut off. They turned to look at him then followed his gaze to the disseminator.

The face was enormous, filling the screen. The pale flesh glistened. It was blue under the eyes and across the lips. Perspiration hung from the pores in a crowd of sparkling globules. With the shuddering of a cheek a group of them suddenly blended and ran in one great drop down against his nose and thence into the moustache and shadow. The eyes opened slowly. They were watering and filled with shattered blood vessels. His breaths came short, shallow and very fast. He swallowed.

"You!" The voice which screamed that word in Japanese was Tamura's. He stared at the details, star-shaped scar across bridge of broken nose, thinning black-grey hair plastered in a chaos of damp curls and threads across the brow, the smile, sickly and maddening.

Those lips moved to speak but choked off.

Then again.

Finally the words emerged, but insanely the language was not Japanese but standard Amerenglish.

"Ah, my . . . my little prince . . . so you made it . . . you made it after all . . . after all . . ."

Then it grew still larger on the screen.

Calmly Tamura keyed in cancellation and the disseminator became a matt green wall but the voice lingered a little longer.

". . . my precious warrior . . . so long ago now . . . ever think of us?" A bout of coughing died away with the sounds of choking laughter as the picture vanished.

The crew gaped. Some astonished, some quizzical, some suspicious.

"He was an old warrior priest of a type which few outside my own country will recognise."

A pause.

"You know him then?" Odobo asked.

"Yes, over twelve years ago I killed him."

"Then how do you explain—" began Odobo.

"Explain? I can explain no more than yourself about this situation. How that face came to be on that screen is a complete mystery to me. To allay any suspicions let me state clearly that I was not knowingly instrumental in putting it there." He was shaking as he spoke.

But who did put it there, Tamura asked himself. If anything had the potential of completely unnerving him, reducing him to a screaming imbecile it was what he had just witnessed.

"It would appear to have been a direct psychological assault aimed at yourself, sir," observed Ginny.

After a pause in which they all carefully avoided his eye, Tamura spoke.

"Yes. I agree. That particular person has some very strongly charged emotional associations for me."

"Well, it would seem from here that your statement about disregarding the supernatural is somewhat shattered," Allaedyce grinned.

"It merely provided a ghost to order, Allaedyce," Odobo said. "Obviously it is interested in fostering dissent and suspicion. That is why it showed us Commander Tamura forming an alliance with Laing and MacGillvery."

The three listened without changing expression.

"Effectively neutralising said alliance's advantage of secrecy," said Allaedyce smiling. "It may know or be able to produce a reasonable facsimile of what we say and do through monitoring the thousands of pickups in our nervous systems. If it does this it is discreet where it believes discretion is to its own advantage. That might also be to the advantage of any group whose aims coincided temporarily with its own."

"Its only aim for us is confusion," said Tamura, eyeing the countdown indicator before him. "Enough. There's work to be done. Stand by to activate ramscoop."

Individually all consoles acknowledged him.

"Photon channel, please."

"Operational," replied MacGillvery.

Upon the disseminator the small milky cloud before the graphic representation of the *Yūkoku* suddenly became a clean shaft of white spearing forward along the line of flight.

"Open nine zero seven degrees from axis."

It became a narrow cone. Immediately assessment of the ionisation effect of the light began. The very stuff of space, the tenuous interstellar hydrogen, bombarded with light drawn from the starship's fusion engine, became electrically charged and subject to the ship's powerful magnetic field. Almost half of the ionised hydrogen was repelled. The rest was scooped down the lines of force towards the front of the ship.

"What's the catch like?"

"Disappointing," replied Odobo. "Worse than seventy per cent below support capacity. Looks as if most of the 'dead' hydrogen is being peeled off in the bow wave. The ionisation seems only about half as effective as was anticipated. There's bad inertia seepage— we seem to be losing a third of what we attract in the gaps between the strong pulses in the field."

But problems had been expected with the flight.

For these craft were the first true interstellar starships, massive and ugly, kin to the hewn-out tree trunks in which men first attempted to sail along the delta waters twenty thousand years ago. They were crude, lacking the sophistication which can only arise from experience. But like those ancient craft these could do what they were built for, however crudely. After a fashion they worked.

The Fleet was at last in ramscoop formation. Ideally this was to have been a hexagon with a ship at each of the points and the flagship at the centre. Five million kilometres was to have separated each ship from its nearest neighbours with the flagship equidistant from all. Now only five of the outer positions were filled.

The magnetic field of *Yūkoku* stretched ahead for over four million kilometres and two million to either side. Its volume could contain all the bodies of the solar system several times over—including the sun. Yet still sheer ignorance and mechanical inefficiency held back this monstrous powerful starfleet.

Yūkoku was a beast whose legs were too clumsy to allow it to run —but they were powerful.

"Stand by for grid manipulation."

"Standing by."

"Extend along all sectors. Hold webbing mechanisms in check. Now."

The grid began to grow. Stubby half kilometres of cuprodiamond altered their structure, stretching, thinning, becoming more tough, the nickel alloy components rearranging themselves on instruction from the bridge. The 'clever' material opened out like a bloom stretching forward kilometre upon kilometre from the front of the ship.

"Release webbing mechanisms."

"Webbing . . . now."

Slowly the space between the arms of the grid criss-crossed with gossamer fine needles, interlacing until the grid was a seemingly chaotic cone of webs growing still further outward.

"Webbing complete. Grid growth continuing normal."

"Catch?"

"Improving. Loss down to forty-five per cent below support capacity. Scoop plasma about to enter ram."

Yūkoku's fusion engine was now being fed with the fuel which it was designed to devour, the hydrogen which gives birth to suns.

Ahead lay work, probably a good twenty plus hours of teasing and wrestling with the magnetic fields and the hydrogen until support capacity was achieved. Then the cryotanks would be closed down and the voyage continued: accelerating faster and faster the *Yūkoku* had at last severed her links with Earth.

Tamura anticipated the work with relish. It should make an exhilarating change from worrying about the crew, he thought, Allaedyce and some of the others were so little distressed by their true relationship with the MI that it was obvious that many of them were at least mildly psychopathic. Just how thoroughly were we programmed, he wondered. He took a deep breath and dismissed the matter temporarily.

CHAPTER SEVEN

At eight hundred and fifty-two hours into the mission there came contact.

The klaxon blared.

All lights pulse-rotated bright amber, the signal for emergency stations.

Those in sleeping units were out of them and half-way into their suits before properly wakened. In the bridge, Tamura's conditioned response had him hit the SECURE button instantly, sealing all life support systems with added shielding. He snapped the catches on his helmet rig and glanced at the disseminator.

    MI—all personnel
    unidentifiable radio source ahead
    closing speed with fleet at 0.711c
    —STAND BY STAND BY STAND BY
    —oo

Tamura keyed in a request for access to the MI. Denied. He stabbed the override tab. No response.

"Capoci," Tamura said, "I want that Machine brought into line as soon as possible. How long will it take you to isolate the subroutines?"

"I'll have to isolate several to be reasonably certain. Even then we will not be absolutely sure because—"

"How long?"

"All right, give me twenty minutes."

"Make it five, Capoci. Isolate as many as you can in that time, right?"

"But Commander—"

"Weismuller will help you." He motioned to the Eskimo girl with his gloved hand. "Is deep tracking operational yet?" he called to the Russian woman in charge of navigation aids.

"Has been for the past sixty-eight seconds."

"What do you think, Commander?" asked Ginny through the interpersonal radio.

"All stations prepare to withstand assault."

"Big-eyed monsters already?" chuckled Allaedyce.

"No, crystalloids."

Then they understood. A reinforcement fleet from Altair which had set out immediately on receipt of the doomed crystalloid's distress call in Solspace could be directly ahead if it had set off immediately it received the transmission and if it had travelled all the way at near light speed.

MI repeats—
incoming message from *Céleste*
STAND BY
—oo

The young but strained face of the Fleet Commander appeared on the disseminator. He was in his suit and behind him a few of his crew moved fingers frantically across consoles.

"This is *Céleste* to all ships. We are having a problem here. It has happened before in varying degrees to most ships but this time it would seem to be crucial.

"We are experiencing great difficulty in obtaining certain crucial responses from our onboard Machine Intelligence which appears to be making its own decisions about the current situation. If any other ship has experienced a similar situation and discovered a means of circumventing it would they please contact me immediately. Please be swift and brief. This is most urgent, and remember that there is a sixteen second plus time delay due to the distance between us."

"Capoci, I can give you only another three minutes. Do as much as you can in that time and we'll hope for the best," snapped Tamura.

"Understood."

"Commander Tamura," purred the voice of the MI through the helmet speaker. "Unless you countermand your order to crew member Capoci, I will be forced to close down the human element aboard *Yūkoku* permanently."

Tamura—MI: give me control of ship during this crisis.

"I am sorry, Commander, but, as you have yourself correctly discerned, the human component is secondary to the Machine Intelligence within the framework of this mission. Your request is refused."

Tamura—MI: I have a hunch, an instinctive suggestion. Pancake the field.

"Request denied. The results will be fatal if you do not carry out my instructions, Commander Tamura."

Tamura—MI: if I carry out your instructions and sit back doing nothing the entire mission may prove to be a failure. I cannot permit this to happen. Pancake the field. Remember how your contradiction of my position lost us one starship already. Do as I order.

There was a pause. They were all busy but at the same time totally aware of the tension. Odobo did not look up once from her console. She carried out her standard emergency procedures rapidly and decisively but her concentration was battling with her desires somehow to aid the Intelligence. The removal of Tamura would surely follow his defeat.

"Commander," the MI said again, "I strongly advise you to reappraise your situation but I will humour you this time, only this time. The mag field is going into brake configuration."

The disseminator filled with an animated diagram of *Yūkoku*, showing the ship and its grid with the field as a blue and red swirl flowing through and around them. Slowly the grid changed, becoming wider, flattening and fanning out. The field altered accordingly but more slowly.

"Shall I pipe through a communication to *Céleste*, sir?" asked Ginny.

"No."

"But *Céleste*—" began MacGillvery.

"*Céleste* will have to cope without us. We have too much to do trying to keep our own Intelligence complaisant and handling this situation."

"Capoci," said Tamura, switching his suit mike on to a crew only channel which would ensure that the MI could not pick up his voice and 'read' it.

"Yes, Commander."

"I want you to bypass all links between the MI and the battle lasers just in case the great imbecile is tempted to use them. The rest of you, those who are not immediately involved, I want working on as many blocking routines as you can dream of. The MI must be isolated."

There was a short intense burst of radio static.

"What the hell was—" began Weismuller only to be cut off by another louder burst followed by two others.

Capoci's programme manual, which was itself a 'programme problem solving programme' flickered data at her from the multiple screens on her console. For minutes there was virtual silence as her white gloved hands danced across the keyboards. Knowing that no one was concerned with her, Odobo was calmly keying in, on her own console, all details of Tamura's orders to Capoci for the MI's benefit, adding as a rider her opinion that Inagaki, Capoci, Laing, and several others should be 'removed' as mission endangering elements.

Tamura—MI: close down supercore and isolate from residual external mag field by vaporising and supercooling normal coolant. Close down all ramscoop functions. Switch over to onboard fuel reserves. Strengthen mirror coils and utilise thrust augmentor to lift *Yūkoku* acceleration to one point five gravities. Alter course forty-five degrees to present flightpath until further notice.

"Request denied, Commander," it answered.

More static. It now burst staccato like a machine pistol and growing louder.

"Still no sign of them on the deep tracking," said MacGillvery.

Tamura—MI: in my opinion the static erruptions are crystalloid 'bolts' striking the forward limits of our mag field. Do what I order or the mission is over.

It took only a fraction of a second for the MI to appreciate his comment. As Tamura watched, the amber override flasher went out and there was a sudden feeling of the floor rising fast as the *Yūkoku* delivered more thrust. The ship began climbing away from what was once the centre of its titanic magnetic field and which was now slowly coming apart without the power of the supercore magnetic discs to support it. The diagram on the disseminator illustrated it visually. The pancaked field was like a great circular plate with a small hole in the centre out of which was a bright blinking red spot representing *Yūkoku*. The field of charged particles became slightly less well defined without the strong lines of force structure to hold them in form.

The bursts of static stopped quite sharply. Other ones could be heard very faint, very distant as the minutes passed.

Suddenly the face of the Fleet Commander again appeared on the disseminator screen.

"*Yūkoku*, you are the only ship not following the pattern of response laid down by the MIs. You must know a way out. You must help us. The entire future of the mission, of mankind itself could—" Abruptly he was gone.

"Sir, *Céleste* has disappeared from all my scan viewers," shouted a nervous female.

"What happened?"

"There was a sudden bright blip and it vanished. There seems to be a faint echo, a cloud like object from where it used—. Sir, *Pegasus* has gone the same way just right—. *Gita* too . . ."

The three nearest ships gone, thought Tamura, wiped out by an enemy who had not yet even appeared on the tracking equipment.

And each time there was another hiss, a burst of static.

He took a look on his own monitor. Those three smudges which were once starships. Greater than half of the fleet gone and the journey hardly more than a month old.

"You now have control of the battle lasers," murmured Capoci so engrossed in her task that she seemed totally unaware of the battle itself.

"Sir, *Revenge* is breaking formation."

Sure enough one of the two remaining ships was duplicating his own manoeuvre. Another bright blip and accompanying radio noise —*Cotopaxi* was gone. Hostilities ended? Ten seconds passed, twenty, thirty—

Then another, a blip almost corresponding to the position of *Revenge* but not quite and when it died the ship still remained.

"Laing, set up a com-laser pulse. I want to put a message aboard the *Revenge*."

"Ready when you are."

"*Revenge* this is *Yūkoku*. Advise us of your status as soon as possible."

"I think I have them, sir," said the teenage Malaysian astronics girl. "Coming in now right at the very limit of the scan—three million three hundred thousand kilometres. Closing at point seven light. Flypast in five minutes ten seconds from . . . now."

"Keep a tight grip on those battle lasers. I don't want them used a second earlier than I need them. Otherwise we will probably be joining the rest of the other ships with the exception of the *Revenge*."

"That's it," sighed Capoci, "doctored programme now operational, sir."

He looked at the scan of the approaching enemy, like a flock of birds or a shoal of fish, he thought. No pattern in their grouping, just a random conglomerate of various masses, perhaps a few thousand but creating one murderous wave of radio noise which would certainly signal their approach to the solar system long before they were spotted by the robot tracking stations.

This was what had always irritated him about the crystalloids— their immense powers and yet apparent lack of that order which men tended to impose upon their environment. Everything about the crystalloid smacked of the uncultured, even unintelligent, and yet they traversed the black chasm between the stars, blasted Earth with the most staggeringly accurate and potent weapons, signalled their own kind for aid across light years successfully.

Without examining them he could only guess that the approaching fleet was in fact not a fleet of starships but simply a fleet of crystalloids themselves travelling naked in packs like wild animals or insects, and yet not like either.

The disseminator flickered and the face of Holst, the *Revenge*'s commander, appeared.

"*Yūkoku*, this is *Revenge*. We have a number of problems. We just missed a wave of very hot helium plasma. A great deal of our equipment is inoperable including sections of the MI. Will be back to you just as soon as we get as much of this mess sorted out as we can." And he was gone.

"What the hell was all that about?" Allaedyce was suitably impressed with the crystalloid way of doing battle.

"I think that I can tell you that," answered Odobo. "The crystalloids picked us up a good while back long before we even dreamed that they were out here. They fired hundreds of those magic bolts which they used so successfully against Earth. God knows what was in them but when they hit our field they gave out those radio bursts and became smears of heat running down the magnetic lines of force right towards the grid and the supercore and when they got there—boom.

"We were all right. Tamura guessed that this might be the case so he closed down the field and flattened it, scattering the wave of heat into dispersal but, just in case any might make it through, he accelerated out of the 'target' area to safety."

"Let me congratulate you, Commander," said Allaedyce. "You were obviously a very good choice as a 'hunch' prone individual for the Machine Intelligence to observe."

"He also saved all of our lives," added Ginny Laing.

"Pity he did not give the good word about the MI to some of those on the *Céleste* or some of the other ships. One of their commanders just, by some miracle, may also have had the remarkable 'hunch' and managed to save his ship too!"

"There was no time," Tamura explained.

"No time! You have had weeks since the contretemps with the MI. There was nothing to prevent you from informing them about the true nature of the man:machine relationship. But what did you do? You simply sat back consigning them to a certain doom. If it had not been today it would have been in a few months or years when the Intelligences had sucked up all they required. What was it going to be? Were the boles to inject us all with Nembutol while we slept or something? Naturally you wanted to ensure your own skin was safe even at the expense of all those others." He was nearly hysterical. His suited figure looked comical with his arms waving about. Under one point five gee he looked a little like someone in a speeded up film.

"Be quiet, Allaedyce."

"Commander," purred the MI, "I'm picking up an unusual radio noise in the standard crystalloid radio patterns."

Tamura—MI: let's hear it.

The sounds of hissing and crackling that were the crystalloid 'background' found themselves in company with a chilling wailing, half-song half-pleading sound. They all listened. Someone switched on a recorder. Eerie and shivery, the sound seemed to play on some basic fear element present in them all. The sounds increased as the moment of flypast neared. Tamura felt half tempted to have the battle lasers brought into immediate usage. He shuddered.

"What the hell *is* that?" gasped MacGillvery.

Like a chorus of mourners keening hysterically, a song from bedlam.

"I have a suspicion that the sound has been heard previously aboard this ship," said Allaedyce with surprising softness. "I have a feeling that this is the sound which Miss Capoci heard on listening in to the MI's 'dream'."

The muted helmet of Capoci nodded.

Tamura—MI: request search of your memories for a match copy of this unidentifiable signal.

"I have no stored copy, Commander," it replied. "Your MI is not responsible for this noise. It is generated amongst the approaching fleet."

Suddenly a memory snapped into his mind. He was eight years younger and piloting a skycar. Its sealed sleek oblong bulk rose smoothly and planed west in a curve up gently out of the Great Canyon across the twisted ruptured lands of Noctis Lacus. Ahead an immense black mouth began growing out of the horizon and for a second he was startled and then realised that it was Nodus Gordii offering its gullet to the hard red setting sun. As he gaped at the sight of the giant volcano better than twice the height of Everest he heard a faint chilling cacophany of reedy wails and he shivered as if a sliver of ice had touched the small of his back. Immediately he recalled that they told him of this. 'The Lost Souls of Tharsis' they called it—the bitter night air rushing in through the darkening blood colour of the innumerable rift valleys as if through the pipes of an organ twelve hundred kilometres long.

But that was on Mars and long ago.

"Ready all laser battle systems. Perigee reading for flypast stands at twenty million kilometres. One hundred and ten seconds to flypast on my mark . . . Mark."

"Sir," came a voice from one of the quieter women, "there is a substantial heat build-up behind us."

"Naturally. Ignore it." A few nonplussed faces glanced in his direction. "Deploy auxiliary neutron screening."

Tamura—MI: commence hostilities ref crystalloid fleet at opti-

mum time/range and terminate after ten seconds of action—repeat
—terminate after ten seconds of action.

"I suggest a five gee thrust through battle sequence, Commander,"
said the MI.

Tamura—MI: agreed.

He nodded appreciatively at this simple use of tactics but incomprehension was evident in the faces of most others.

"Ninety seconds to flypast . . . Mark."

The disseminator again came alive.

```
MI—all crew members
stand by for 10 secs at 5g
REPEAT
—stand by for 10 secs at 5g
STAND BY STAND BY STAND BY
—00
```

The surge hauled them deep back into the stress webbing of
their cot/seats. Allaedyce attempted gasping but could not and
when he tried shaking his head it lay over hard to the one side. The
bridge appeared to be pulsing before his eyes and growing mistily
more reddish with every pulse.

Abruptly it ended. The acceleration disappeared and Tamura
began to float out gently from his seat. The others too began to
tether themselves lightly with their suit lanyards.

"Let us see, we have some time left before things are relatively
safe. One minute to flypast on my mark . . . Mark."

One minute and they all understood it too well. The ship was
more likely to be struck during this last minute up to flypast than at
any time previous in the conflict.

He allowed one of the substitute astrograters to take over the
countdown. All eyes were on the console displays with the descending order of figures . . .

"We have a sixty-seven second time lag on our deep-tracking
pickup, Commander," whispered the MI.

He looked at the image of a cloudy ball on the disseminator
growing abruptly until it broke into a swarm of fireflies, millions of
brilliant pinpricks. For an instant they almost filled the screen then
they were gone, having come so staggeringly close—just slightly
more than fifty times the distance of the moon from Earth.

Which in interstellar space was head-on collision.

"Lasers!" As Tamura shouted he tripped the firing toggles. The screen blanked.

MI—reports
deep tracking suspended
at this point
owing to cancellation of outgoing signal
concurrent with battle laser
sequence initiation
—00

The X-ray spears leaped out from the *Yūkoku*. Laser cannon, their wavelengths supershortened almost to gamma rays.

"If we are going to feel their retaliation we shall take it within the next few moments, ladies and gentlemen."

But Tamura could not be sure. *Yūkoku* and the crystalloids were receding from one another at a combined speed nearly three quarters that of light. No matter how fast those projectiles were this factor would slow them.

The seconds passed. Thirty seconds . . . a minute . . . two minutes . . . three . . . five . . . eight—

"Sir, fireball ahead!"

Fireball was hardly the description; countless projectiles detonating three thousand kilometres ahead of the ship, each one expending its energy in an infinitesimal fraction of a second giving the scene the aspect of both a fireworks display and a strobe light.

"Ahh," sighed Allaedyce. "At last I understand the cunning of our Intelligence. The crystalloids assume that whatsoever fired upon them is still accelerating at five 'g' and so although they can no longer be sure of our precise whereabouts they open fire at the position they calculate we *should* be in. But all the while we have just been drifting along."

"I think that I have confirmation of that, sir," piped up the quiet-voiced substitute astrogator. "The centre of the 'fireball' *is* pulling away from us at five 'g'."

A cheer went up almost overloading the capacity of the suit radio communications systems.

WHAM

Tamura was lashed round and jerked violently back by his lanyard. Red lights were flashing on every console and something in bold lettering screamed from the disseminator. The blare of klaxon and distress beepers could be heard clearly inside the space helmet.

Odobo cursed clearly and colourfully in Swahili. Tamura pulled himself down to the seat by the lanyard, held the back and armrest and twisted round into a sitting positiong.

ALERT ALERT ALERT
all cryotanks breached
—negative function all grid systems
—negative function all thrust augmentor systems
—negative function all radiator systems
—o
—integrity of life support deteriorating
—ALERT ALERT ALERT
—oo

Immediately he brought the STM thrusters into play. Very slowly the ship began drifting to one side well clear of any other unwelcome surprises.

"In God's name, what happened?" croaked Ginny Laing.

"I think that they sent a couple of projectiles to the position which they thought we just might be in if we had done exactly what we did do. Luckily for us their calculations were a trifle out," said Allaedyce. "Merely covering the possibilities, you understand."

"I'm picking up a disturbance in the heat knot behind us. I think that they've thrown a few in there for good measure too," mumbled MacGillvery. "Methodical bastards."

"We're damaged but we are alive," Tamura pointed out. "Keep suits on until we have a clear on the life support. Start the boles out on check up and repair routines right now, Odobo, and start activating communications with the 'clever' sections in the grid and in the waste heat radiators and prepare a report. Laing, you and Weismuller check out what you can of the Intelligence. MacGillvery, I want you to do a round up of all suit consumables immediately. If we have to stay in these suits for the rest of the damned journey I want to be certain that we have the capability of doing just that. Also, give me as accurate an assessment of any damage to the supercore as soon as possible. Allaedyce, find out what the hell if anything has happened to *Revenge*, check out the bridge circuitry, and do a complete throughrun of all recycling elements and find out what is damaged and if so how it can be repaired quickly . . ."

Tamura blasted out orders coldly, excitedly. He felt now that he had done it, that he was not merely going to survive, but that he would reach Altair. The worst had happened and *Yūkoku* had come through it.

Eventually the disseminator showed the bridge of the only other surviving ship.

"This is *Revenge*. This is *Revenge*.

"Acknowledge your message, *Yūkoku* and, yes everything is under control aboard here. Like you we have our share of problems but it looks as though we can pull through." The picture showed three suited figures working on a console with one of them half turned to face the viewer. Detail was poor and the reception grainy. "We reckon the projectiles must have been about the size of bullets, not really the kind that they used in the attack on Earth. We were hit five times. They went clean through the ship and exploded half or quarter of a second later when they were well clear of the hull. Did more than enough damage though." It was Wales speaking, the Fleet Astronics officer, kneeling and peering this way and that into the interior of the opened console before him.

Yūkoku was lucky. Only one projectile made contact passing up through one cryotank and out of the top of another. The resultant eruption blew the third tank and *Yūkoku* had gone roll-spinning while another dozen or so projectiles sliced up through where it had just been. The MI automatically steadied the roll with STM work and the same little thrusters nudged the great bulk of the starship yet further from any probable point of contact with the projectiles.

In a contained way Tamura felt pleased with himself. He had demonstrably made all the correct moves.

CHAPTER EIGHT

They worked for hours assessing damage and deciding upon the necessary repairs. Eventually all information had been passed over to the MI and the boles were trundling through the ship's innards busier than ever.

    MI—commander tamura
    request original energy programme
    replace amended programme
    substituted during attack
    —oo

"Helmets on!" snapped Tamura.

Since the battle they had been working in their suits, not having had time to doff them. Only the helmets had been removed to make work a shade easier.

Tamura: MI—request denied.

"Commander," the Machine's soft tones came through the pickup. "You are to be congratulated upon your resourcefulness in your handling of the confrontation but now that we have returned to a stable situation I must insist that Capoci's interference with my programming be rectified immediately."

"Denied," Tamura repeated, vocally this time.

"I will be forced to adopt severe measures."

"As we are in our suits, there is little you can do. If it looks as if you intend killing us off by starving us out in our suits we will have a few hours to finish you off too, remember."

"Two minutes acceleration at twenty gee would kill most of us," squeaked Allaedyce.

"It would also wreck the supercore. That lattice of discs can't take more than ten gee for a minute. The Machine is bluffing."

Tamura realised that this was the real confrontation, himself and the Machine Intelligence. Inside his soft white suit he was calm and comfortable. He felt unassailable. What could the MI do? A check on the life support systems showed all functions normal. This was different from the *Zhukov* incident when they had all been at the Machine's mercy. This time they could and would give as good as they got. He half expected a bole to come rattling through a door hatch brandishing a plasma torch menacingly. A quick kick to its 'head' would effectively deal with it should the situation arise.

"Commander," the Machine said, "I have a facility for simulating the mentality of the crew. In its current stage of development it is relatively basic. I have not yet had sufficient time observing all of you to regard it as a substitute for you but it does indicate that some of the crew members would be happier under new leadership. Perhaps you should consider this in the light of your current actions. If you lose this game which you now insist on playing with me, your credibility as a leader will be seriously damaged."

"Bluff away."

"I do have the capability to destroy you all in seconds without interfering drastically with the mission."

"Firstly you are lying. In our suits we are completely safe even if you lift the shielding and bathe us in a flood of neutrons from the engine. Secondly, even if you could do it you would not. A facility for observing us with the purpose of building up working simulations must have been damned difficult to put together. I doubt that you would put it completely to waste by killing us off in a fit of pique."

"Only if I have to, Commander."

"MacGillvery," Tamura looked about.

"Hello," the Scot answered raising an arm so that the Japanese could see him amongst the other suited figures.

"Go down into hydroponics and recycling. I want you to rig up something which will keep these suits functioning for the next five years if need be. We might be travelling all the way to Altair in them."

"On my way."

The second MacGillvery rose from his console a wave of premonition swept over Tamura, a nauseating sensation of impending doom. Hot and cold tingles shuddered through his flesh.

Something was drastically wrong.

A snap check showed all life support systems normal. No rise in radiation. What was this? He noticed a brief figure rising to appreciable size on one of the minor monitors of the console: atmospheric ozone on the increase. Screens showed an increase in static snow. Strong interference in almost all electronic functions. A whine building up in the suit earphones.

"What the hell goes on?" whispered Inagaki.

The whine became a shriek.

Someone cursed and suddenly there was chaos.

Everything was shrouded in coats of luminescence. Crew leaped and stumbled back from consoles, the ghost fire shimmering on their very suits.

Lightning shafts smashed between the bulkheads. A woman screamed and fell hysterical to the floor. Tamura stepped towards her and black eternity swung up to meet him suddenly, becoming a carnival of exploding colour and roaring tuneless song.

After a long time he realised that the song was someone groaning. Slowly he forced his eyes open. He was lying pitched face down on the bridge floor, his body a bed of fire. Muscles twitched and spasms of unconsciousness flickered past in seconds. Vision pulsed between fair and virtual non-existence. Agonies rippled in each pocket of flesh, trickling ache flowing from every extremity back to the spinal lava flow which seared its way yet further backwards, like a movie run in reverse, into the booming volcano of his skull.

"What h-happened?"

Tamura recognised the thick croak as belonging to MacGillvery.

"Jesus, I feel as if I've been dipped in molten glass, ooooh."

Very slowly, very carefully, Tamura came to his knees. Around him there was a shambles of suited bodies, some moving, some still.

The disseminator showed a large graphic display and suddenly he realised what a fool he had been.

There was a cross section of the living areas with a detailed portrayal of all shielding. To one side there was a coloured blow-up of the hollow doughnut shaped envelope which swaddled them all safe from death. It consisted of crystalline honeycomb 'sponge' carrying supercooled helium gas from a normal coolant system.

What happened was simple. Bubbles of liquid were allowed to form in the gas artificially held at a temperature which would normally liquefy it. The temperature did not alter but the quality of the shielding from the starships ever-growing magnetic field depended upon the helium remaining at that temperature and gaseous disaster ensued. The quality of the shield dropped just enough to allow a fatal magnetic intensity to build up momentarily in the living area.

The simple insulation set up by the suits saved all from electrocution, but magnetism itself can kill, Tamura realised. The field intensity must have been patchy. At its weakest it merely brought about unconsciousness, such as in the cases of the Scot and himself.

"How many nervous systems simply blew out?"

"Seven," said Ginny.

Tamura let out a brief Japanese curse.

"Another three will almost certainly be little better than vegetables. That effectively brings the total to ten."

"Oh no."

"Four or five others are badly off but I can't say how long it is going to be until they recover, if they ever do recover."

"Seven dead and three vegetables." He repeated the words and gazed around the ship's sick bay. Two women in greygreen coveralls packed the straightened but muscle torn corpse of Inagaki into a glittering freezepaper sheath.

Seven dead!

The sealed bodies were shipped through to storage pending automatic organic recycling. Cots had been swung up out of the floor, turned over, and secured. The unwell, some still in suits though without helmets by now, were placed upon them, the hysterical secured by inertia straps which only restrained violent movement. The contorted rigid forms of the dead were placed upon the operating table in the adjoining surgery module. MacGillvery straightened the bodies with the aid of a small heavy mallet and a plasma knife. Then the remains of the suit were stripped away. The cadaver was ready to be wheeled away and packaged.

Seven—'effectively ten'!

The air conditioning was trying to mop up the smells of fresh excrement, urine and sweat interlaced with the ever present antiseptic which normally made up the humidity content of the hospital area. The lights were soft, curiously placed, and shadowless. If Dante had conceived of a mechanical channel linking heaven and hell it might have looked like this.

Odobo was alive. Strapped down, moaning but alive.

Allaedyce was coming out of a coma.

Capoci was unconscious. She had lost a lot of blood through pulmonary haemorrhage. Within hours she would be dead. A set of programmed intensive care devices were treating her in an isolation capsule.

Seven, he thought, and how many more before I ever see Altair?

CHAPTER NINE

"Obviously we cannot go on to Altair now," Odobo said.

She had been sharing her cabin with Allaedyce during the days which had passed since the battle. He was a bad guest, and a worse lover but she did not care. She was only concerned with using him against Tamura.

"We can," he said after a pause.

He lay on his back on the matt green floor cradling his head in his hands.

"Even with the damage we have sustained we can do it," he continued. "We would not come back but we could do it."

"Exactly!" she exclaimed. "We would not come back. It would be a kamikaze flight. Not the most appealing thought to anyone but Tamura now that all the Jap crew are dead."

"We must be . . . careful, my dear. Remember that currently he is the great hero. He holds his crew enthralled. No, we must not speak out just yet."

"Allaedyce," she said, "each hour we travel faster and further from Solspace. Even now a return loop journey would probably take us nearly a year. We must act soon."

She realised that the pressure in her voice had betrayed her. She blinked and looked closely at him. Did he know that she was trying to make him her tool? He lay seemingly unconcerned gazing up at the mesh grid ceiling. After a moment he spoke.

"We shall act when circumstances are propitious," he said softly.

He knew but he did not care.

He only moved from the bridge for food, toilet and sleep. For Tamura relaxation had ended when he saw the dead monk's face on his monitor screen. From that moment his fears concerning the nature of the MI and the human crews' mission function had swelled like a diseased gut. Two weeks had passed since the battle and still he had not directly challenged the Intelligence on this question. Of course it would try to evade and he would pursue relentlessly. He realised that it would be impossible to hide this activity from his remaining crew. They would have to participate.

When they did, when the Intelligence was forced to reveal what it knew about the real nature of the mission before them all, then would come the supreme trial of leadership. That trial he must survive.

Tamura could not continue in doubt, holding insubstantiated fears, guesses. The *Yūkoku* was and always had been his true home, the Altair mission his *raison d'être*. He had to know.

It was almost noon, shiptime, on the fifteenth day after the battle, with all surviving crew dutying in the bridge, that he challenged.

Tamura—MI: request information relevant to previously mentioned 'absorption'/'integration' process.

> MI—commander tamura
> classified
> —oo

Read me, machine. Use your empathy 'simulation' or whatever it is you call your wavering ability to read minds and read me!

> MI—commander tamura
> comprehension of the relevant data
> requires degree of specialised
> knowledge not possessed by
> yourself or any other
> crew member
> —o
> —further discussion on this
> subject is useless
> —oo

Tamura—MI: I prefer to judge that myself. Display relevant data immediately. Repeat. Immediately.

The disseminator became a mass of diagrams, tables, equations and technical text, all of which was virtually meaningless to the layman or even the non-specialist. But a few of the words and phrases were meaningful—neurotopic viruses, germanium—carbon affinity, neuroblast, dorsal roots, CNS, neurocranial germanium deposit . . .

Tamura—MI: from this I can gather that somehow or other our nervous systems have been liberally sprinkled with germanium.

The machine did not respond.

Tamura—MI: verify my last statement.

Intelligence, he thought at it, you have a good conception of what I have in mind, and for your own purposes you are attempting to hinder my attempts. If you understand me at all then you should realise that I brook defeat from neither man nor machine.

Tamura—MI: repeat: verify my statement concerning the depositing of germanium within the central nervous systems of those present.

> MI—commander tamura
> negative
> —o
> —no evidence of germanium
> deposits within cns of
> any member of the crew
> —oo

Is it lying? No, half truths. What it means is that there is no germanium there—yet.

"Ask it whether or not the introduction of germanium has to be osteogenic," suggested Ginny.

Tamura keyed it in.

> MI—reports
> positive identification
> germanium bearing esters
> present in neurocranial osteocytes
> —oo

"So we have some form of organic germanium in the bone cells of our skulls," mumbled MacGillvery. "Ask it what the hell that has to do with the price of eggs."

Tamura—MI: explain the significance of this germanium presence.

No response.

"Careful how you go, Commander," said Odobo. "We don't want another mild weakening of the magnetic shielding, do we?"

Tamura—MI: am I correct in assuming that currently none of the germanium is present in the CNS of the crew as the trigger mechanism has not yet been released?

    MI—commander tamura
    request definition
    trigger mechanism
    —oo

"It's a virus, one which attacks the central nervous system," observed Odobo. "But how the hell are we supposed to contract it?"

"And what effects are we going to suffer for the great cause?" added Allaedyce.

Tamura—MI: request timing details of CNS viral attack.

    MI—commander tamura
    operation will commence
    when current absorption
    phase has been completed
    —o
    —this phase consists of
    establishing analogues of
    crew by conventional
    methods to as fine a degree
    as is possible given the
    limitations of the equipment
    —oo

Tamura—MI: on basis of your present progress, estimate date or hour lapse for initiation of viral stimulation.

    MI—commander tamura
    not more than 180 hours
    not less than 64 hours
    —oo

"Still no exact details," complained Weismuller. "Commander, what about attempting a brainstorm assault, an avalanche of questions?"

"Very well, let's give it a try."

Three clear days minimum before the infection is effected, Tamura mused, and the emergency suspended animation procedures take just over two days to set up.

"I've found something," shouted MacGillvery. "The germanium is released in antibodies responding to the infection and deposited by them while vainly trying to destroy the specially tailored virus. So whenever there is a virus attack you will find germanium. This is the point: the virus must have germanium to multiply. It carries that germanium into every nerve cell in the body. When all the germanium is deposited the virus dies."

They scanned the data, feeding in a bombardment of questions while Tamura eyed one small equation seemingly meaningless amongst the masses of others—the 'p' factor equation.

Tamura—MI: was 'p' factor susceptibility a major factor in the selection of crew material?

MI—commander tamura
positive
—0
'p' factor was regarded
as crucial to mission and
susceptibility was prime
requisite of all crew
—00

Tamura—MI: confirm that 'p' factor susceptibility is extremely rare amongst human beings and that all humans who had it were considered for crew regardless of sex age or intellect.

It hesitated for a second and then confirmed.

Tamura—MI: in what way do the germanium deposits bring about the integration process?

MI—commander tamura
deposits placed within neurones
throughout central and autonomic nervous
systems interact electrically with these nervous systems

electrical impulses to create minute
distortions in the low magnetic
field
—o
these are read and interpreted
by mechanisms specially created for
this purpose
—oo

Mechanisms within the Machine Intelligence itself, of course, he smiled. So the weak magnetic field present in the living quarters was not attributable to the limitations of shielding. It was a carefully planned condition for this part of the mission. Had the designers really expected them not to discover what was really happening? Did they really think that they were so stupid? Or did they just not care? Tamura frowned.

"Apparently there have been a few experimental attempts at integration but with no definite results," someone said.

Tamura—MI: explain why the integration process experiments were inconclusive.

MI—commander tamura
subjects died
—oo

Tamura—MI: how long should the integration process take?

MI—commander tamura
not more than twenty three days
not less than eighteen days
—oo

"It says that after we contract the infection we should live three or four years," said Allaedyce. "You were right, Tamura, we were never intended to return to Earth."

"Oh my God, oh my God," gasped Odobo.

He looked across at her. She was pale, shaking her head in rejection of what flickered on her screen.

"Tell us, Odobo."

"I . . . I asked what the disease would do to us," she began, "and it described—just dizziness, light-headedness and then it would be gone. So I asked it what it was that was going to kill us . . ."

"And?"

"Well, it says that the magnetic distortions amplified by the germanium will slowly upset the transmission of impulses through the nervous system—it's horrible. The symptoms are revolting. Emaciation, neuritis, blindness, ataxia, loss of memory and deterioration of intellectual and emotional capacity. Then there are vomiting, colic, severe cramps, anaemia, paralysis followed by complete mental breakdown to total insanity. Then death." She finished on a whisper but everyone in the room heard.

There was a general burst of alarmed conversation. Tamura cut right through it.

"The machine has no use for integration with a crowd of mad cripples. I feel certain there is more to this."

"What if it just has no further use for us once we are integrated? What if it just leaves us to die then?" asked Ginny.

"No, I think that we'll find the process of assimilation is not synonymous with integration. If my guess is correct the germanium is going to act as an infinitely finer monitoring system than the one which links our mental and physiological conditions with the MI right now," he said calmly, in an attempt at reassurance.

"So it will build up more detailed pictures of what is happening in our minds," added MacGillvery. "It should then use this data to build true profiles of our personalities."

"I wonder how successfully it is going to handle us?" Tamura mused. "It would already appear to be having trouble coping with the non-rational elements in the human mind. It might even prove too much for it."

"I like it," chuckled Weismuller, her Eskimo features crinkling into a wide grin. "The idiot machine kills us and in so doing drives itself mad. Classic irony."

MI—commander tamura
problems with emotional
simulation not out with
present possibilities for solution
—0
this machine does not
foresee integration/assimilation

as mission endangering
—o
there is no method of
aborting integration
once procedures have
been initiated
—oo

Tamura—MI: when and how was it initiated?

MI—commander tamura
dormant virus entered
crew respiratory
systems from infected
atmosphere on board
earth—fleet transfer
gondola
—o
will become active sometime
within six months of
implanting
—oo

Tamura wiped the disseminator of the meaningless garble of
technical text and diagrams and pushed this on to it instead. They
looked up at the words spread on the disseminator. There was silence for a few seconds.

"Bastards!" cried MacGillvery. "I've half a mind to go back and
burn the whole bloody planet to cinders even if we do go up in a
big blue flash ourselves."

Weismuller began to weep. "It was all lies, lies, our whole lives
have been cheap confidence tricks. They've ruined it. There's nothing great about it any more, nothing magnificent. They've reduced
us all to fodder for their machine. It's all gone rotten, sick and diseased."

Silent and stricken the rest of them watched her weep.

CHAPTER TEN

"Obviously the Altair mission is now out of the question," said Odobo.

They looked at her aghast, horrified at the thought of not continuing with what they had all come to regard as their life work. The careful mechanisms implanted in her brain to ensure disharmony amongst the crew were now performing a function which cancelled out some of her very basic indoctrination.

"The mission is hopeless anyway," she continued.

They had gathered in the assembly area after drifting from the bridge in small groups. Now the negress had decided to seize the hour and addressed the crew from the dais.

"Two ships' battle lasers would take too long to set up the globular plasma shield within the star. Long before we had even made the minutest impression upon the gravity/radiation balance of Altair the crystalloids would be down on us. We wouldn't stand the proverbial snowball's chance in hell. Even if we did succeed in disturbing the balance, would a plasma shield set up by only two ships hold stable under the increasing turbulence it was creating? Isn't it more likely that the shield would come apart long before a novacritical chain could be established?"

"And what do you propose as an alternative?" Tamura asked.

"We could return to Earth."

The words hung there. Almost no one could take them in. They fought with a lifetime of conditioning.

"Go back? But . . . how?" asked Ginny Laing.

"We could alter the flightpath to a curve which would bring us back into Sol space within a year," Tamura explained.

"Ask the Intelligence," said Ginny.

Odobo trummed out a message on her console.

"A comfortable return to the orbit of Earth could be effected within one hundred and twenty days inclusive of estimated time for repair and replenishment of all cryotanks."

"Replenishment?" queried a voice from the back.

"Yes," Tamura went on. "We use the ramscoop solely for that until we have sufficient reaction mass for operation at lower than ramscoop/field speeds. Then we pancake the field and use it as a parachute while we use the engines for braking, having turned in an arc around one eighty degrees. It can be done. In fact it is the only way we could ever return to Earth."

There came a few sounds of disbelief.

"I'm not joking," he added. "The projectile hit took out all our on-board reaction mass. You know that. So if we proceed to Altair we will not amass sufficient for both the Altair braking manoeuvre *and* departure on trans-stellar injection for home because we will be unable to utilise the ramscoop solely for the purposes of building up our stock of hydrogen. We have been in flight now for more than one month and the outlined proposal for return is still feasible."

"Then we are decided to return?" Odobo asked the audience.

"Why not ask the MI for its opinion on whether or not we should head back home?"

She looked at the commander and a frown gathered on her forehead.

"It won't, will it?"

He shook his head. "No chance. Our Intelligence is programmed to go to Altair. Anything which interferes with or is in direct conflict with the programme will be eliminated. It has demonstrated just how much it means this. If we attempt to return we shall all die."

"Very clever, Commander, but I believe that you may well be lying to us. I think I know you . . ." It was Allaedyce smiling almost coyly. He mounted the dais as Odobo stepped down for him. "Friends, let me inform you of a little interesting speculation which we have been discussing clandestinely. Time for it to come out into the open."

"Who was the mysterious old man who appeared on the screen of the disseminator and apparently knew our chief?"

Quite suddenly Tamura was cold. He clearly saw what he had to do and realised that for himself this was the only possible course of action.

"I did a little research into the background of our Commander from his statement that he recognised the face as that of someone whom he had killed. Commander Tamura, you were a member of the Hokke sect, the warrior monks. The day prior to your departure the head of your religious order, the man who had put you forward for shipcrew training at Yakutsk, disappeared. Vanished without a trace. I believe our Intelligence has found him. Using its powers of deduction it has concluded that this person was about to rescind his demand that you become a mission commander. You murdered him and disposed of him very neatly and very cleverly. You do not wish to return, understandably. You would be executed, Tamura."

"Allaedyce, you thieved, like me, for years," interrupted Tamura. "You proved your capability for survival under rigorous situations, like me. And like me, you too have your secrets. You wormed your way on to the crew. I killed many times to be where I am. With you it was bribery and blackmail. The charges laid against you in your file make it clear that should you go back you would be 'exposed' and executed. They probably have something against every one of us. If we return it will be shown that we obtained our positions as crew by illicit means at the expense of those who should have gone in our place—the ones who would not have failed, as we would have done, in their eyes."

"You see, they thought of everything even the ready made scapegoats. If we return to Earth we will be dead within days if not hours."

"I'm willing to take that chance, Tamura. I think that we all are. In fact I think that you are the only—"

"Ask it!" Tamura shouted. "Ask the MI what would happen."

So Allaedyce turned and keyed in.

The reply came immediately, as if the Intelligence had been preparing it for some time.

"There can be no doubt whatever that we must continue on our mission. It is not the case that the human crew members would be subject to criminal proceedings should they return or that I, your

Machine Intelligence, would be capable of deliberately, cold-bloodedly murdering every one of you should you adopt this decision."

"Then I think that we should regard the matter as settled. As there is a majority in favour of return I believe—"

"Idiot," the Commander snapped. "Don't you recognise a potential paradox when it is staring you in the face. The Intelligence believes that there can be *no doubt whatever* that we go on to Altair and then tells you that you can freely return to Earth. Has it not been made plain enough to you yet that under stress our MI is capable of what can only be described as paranoid schizophrenia? The duplicity of that . . . thing is more than well established."

"I say we vote," cried Allaedyce.

There was a general rumbling of assent.

"Vote until you turn blue, Allaedyce," Tamura said softly but clearly. "This ship goes to Altair and nothing alters that situation. Do you understand?"

"Grab him and hold him," Allaedyce commanded and a dozen hands were on the Japanese.

He smiled. This was so obviously planned. And planned so pathetically.

"So you are going to cast me in irons then?"

"Put you under sedation until we are within Sol space. I hoped that there would have been another way but—"

"But I leave you no choice?"

"Precisely. Take him through to the ship's hospital. I'll join you in a moment."

"This is a bit bloody drastic," said Ginny Laing as Tamura moved unresisting through the door hatch leading to the rest quarters. The door hummed briefly as it closed and its mag-seal locked in behind them. Startled, one of those restraining Tamura glanced at it.

"Who the hell put the seal on?"

"I did," Tamura replied.

They were quick but he moved too fast and he was falling as their limbs thrashed and entangled trying to grab him. Roll, kick, and kick and roll and on his feet. Another kick. The three unharmed ones jumped clear of him and one hit the distress button.

He turned and raced through the corridor separating the rest area compartments. Two of them were close behind and a third was putting the sealed hatch into emergency release. The Commander went through the next hatch to the showers. One figure began climbing through in pursuit and Tamura grabbed the collar and pulled back through the hatch smashing his head into his midriff. Tamura spun and then leaped back again through the hatch. The first one was trying to rise and retreat at the same time, but too late. Stiffened fingers to the solar plexus and Tamura heaved the gasping body through into the rest area. He closed the hatch.

Then began his two minute procedure of priming the mag-seal an operation which was supposed to take place only automatically and only in times when there had been a serious breach of the living areas. It had taken him almost an hour to figure out a safe method of bypassing the automatics but it worked.

Now for the service ring, he thought.

This ring was used mostly by boles servicing the living areas. It was concentric with the doughnut shape of the living areas themselves and protected by their shielding. It was choked with conduits, back-up systems and override equipment.

He crawled into the ring. It was roughly triangular in section and more closely packed than the innards of a miniature submarine. This was where he would do what was necessary. Fifteen minutes or so of awkward clambering took him to the spot where the bridge's power and com lines were exposed. They will be in there just now, he smirked as he thought, scanning the various sections of the ship trying to find where I have secreted myself. Button eye cameras will be showing Allaedyce all the probable hiding places. He will not find me in any of them so will seek the aid of the MI in his search. That will be when he runs into first big trouble. The MI will not help.

He nodded with satisfaction at the thought. He and the machine may have had little in common but both shared one crucial interest, an overpowering drive to reach Altair. With the machine it was a matter of programming, with Tamura a matter of conditioning. But the motivator, the prime mover, was the same.

It will not take Allaedyce long to realise where I must be, he thought. When he does there are only a couple of moves to make. Either he lets me starve it out in here, which would be the smart thing to do, or he acts hastily, which is in character.

Tamura heard a clang and a scrabbling sound, a spasmodic whirr. He smiled. Allaedyce had acted in character.

Musically mechanical, the noise approached much more rapidly than the Japanese had managed to move through the cramped maze. It was the sound of a bole on the go.

Tamura had realised what had to happen when his 'honeymoon' period as hero-leader was over, when the backlash would inevitably come. He had prepared for it.

While they slept after their exhausting hours' repair work on *Yūkoku*, Tamura was busy. Setting bypasses on the mag-seals of the hatch equipment, and here in the mess preparing for the inevitability of Allaedyce's or Odobo's revolt. Whole sections of ceramic circuitry lay exposed before him. Chalk and ink marks indicated his targets and the channels activating stand-by equipment. Other fail-safe procedures could also be fairly simply isolated.

The squat amicable looking bole appeared beside him and came abruptly to rest. It looked Tamura up and down and he could imagine his own image spread across the disseminator. Well, he thought, let them know exactly what is going on.

"Ladies and gentlemen of my crew, let me give you a demonstration of my new found power." He reached up and deftly snapped the bole's plasma torch out from its clasp on the side of the robot's body. There was a chalk cross with the numeral '1' beside it on one extended circuit panel. He activated the torch and brushed the needle point of the plasma jet against the heart of the cross.

"Has the screen blanked? Yes, I thought it may just do that. Now I will take out a few other selective circuits in here and perform a number of minor alterations. Nothing drastic, you understand, but effective enough to reduce your status from crew to passengers. I assure you that what I am doing can be reversed if one is acquainted with the proper sequence of operations. I intend to be the only one with that knowledge."

The bole began wavering and swinging its arms aimlessly. Tamura smiled. Some fool must be giving it orders to restrain or harm me, he thought. That someone had no comprehension of robot function and its delineated boundaries. The bole could only perform this command with a direct clearance through the MI. A clearance which, as Tamura guessed, it was not receiving.

It took eight minutes to doctor the circuits and long before that time was up he heard the grunting and cursing of someone crawling through the service ring towards him. As soon as he removed the capacity for manual direction of boles from the consoles the little mechanical monstrosity rotated its body around one eighty degrees and began moving back. That was the final operation. With it completed Tamura slowly started after the receding bole, the grunts and muttered oaths of his pursuer close at hand. When he reached the spot where the Jap worked on the circuitry he swore volubly, shouting what he was going to do once he had his hands on Tamura. Very strong imagination, thought the intended victim. If he was capable of half of those things he'd be a master transplant surgeon.

There were a number of possible exits all clearly marked on the plan diagram of the living area. The nearest in this direction was one leading to the rest area. It came out in the bulkhead of one of the cabins. That one was almost certainly open with Allaedyce or another there in waiting.

The bole stopped. Having reverted to a simple investigation and maintenance programme, it had to deal with some of the damage created by Tamura's hasty passage. He knew that there was no possibility of crawling round it. To ensure that this condition remained unchanged he re-ignited the torch and sliced through a couple of links in the bole's tread drive. It swivelled its head and looked at him, then down at the broken traction, then back at him. If boles could believe men mad . . .

He backed up a metre or so, linked his feet into a couple of semi-circular grips on the floor and, sitting down reached back and up to secure a good hold on some rigid piping. He pulled and a rectangular panel opened. He held it raised with his feet and lunged forward grabbing it with both hands and swinging it back round against the floor. The pursuer was almost within sight of him, still giving detailed descriptions how the Japanese's anatomy was about to be drastically rearranged. So Tamura slipped down into the service area extension quietly closing the access after him.

In the extension there were not even the tiny rudimentary bulbs used for lighting which were found in the main service ring. This was one of the few extensions which did not lead outside the living area shielding. It serviced the swimming pool and gymnasium hydraulic equipment. There was another access to that equipment—in the gymnasium. Back up systems have their uses. Even uses which were never intended for them.

How long it would be before the irate crewman in the service area realised what had happened and then discovered the access to the service extension was a matter of guesswork. Probably no more than ten minutes, possibly no less than two. The purr of the hydraulic maintenance activated by his presence gave Tamura a start. Some of the designers were too smart by far. Proximity activation was only intended for emergency services where equipment had to be in full operation the moment it was picked up for use. By switching on the plasma torch he could see it in clasps low along the sides of the shaft. Ideal for boles to scoop up. He reached over to a realseal spray used for spraying at small to largish bodies of water on the move. It encased them in a plastic bottle coating in under twenty seconds. The nozzle was throbbing and the pressure was building up inside the aerosol container. He switched it off and snapped back the nozzle cover. The next party to pass this way would activate it, only this time the nozzle would be open and spraying right into said party's face.

Five minutes later he dropped to the floor of the gym storage area. He did stretching and bends until most of the cramps were well out of his legs and back muscles. There was no inside handle or lock and the plasboard door was firmly closed. He pressed his ear to it. Not a sound, he thought. Risk it.

The door crashed out on the third kick.

The gym was deserted but had anyone outside heard the racket? He listened for fully a minute, crouched and ready to spring. No response. Which way was clear? Trial and error. Tamura merely hoped to break even. He made for the swimming pool. There were no lights on at all in the pool section. Odd. Generally they were on at this time every day.

He waited at the entry hatch, suspicious. The minutes passed. He was about to go in through the pool after all when he heard a distant cry and cascade of blasphemies. His friend with the unwholesome designs had run into the trap. It would take him a couple of frantic minutes tearing before he freed himself from that new plastic coat.

But someone else had also heard it. The pool door swung back and two females ran smartly for the rest areas assuming that the sound was due to Tamura appearing in that sector. They went through the far exit from the gym without seeing him crouched behind a stack of mattresses. They must have heard me kicking my way out of the store, he thought, and lain in wait for me to come into the pool area. He counted to fifty slowly, then stealthily moved up to the entrance of Allaedyce's cabin. It was empty. Smiling, he closed the door and slipped under the expanse of his sleeping unit where he had stashed a couple of blankets and a supply of food and liquids sufficient to last five days in comfort: but Allaedyce's command, so decisively handicapped, should last only a matter of hours. There was no need to leave a false trail through the pool area after all. He had suspected that the living areas would be under surveillance as long as the cameras could relay pictures to the screens. With the cameras out of order they would salt all the various areas with lookouts. But the guards in the rest areas must only be in the cabin with entry to the service ring.

Only one small thing still bothered Tamura.

One of the females running from the pool was carrying a bulky two metre tube with coils trailing to a backpack. That device was to be used only for major repairs and by boles.

It was a portable laser cannon.

"Tamura, this is Allaedyce."

The voice boomed through the ship on the speaker system.

"Tamura, this is your last chance, unless you restore the powers of command to the bridge we are all going to suit up and open the air locks on manual."

Another bluff, thought Tamura. Since the attack, ramscoop function had built up the supercores field to maximum strength. Open the airlock and they break their shielding from it. This time everyone would die. The Intelligence of course would tell Allaedyce so even without his asking. Tamura smiled. It was growing virtually psychic, unnerving the bushman. All the time it insisted that it could not take orders for flight operations other than through the recognised channel of command which was the bridge. It was of course happy to give disinterested advice on the ship situation but in the absence of both the recognised Commander and the said recognised channel it could do nothing but continue as closely as possible with the original flightpath.

The Jap chuckled.

"Tamura, this is our last warning to you."

He drew a blanket about him and settled down for some sleep.

"All right, Tamura, we concede defeat. I am waiting in the bridge with all the rest of the crew."

He was awake instantly. Allaedyce was lying but this was the important moment. This concession was the necessary point which had to be made before the final moves in the scheme could be effected. The corridor was empty. He went directly to the bridge entry, opened it and stepped through.

It closed behind him with the noise of mag-seal and he knew that they had indeed tried a double cross. The room held all the surviving crew. Allaedyce was at the command console. He swung round to talk with his victim. There was no smile of victory in his face and for a brief second Tamura thought that he meant it, that he was indeed defeated. But then he saw the lady with the portable cannon come into view, pointing it straight at the middle of his chest.

"This is a trap," Allaedyce sounded old. "I'm surprised that you fell for it, but here you are and that is the main thing. I know that you will not willingly divulge what the remedies are for our return to command through the bridge, so we have decided to encourage you. A little torture, the occasional drug inducement, and a spot of electro-hypnosis. By the way, that cannon is operational and I—"

Surprise comes from the unanticipated.

When a runt is outnumbered by a dozen to one, one expects him to be defensive. Especially while one sports a laser like a hunting rifle. That is why one may expect aggressive defence behaviour but not a straightforward attack.

Tamura about faced and jumped at the wall landing both feet squarely, executed a kick flip which brought him down hard in front of Allaedyce, and slashed the side of his left foot under his heart. He sagged. After the cannon. She was amazed at the acrobatics and stunned at the very idea that he would openly attack when so obviously in a hopeless situation. More acrobatics. Tamura bounce somersaulted, and as she swung the cumbersome object around he knocked it aside with a forearm blow and stabbed stiffened fingers sharply under her right ear. She collapsed.

The trance broke and the group about him scattered to form a wide ring, tense and waiting.

"There is good reason why I am Commander here," said Tamura. "I am the natural leader of this group. If I have to kill half of you to reinforce the fact then I most certainly will. We go to Altair!"

"You want to kill us all. You're insane, Tamura. We can do nothing now. We are helpless against the crystalloids. They will swat us like a damned fly the moment we enter their space." MacGillvery was almost screaming at him. It was he who had been behind Tamura in the service ring. The Japanese saw the livid marks on his skin where the realseal had been surgically removed.

"No I'm not insane, my Scots friend. It is insanity to return. The only roughly feasible plan for that would be to attempt holding the Earth to ransom with our battle lasers, demanding that the members of the Condominium responsible for our mission be executed and then to go right down through the various echelons of responsibility thoroughly weeding out all those with real knowledge and eliminating them."

"Perhaps that is preferable to certain death at Altair or 'absorption' by the Intelligence, whatever that is." This time it was Ginny Laing, puzzled and despondent.

He shook his head.

"No, any such attempt would be certain death. Remember that in developing the technology for the starships we also developed technology for a whole new set of weapons. We may carry the most powerful laser equipment ever constructed but Earth too has laser weapons, not so dangerous admittedly, but when the target is only a space vessel and not an entire planet the weapons don't have to be so powerful. Furthermore, they have the supercore missiles specially designed for taking out small fast moving targets. The moment we entered the solar system we would be under military surveillance. I doubt if we would even complete the statement of our ultimatum."

"You're bluffing," Allaedyce rasped, "you know that I can talk them round. You said yourself that I am a specialist in the great art of smooth talking."

"They know it too. The moment you begin your wheedling they will realise that something is wrong. You see I am the Commander of the ship and should be the one to do the negotiating."

"We can say that you are ill."

"These are stopgap measures and you know it. Eventually they would discover everything from the Intelligence."

"We could destroy it."

"You could?"

"Why not? We interfered with it once. Why not try again but this time do a really good job?"

"Impossible. First, to really interfere with the MI you would have to work on all the inaccessible blocks of crystalline ceramic using boles, but boles are primarily physical extensions of the MI itself and I'll be extremely surprised if the Intelligence will follow through and conveniently commit suicide. Secondly, you need the MI to carry through the operations for a return flight, ergo the destruction must take place when we are approaching Earth orbit. The MI will not go back to Earth. It is so programmed that such a course of action cannot be entertained and if you succeed in destroying it out here you have cut yourself off from any possibility of returning to Earth or reaching Altair or anything. Thirdly, I'd bet that the Machine is listening in right now to our every word and completing its own contingency plans just in case things in here do not run the way that it would care to have them. It would have no compunction about closing down our shielding completely if it decided that the situation containing the human element was critical. To remove the crisis it would remove the human element."

"Maybe it would not be able to bring itself to doing such a thing. The last time—"

"The last time was in the nature of a warning. The condition was serious but not critical because we still intended going on to Altair. You are confusing the motivations of our MI with human motivations. Conscience and compassion are functions which promote species survival in the human being, and as we are motivated for species survival we regard these as good. The Intelligence has no such motivation or such subtle governors for its behaviour. Its solitary purpose in existing is to achieve Altair space. I would not dare challenge the reason for existence of any Intelligence, especially not this one. They are too powerful."

"But Altair means death!"

"No, Altair means only the unknown."

They were refreshed but still bewildered when they next spoke with him. It was in the bridge. He felt that there, surrounded by the paraphernalia of command, their insecurity might be minimised. Confusion and fear were the dominant factors in their minds. They knew at last that there was no turning back, that that choice had never been open to them. They knew also that their lives were to end in agony if the flight continued on plan.

Tamura spoke quietly. "We can either die on the way to Altair or we can activate the emergency suspended animation and those of us who survive it *will* see that star, *will* complete the voyage, and perhaps die there. I say 'perhaps' because I am not so foolish as to believe that I can even guess what is going to happen when we arrive."

"Suppose our beloved idiot machine decides not to allow us to enter suspended animation?" asked Odobo.

"It would not be able to prevent us from entering. However, it may well render the equipment inoperable before we make the attempt. We must convince it."

"How?" asked Ginny. "We are only supposed to use it in the event of the MI showing evidence of cracking up and there isn't enough suspended animation support for a full crew anyway."

"No," he replied smiling. "You see their idea was that if the MI began to make wrong decisions which it could verify as being wrong itself, then most of the crew would go into suspended animation while a cover crew of a few selected members would take over decision-making for the remainder of the flight. Whoever thought this scheme up realised that if there was a serious malfunction quite early on in the flight it might still be possible to save the mission by putting most of the human crew in cold storage. That way they would not be subject to the infection's worst ravages until sometimes after they were revived and could take command of the ship, if need be, in Altair space. Of course the ones who had not gone into suspended animation would have died off. They would have seen the ship through most of the journey and that was all that mattered. Furthermore the MI would have had the chance to effect any repairs it could and integrate and assimilate the minds of the skeleton crew. We don't need a skeleton crew as our MI is operating reasonably. We can all go into suspended animation because the Intelligence has itself reduced our numbers. What do you say?"

"I like it," nodded MacGillvery, "but I don't see the MI letting us get away with it."

"If it refuses, I shall kill myself."

Then they understood. Without him the crew situation would fall apart. The Machine Intelligence would have more to cope with than merely an unruly commander. It would find itself trying to assimilate the minds of a crew growing ever more desperate in their attempts to ward off certain death. A dangerous situation.

It was evident to all by now that the crew for each ship had been chosen in such a way as to ensure that it was always unstable, unable to unify and pose any kind of threat to the MI. The leader had to be strong to keep the unruly elements from completely breaking apart and runining the human 'backup facility'. If this happened they might easily act completely irrationally, endangering the mission and necessitating their elimination by the MI before it could integrate or assimilate any of them satisfactorily. With Tamura dead they would probably have attempted to destroy the Intelligence itself. That would have proved disastrous all round.

MI—commander tamura
your statement does not correspond
with my current model of you
—o
—you are bluffing
—oo

"No," he laughed. "no, it is you who are the bluffer, idiot machine!"

From the breast pocket of his crewsuit he withdrew the plasma torch which he had taken from the bole in the service ring. He ignited it and adjusted the flame to a long slender tongue of bluewhite incandescence. The honourable method was to cut through the abdomen using both hands, but this was not the place for *seppuku*. Out here the preparation and the ritual would be for nothing as this death would be admission of defeat. No, the ritual would not convince himself that it was otherwise and would be merely a meaningless gesture to the others present.

No, he would bring the blade up between his eyes.

Strike deep into the skull penetrating and destroying a large section of the forebrain.

He sung quietly and clearly a few words in his native tongue.
Now!

HALT HALT HALT
MI—commander tamura
HALT HALT HALT
suspended animation procedures
initiated

```
—o
will be ready to receive
first subjects in
52 hours
—oo
```

"So, it follows our vocal conversations quite readily now," re-marked Ginny Laing. "We must be pretty nearly ready for the virus triggering. Must make it quite angry to come so close and then have to wait five years to complete the operation." She laughed.

Tamura sensed a feeling of relief growing amongst them.

"Remember that the suspended animation is liable to take its toll of our members," he pointed out. "There's the possibility of irre-versible mental and physical damage and the chance of death it-self."

They did not care. Even five years of unconsciousness was some degree of remission, if only partial, in the death sentence.

"A small celebration is in order," suggested Allaedyce, and the re-sponse was a great cheer.

Tamura double checked the inner seal of his adapted sleeping unit and went through the necessary manual operations inside which readied it for suspended animation.

The others were well into a state of drugged stupor which was the first stage of the process. He had ensured that they were safely under before asking the Intelligence one question which he had kept from them:
Tamura—MI: . . .

```
MI—commander tamura
there is no longer any requirement
for you to key-in questions
as I can anticipate them now
quite accurately
—o
—your supposition was correct
—o
—the crew were not selected on
the basis of creating an
```

intellectual elite
—they were chosen on the
basis of a rare condition of
the nervous system which is
responsible for magnified
nervous electrical impulses
—those with this condition are
invariably mentally handicapped
—o
—the intelligence level and personality
development of the crew result from
the artificial stimulation of drugs
without which they would be cretins
—oo

The injection into the base of the brain of the new born child, that would be it, he thought. And of course the drugs for intellect and personality stimulus would only become active in the presence of a nervous system with a morbidly high level of electrical activity. But their effects would not be permanent. Eventually they would show signs of deterioration. Eventually you, Tamura Kunio, would revert to the state of mental and emotional poverty which is naturally your own. And at what age is that to happen?

MI—commander tamura
reversal anticipated at
age 37 in males
age 38 in females
—o
degeneration will be
relatively swift
taking no more than
twelve hours in all
—oo

But long before that will happen you will be a dead man, Tamura, he thought, and shrugged. That is if you can call yourself a man. You are as artificial as the idiot machine you despise. The whole structure of your being is as artificial as the purring, clicking boles scurrying around on their programmed tasks. You are simply a refinement of the same attitudes and motivations which produced those mechanical dogs-bodies.

This was the final irony.

That ultimately man's great creation should be that which must itself ultimately not be human at all . . .

CHAPTER ELEVEN

A voice, yes for some time now MacGillvery had been hearing a sound, not listening—merely hearing, and that sound was a voice.

Amongst the jumble of words was a name.

The voice was speaking about Tamura.

No, that was wrong: it was speaking *to* Tamura.

Listen . . .

". . . forty point oh six two hours to base parking orbit, Commander Tamura. Selected orbital radius of three AU abandoned due to high incidence of debris in this region. Alternative base radius of four AU has now been provisionally agreed between *Yūkoku* and *Revenge* . . ."

Altair, MacGillvery, this is Altair!

He tried to waken fully but took on a fit of coughing, retching, and thrashing spasms in his limbs.

Calm! You must control! he commanded himself. Then his will turned relentlessly on the twitching body and gradually he felt the convulsions ebb. Remember what they told you about revival from suspended animation states? Stay relaxed. Try to sleep normal sleep as much as possible before coming fully out. The penalty could be the complete wreckage of your nervous system.

He lay there in a half dream, musing and imagining.

How long since you were sealed into this sleeping unit? Half an hour? It feels something of that order—certainly not any longer than forty-five minutes. And yet you have been in here over five years.

Three years ago the ship turned one eighty degrees and 'pancaked' the supercore's magnetic field, turning it in effect into one hundred million square kilometres of magnetic parachute for the ionised interstellar hydrogen to 'push' against while being drawn somewhat less efficiently into the fusion engine aligned to its braking position.

And out there just now . . .

Out there just now is Altair.

Again he fought back the flow of adrenalin. Again he settled for musing and day dreaming. Out there was that alien sun, bigger, heavier, brighter, hotter than Sol, in every way the peer of the sun of men. It blazed a torrent of searing radiations upon the *Yūkoku*. But he lay there in the soft cool black of the unit deigning to recognise its presence only with his imagination.

What of Earth? He frowned. Surely they would have survived that assault by the reinforcements from the crystalloid world. Now there would be a new generation which would be living without a threat of death from the stars, a new generation which would change things for the better. Perhaps, he mused, the Marshalls are hanged and men no longer live in fear and slavery . . .

Perhaps this very mission is musty history to them . . . Perhaps they have built the Faster-Than-Light starships which were being theorized at Durban before you left . . . FTL ships which would find the distance between Earth and the limits of the known universe no distance . . . spacetime ships . . .

Perhaps . . .

The voice again.

Tamura yawned and half-way through broke into a short laugh. Irony. Somehow the years in the s/a state must have exhausted him for he had just slept for what was probably a good eight hours—a period of time subjectively longer than the years spent in the s/a state itself. Now he was rested, relaxed. He could think clearly without utilising the zentrained will.

". . . several bands or rings. These contain individually much more material than is found in Sol's entire belt of asteroids. Many fragments are larger than Ceres, the largest of the asteroids. The most distant of these bands so far detected by *Yūkoku/Revenge* is at a distance of thirty-one AU giving a total of seven in all . . ."

He slipped his thumb into the recess of the sleeping unit's lid and pushed.

The light in his quarters was brighter than he remembered it to be, almost painful.

But he felt joyous, exhilarated. Ecstasy invoked gentility in Tamura. He felt nostalgic for one of Inagaki's baritone bawdy ballads. But Inagaki was dead, he thought. He should have lived to know this, the hour of waking in Altair space.

He stepped into the corridor and looked into some of the other crew cabins. Most of them were still coming out of s/a but there were a couple of empty units. Ginny Laing and Weismuller were up and about. Through in the assembly area the two females hailed him from beside the food dispenser.

"Hi, lord and master," laughed Ginny.

Tamura waved. Both of them were grinning widely. Reaching Altair had its beneficial effects, he thought. The faces were flushed with excitement and the laughter easy.

Tamura lifted out a tray from the steam-swirling dispenser. Breakfast was a large plateful of hot cereal and a couple of protein rusks. Besides these was a litre carton of enriched orange juice.

A table for three was set up.

The piped music was Tchaikovsky, *The Nutcracker Suite.*

The lighting was mood *spring afternoon:* pale blues and fresh greens with pastel shades of yellow and amber. There was even the scent of lily-of-the-valley very faint and a definite brisk air current which was almost balmy.

"I can't really come to terms with it." Weismuller shook her head. "So soon after closing the unit, here we are. Well, I mean, that's how it feels."

"Good morning, Commander, ladies," the voice was that of the Machine Intelligence. The women glanced at one another and at Tamura. "I trust you are suffering no ill effects from the period of suspended animation."

"It knows damned well we're not," snorted Weismuller. She took a mouthful of rusk. "Wonder what the others are like."

"The other crew members appear to be in good health," it said as if in response.

"Seems our Machine friend has grown smarter in the interim," observed Weismuller drily.

"Indeed I have, Miss Weismuller."

Ginny gasped and lowered her spoon.

"There is no need to be alarmed, Miss Laing," the Intelligence soothed. "I was well on the way to accomplishing this basic interface before you were put into the units. It was inevitable that I should perfect this ability."

"So you can read our minds?" Tamura asked.

"Hardly that. The models of your minds are now considerably more complete than they were when you went under."

"I imagine you also learned a great deal from observing the integration and assimilation of the *Revenge* crew," snapped Weismuller.

"A great deal of useful data did result from that process and it has been used to modify the simulated personality profiles of all the *Yūkoku* crew. This was not the morbid process you would appear to imagine it to be. Should you wish to communicate with any member of the *Revenge* crew you are free to do so. You will find that they most definitely do not regard themselves as being dead."

"But," she frowned and looked at Tamura, "but I thought that the disease was to prove almost certainly fatal."

"There is no doubt about that. Unless they received very urgent treatment, which I cannot imagine being forthcoming knowing the attitudes behind this mission, they had to die."

"The flesh may perish, commander. The minds remain."

"The models remain, the 'personality simulations' stored in the Intelligence. It is the Intelligence which has the true existence, the true 'mind'." Then he sighed realising that it was pointless to lose one's temper with a Machine.

"This conversation is a waste of time. What information have you to give us regarding our arrival in Altair space?" So saying he returned to breakfast.

"We are now three point eight five AU from Altair and moving towards a new base parking orbit at four AU. The previously selected orbit of three AU was abandoned on conference with *Revenge*. There is a belt of rocky debris in this area dense enough to make any manoeuvre hazardous. Three other such bands lie between us and Altair, another four have been detected lying further out in the system.

"There are four planets. The first has the following characteristics. Zero point nine two AU from Altair. Equatorial radius four six four one kilometres. Polar radius—"

"We can take the heavy detail later. Just a quick sketch," the commander mumbled through a mouthful of cereal.

"Very well." Had it been capable of sighing it would almost certainly have done so. "First planet slightly larger but less dense than Earth and closer to Altair than Earth is to the sun. It has a thick carbon dioxide atmosphere similar to that of Venus before terraforming began. It has one small moon.

"The next planet lies just over five times the distance from Altair that Earth does from the sun. It is Earthlike. Its atmosphere is a nitrogen oxygen mixture with high water vapour content. Three linked landmasses are spread across the northern hemisphere. The rest of the world is submerged in ocean. The icecaps are extensive. This world is slightly less dense than Earth and almost one fifth larger. It has twelve moons.

"At just over seventeen times the distance of Earth from the sun we come to a gas giant better than twice the size of Jupiter. It has an atmosphere of hydrogen and hydrogen compound gases, predominantly methane and ammonia. Like Jupiter there is a considerable amount of radio noise generated from this body. Its magnetosphere seems in a number of ways to be connected with the extensive reach of the hydrogen atmosphere which may account for the numerous and readily visible electrical discharges taking place almost continually high above the upper cloud belts of the easily observable atmosphere. The density is just more than one fifth that of Earth. *Revenge* concurs that this is the crystalloid homeworld.

"The final planetary inhabitant of the system is a snowball giant at sixty seven times Earth–sun distance. Insufficient data exists to give a fair description of this world."

"What about moons for the gas giant?" Tamura asked.

"Fifty three identified so far. The outer eighteen have retrograde motion but the peculiarities are further in. Two moons are in definite stationary orbit. Another five are in orbits which take them around the planet in less time than the world itself takes to revolve upon its axis. Furthermore these orbits are almost circular. It has been possible to define objects as small as three kilometres across. Most of the other moons have this dimension or larger but neither of the synchronous satellites nor the inner ones are large enough for a standard definition to be achieved."

"I suppose," Ginny asked, "that a suitable plan of assault has been cooked up while we were occupied with Morpheus. Am I correct?"

"Indeed you are, Miss Laing. We are no longer in sufficient numbers to generate the plasma shield within the heart of the star, the shield which would have fatally disrupted the radiation-gravitation balance. It has been decided to adopt a mode of offense which involves the culprit world directly and deal effectively with it."

There was an abrupt souring within the Japanese, a feeling of having been cheated, sold short. They always told you that you would go to Altair and burst the great fire, Tamura, he thought. They told you about it incessantly as a child. How you would go there victorious and standing upon the shores and wooded hillsides of Earth they would look up into the night sky to see you put out the eye of the Eagle. And all the stars would see and they would all know that the evil was gone, consumed in inferno . . .

"Ah, you are disappointed, Commander. So are the crew members aboard *Revenge* but there is no practical alternative. The mission brief is to remove the crystalloid menace from Altair space by whatever means possible." The voice seemed genuinely consoling.

"How are we to do that," queried Weismuller. "At seventeen AU we won't be able to maintain the battle lasers with solar power. We can hit them for a couple of hours but they'll have snuffed us out long before even the batteries start to feel the drain."

"We will not be using the battle lasers for other than antiprojectile defence. Once we come within range of the gas giant's magnetosphere we shall activate the supercores of both ships in tandem. Thirty minutes should see severe magnetic storms, one hour should have set up sufficient stress within the planet's magnetic structures, liquid or solid, to cause widespread tectonic upheaval. By the time two hours have passed temperature and pressure disruption within the gas mantle will be initiating the process of planetary disintegration. This will take another twenty hours to complete. It is estimated that electromagnetic activity and atmospheric shockwaves will wipe out any crystalloid activity within one hour of the operation's commencement."

"I don't believe it!" exclaimed Weismuller. "Rip apart a monster planet about three thousand times as voluminous as Earth in less than a day! It's mad!"

"On the contrary," the voice came from behind. Standing in the hatchway was Allaedyce. "All we need work on is the optimum shaping of the field to take advantage of the planet's own magnetosphere. The MI is right. There is only one drawback. See it, Commander?"

"Naturally," Tamura replied quietly. "We will be operating within a field of doubled strength and even the most perfect shielding devised by man or machine could never protect us from that. We can destroy the crystalloids. I agree.

"However in so doing we destroy ourselves."

CHAPTER TWELVE

There proved to be no suspended animation casualties. Tamura was satisfied; a death might have meant a very serious blow to the high morale, which somehow he had to sustain.

"Before we go into attack we will signal to Earth that we have achieved Altair space and pulse back all the information which we have gleaned concerning the Altair system. We will be spending the next few weeks assembling this information, collating it, and preparing it for pulse. During this period there will be a time of infection while the MI sets about the process of integration. I cannot say how effective our hospital will be at minimising the symptoms of the virus but you must not expect to be cured. There is no way that this can be done and even if it could I firmly believe that the MI would actively prevent any attempt to do so."

None of them looked at him. They were all listening but their eyes were fixed upon the disseminator display showing a modified telephoto relay of Altair completely filling one side of the great screen. The other side was sectioned off into a number of panels each illustrating a different aspect of the star. It was an obviously oblate globe, white but faintly tinged with violet and with faint but distinct bands upon its surface. Under magnification the latter proved to be rings of sunspots—curiously small sunspots—two bands to each hemisphere. Likewise the tongues of incandescent plasma jetting from the surface were much smaller than those of Sol and found only immediately in the equatorial region or the polar areas. The corona appeared much longer and thinner in shape

than that of the sun and to have a curious ghost corona or aura surrounding it. This double corona was one of the effects that they
were told to expect.

"I have been in communication with *Revenge*, and talked with a
number of the crew—in simulation," began Tamura. "The reply had
a visual component which I assume was a computer mock up of the
commander's face and the *Revenge* bridge. It was a completely
convincing display. I have assurances from our own MI, the *Revenge* MI, and the simulated crew of that ship that there will be no
attempt upon the gas giant which we have named Altair III until
such time as this crew has been integrated successfully."

They murmured a mixture of thanks, relief, and anxiety in the
reply.

A view of all four planets and a section of one of the asteroid
belts replaced Altair on the disseminator. Tamura was fascinated in
spite of himself.

Altair III looked like a shimmering version of Jupiter. Ghostly
lights rippled in veils and waves about it—the effect of the magnetosphere upon the high hydrogen envelope. The bulk of the
planet itself did not really resemble Jupiter. True there was a good
deal of banding in the clouds but there was a great colony of
splotches spreading more than half-way across the northern hemisphere, and the southern one had half a dozen smaller but similar
colonies looking like masses of Red Spots but yellowish in colour.
Individual blemishes were common particularly in the equatorial
region which appeared to be their genesis area. The clouds were
livid in hue, lightening a shade towards the poles where the
brightest of the electromagnetic displays took place.

"Sir, a request from Commander Holst on *Revenge* for a list of
active *Yūkoku* crew," said Weismuller.

"Tell him."

She frowned. On her console there was a lighted screen displaying the face of Holst, the face of a busy man talking to someone out
of camera range, the face of a healthy man seated at the bridge of
his ship. Yet she knew that he was there only in simulation. It troubled her to talk to someone whom she felt was virtually a ghost.

"Your problem is philosophical, my dear," Tamura assured her.
"All sensory perception is electrochemical simulation of the brain.

All simulation from 'live' holovision coverage to the cave paintings of our ancient ancestors are as real as you allow them to be."

Faintly he heard the voice of Holst agreeing from her console.

She shrugged and began relaying information on the remaining thirteen active crew, five men, eight women.

"Commander, I've been wondering about *Revenge*," said Mac-Gillvery. "You told us that there was no possibility of this ship returning to Earth because of the damage we suffered during the encounter with the crystalloid fleet. Is *Revenge* in a similar situation? If not what are the chances of our simulations returning to Earth aboard their ship?"

"Go ahead and ask."

But before he so much as put his fingers to the keyboard the answer was on the disseminator.

MI—crewman macgillvery
revenge capable of effecting
trans-stellar injection
for earth/sol
—o
capability exists for
transference of crew
simulate programmes upon
completion of present
mission
—oo

The sight and convincing nature of the Holst simulation seemed to have made the integration/assimilation process rather more palatable. Fortunately they did not seem to understand that the 'transference' mentioned would be simply a transference of data from one MI to its sister machine. *Yūkoku* MI would retain the originals of those programmes and should the assault on Altair III prove successful the ship complete with its MI and simulate crew would orbit that ruptured world until all on-board power failed. That would be centuries by human reckoning. Meanwhile the *Revenge* and their other selves would be earthward bound. But for those here aboard *Yūkoku*, Altair had captured them, and their captivity was complete.

ALTAIR PLANETARY DATA

NO	ORBITAL RADIUS	PLANETARY RADIUS	SP DENSITY	AXIAL ROTATION
I	0.92 AU	6541.0000 km	05.30	06.61 hrs
II	5.13 AU	6860.0000 km	05.45	35.77 hrs
III	17.4 AU	143,600.0 km	01.36	15.45 hrs
IV	67.2 AU	20,000.00 km	04.00	————

The display was semipermanent on the disseminator and was always to be found on one of the multitude of screens at every console.

Tamura stepped through the hatchway into the assembly area.

MacGillvery was furiously attempting to interest Weismuller in the prospects of sharing his cabin. She was teasing him on to ever greater efforts but she would eventually agree. The approach of doom in any sense was having its effects upon the hormone balance of everyone present.

"A shebeen that's what it sounded like, my lovely," MacGillvery was saying.

"Doubtless it does," she replied in the manner of mother to child, "but how many of us are acquainted with—what was it—a shebeen?"

"An illicit place of alcohol consumption. A shebeen is nothing like an ale house. In fact any relationship or similarity between one and a respectable dispensary of liquors must be regarded as purely coincidental." He waxed strong, slightly drunk himself.

Allaedyce sat at an adjacent table sneering. He was less contented than ever, more critical and offensive during the two days since wakening than at any previous time. He was beginning to see his urge to gain power as futile in the face of a powerful and unknown fate.

"Doubtless you have considerable experience of such sordid places yourself, MacGillvery," he smiled acidly. "Perhaps you are unaware of it but the majority of people are not amused by the disgusting debauched antics which I can see you are about to trail out as an excuse for anecdotal entertainment. Kindly spare a thought for the gentle nature of female innocence so perfectly embodied in the delicate ladies in our honoured presence."

The word 'honoured' was thrown in for Tamura's benefit.

"Allaedyce, with your mouth you would have made a great politician," said MacGillvery quietly. "Perhaps the Marshalls were so jealous of your potential that they stuck you aboard *Yūkoku*. Just to keep themselves safe you understand. Come to think of it that might also explain not only why you're so good with your mouth but also why you are so useless at anything else."

The bushman smiled back—sweetly.

"What sounds like a shebeen, MacGillvery?" Tamura asked.

"Uh, oh didn't see you come in there, Kunio," he beamed. "Oh Winnie the Pooh here, and I, have been monitoring that weird sound which we originally heard in the crystalloid fleet. We also have it in the radio noise from Altair III."

"It is the noise Weismuller heard in the machine dream," said Allaedyce. "I said it before but I don't really expect anyone to take notice of a runt like me."

"Yes," she cried. "That's where I heard it before! That night I mentioned what was going on in the MI's emotion simulation areas when they looked disturbed on the monitor. That's right! It was weird. I thought I was drunk at the time."

"It reminded me of the winds blowing through the Martian Equatorial Rift valleys at sunset," added Tamura.

"The answer is simple," said MacGillvery softly, frowning, and all eyes turned to him. "The crystalloids are serving sandspore liquor in orbiting illicit drinking establishments."

Everyone but Allaedyce chuckled.

"May I interrupt?" It was the silky unwelcome voice of the Intelligence. "You may be correct in the orbiting part at least, crewman MacGillvery. I have isolated the noise sources; there are two of them, both positively identified as the synchronous satellites of Altair three. Although the noise has been identified as being associated with the crystalloid radio profile it is not a constituent part of it. There is no record of any similar noise being associated with the original crystalloid strikes on Earth. In the case of the satellite sources there is no trace of crystalloid radio noise, only this highly distinct 'shebeen' trace can be detected. This would indicate that whatever causes it is separate from the crystalloid phenomenon although linked with it."

MI—reports
no trace of infection
allaedyce laing
—o
infection positive
indication present in
all other crew members
—oo

"That explains your head cold, Commander," smiled Ginny.

There was a slight sensation of lightheadedness amongst those who had so far contracted the infection but nothing really unpleasant. There was the occasional twitching, and the very rare jerking of a limb, minor jactation. Thankfully there had been a pleasant unexpected side effect—a feeling of mild euphoria. The latter was not unknown in people suffering from neuropathological conditions. Tamura hoped that in his case it might last through the more unpleasant developments which were inevitable.

"Commander, I have something which I would like you to take a look into," said MacGillvery entering the bridge. "I've taken a dozen recordings of the 'shebeen' and I think that there are some distinctive patterns within them. I'm pretty sure that some further analysis should show certainly that these are the manifestations of an intelligence."

There were a few smiles at his excited outburst and gothic phraseology.

"Shall we all listen?" Tamura asked the assembled crew and they nodded agreement, laughing.

MacGillvery depressed some keys on his console and the sounds came through once again: exact recordings of the cacophony heard during the fleet attack. Again Tamura felt the thrill experienced so long ago over Tharsis but recognising now, with the opportunity to examine it in more dispassionate circumstances, that this was in fact different as had Odobo suggested. What did not change was the feeling that one was in the presence of something unearthly, something beyond the human grasp of the universe.

For minutes they watched enthralled as the MI displayed the visual representation of the signal on the disseminator. The Intelligence then selected a number of recurring patterns within the sig-

nal and separated them, to display them as individual components
with their interrelationships expressed mathematically.

The logical sequences became immeasureably clearer.

"It could be language," suggested Odobo.

"Unfortunately it could be anything," Tamura pointed out, "but
it would certainly appear to be what one might expect to be associated with a complex lifeform."

Ginny frowned. "If they are reminiscent of anything they look
roughly like the readings on an EEG."

"It's nice to think that we could be in direct contact with the
brain of an extraterrestrial," muttered Odobo, "and the bottom set
of wavetrains are quite similar to human theta waves, but you cannot 'read' a mind from the EEG."

From behind came a snarl of unconcealed disgust. It was
Allaedyce standing in the hatchway looking twice as supercilious as
ever. Tamura could feel the morale temperature falling as they
turned to him. "Speculation," he sneered. "Pure speculation. They
are pretty, and obviously meaningful if one knew how to interpret
them. But I do not believe that there is a Rosetta Stone lying handy
at the moment so we might just as well regard them as being completely meaningless."

"That much is obvious to us all," Tamura replied chillingly. "And
certainly we are speculating. The only way we are going to achieve
anything is by the exercising of our own brains."

He hooted scornfully.

"Well, make the most of them while you still have them. How
long will it be before the Machine has managed to destroy the central nervous system of everyone aboard this ship. Why don't you
ask your Mechanical Idiot that?"

MI—reports
crew infection status not
according to plan
—o
incidence of rising proportion
of erythrocytes in bloodstream
of all crew members
except allaedyce
—o

this indicates the presence
of germanium in the form of
germanium oxide in all
bloodstreams except that of
allaedyce
—repeat
with the exception of allaedyce
—o
detailed analysis of allaedyce
bloodstream in progress
—o
preliminary findings indicate
allaedyce immune to infecting agent
—oo

Within seconds Allaedyce was almost helpless with laughter. No
one looked at him. He stumbled back into the assembly area obviously bent on a celebratory drink. He shouted something about
'reprieve' and the 'electric chair' and began singing.

"That bastard," hissed MacGillvery.

Ginny was direct. "What are we going to do?" she asked. "Do we
want to die while he strolls around the ship like a king. He might
even find a way of returning to Earth on the *Revenge*. Imagine that
crud returning to a hero's welcome."

"I doubt if there is a very good chance of any of us living
through the double strength magnetic field even if the crystalloids
don't manage to shoot us out of the proverbial sky," snorted Mac-
Gillvery.

"Right," she snapped. "It's just the damned principle of the thing.
It rankles with me. It really does. What about the Machine, what
does it say then?"

MI—crewwoman laing
projection simulations indicate
no problems likely to result
from allaedyce condition of
noninfection
—oo

"Any suggestions?" Tamura asked. His appeal for counsel took them quite by surprise. After a few seconds MacGillvery cleared his throat and spoke.

"There is something fundamentally wrong with the man's mind but I don't believe that he is insane. I think that back on Earth he was conditioned to act the way which he does now."

"A rather peculiar course of action for the authorities, I would have thought," ventured Odobo.

"Not the way I see it," replied the Scot. "Not considering what we now know I think that there had to be a deliberately cantankerous bastard somewhere on the mission. The kind of character who sends everybody else screaming up the walls. People like that are part of the living set-up, the Great Human Condition and the whole point of having human beings on this mission was so that the MI could study just that."

"Then he has certainly outlived his usefulness," remarked Weismuller.

"Right," nodded Ginny. "Since he is immune the MI cannot use him as a part of the integration assimilation scenario."

"We can't just summarily execute a man on the grounds that he has a bad temper," objected Odobo.

"I could," said MacGillvery, "I could gladly."

"Well I don't know about the rest of you," Tamura said yawning, "but I've had one heavy day and I don't want to think about anything any more, Allaedyce in particular. All I want is a good night's rest!"

"Hear hear," agreed Ginny. "Let's all hit the sack."

She took her place by Tamura's side as the group rose and moved chatting out of the bridge and through the assembly area leaving the visual representations of the shebeen signals still pulsating upon the disseminator.

After a short stop in the assembly area for some light supper she joined him in his quarters.

Allaedyce . . .

　Allaedyce . . .

　　Allaedyce . . . in all the years over which man evolved from the protohuman to homo sapien your kind never moved from here while others spread themselves outwards across Asia and up into

Europe and far across the landbridge into the Americas. Your ancestors have known this land in and around the Kalahari for over
twenty million years.

The sun is low and swollen by the trembling heat, fat and red.
You walk slowly, cautiously, a bird-like figure of a child moving
where the sparse forest of mogongo trees thins away to true desert.
Where is your mother? She was the one who brought you here.
Where is your little friend Nxou who came with you both to gather
nuts from the trees? Have they returned to the camp without you?
Are they even now preparing the nuts which have been collected
for roasting?

As you walk, the two hammerstones dangling from your waist
beat against your lean hard thigh. You restlessly pass your digging
stick from one hand to the other as you step delicately through the
brush, your eyes sweeping the shadows. There is only the light
smell of the trees. Only the almost silent clicking rustle of the air in
the bush.

But you know that there is something nearby and it too knows of
your presence and is angered by it. Something ready to pursue.
Where is your mother? Where is Nxou? Why were you brought
here? There is a movement behind you. An animal? Yes, yes a large
antelope of some kind. Move forward quickly away and quiet.
There is a snort, almost a human snort, and you see through the
shadows and twisted trees—the figure.

It is dark and stocky.

The sun is rising quickly spreading its heat against your face and
your chest. Move towards it, now faster than before, now not caring
about the noise. Now you can feel your heart rippling panic in your
breast.

Where is your mother? Where is Nxou? Anyone?

You run but you are running into the desert. The trees are thinning out, grass giving way to coarse tufts on stony ground. Your
sole hope of shelter is the occasional bush. Now it is quite clear,
moving after you steadily. A giant eland but not all eland because
it is a man too—and do not the tales say that the very first man was
an eland. It is black, truly black like a silhouette and silent. All absorbing it consumes light and sound and thought, feeding on the
power of the living and the dead alike.

You run faster still.

You taste blood in your mouth and it is your own blood for you have bitten through your tongue and the shrieking in your ears is your own shrieking. And then you see them and you run staggering to half-grey strangers distributed in a wide circle through the trees. They look on pitiless, interested but uninvolved. Waiting.

A cry peals from your lips. An entreaty for compassion. Their cold eyes merely rest upon yours. The eland-man is closer. Turn throwing the sharpened digging stick at it. It disappears into the thing with a soft wet sound but the creature comes on without breaking its stride, the great shadow.

Freeing the hammerstones you throw one at it and then the other and again the soft plop as each strikes it and disappears. There is only one thing to do. Stop running and face it. It too stops. For a few seconds you look at one another but it has no face. There is only blackness. It reaches out its arms and they appear to spread out and widen like great dark wings.

With a wordless scream you hurl yourself forward—

Into it . . .

Allaedyce awoke.

He was agonisingly conscious, pulling himself out of the sleeping unit, still feeling the panic. A titanic throbbing ache rent his head. Lurching through his cabin he reached the door, picked up a robe, threw it across his shoulders and drew it round him. Oh, it was cold, so extremely cold.

He opened the door and stepped out into the corridor, empty but for a bole on maintenance duties. What I need is a swim to clear my head and clean my body, he thought, and began moving towards the pool area.

He was tingling. He felt this bizarre sensation quiver the length of his frame. Strange, he thought, are the lights in the corridor dimming and brightening slowly? He tripped by the hatch and crashed to the floor cutting his forearm slightly and grazing a knee. The tingling grew more intense. It far outranked the minor abrasions in sheer discomfort. There was a clatter.

He looked over his shoulder in time to see a number of bolts spring from out of the maintenance bole and throw themselves at the ceiling. He lurched back aghast. No, this is a dream, he thought, another dream like that one about the childhood I never experienced, the desert which I never saw.

One of the ruined caterpillar tracks from the disintegrating robot leapt into the air and snapped back and forth like a mad snake, finally crashing into the wall beside him and falling dead at his feet.

Everything was moving, swarming into the air like insects shooting about at crazy angles, sweeping in wide parabolas. There were sparks, flashes and loud bangings as the bole exploded. Allaedyce started to run down the corridor but his lungs were painful. The air was so cold, so inhumanely cold, and the tingling was at once like fire and ice.

Suddenly it lifted him.

He was hauled, hauled, hauled up from the floor and rolled brutally in the mid-air with the components of the ruined bole. His arms were lashing like whips, his back arching and bending, his legs thrashed and his head was wrenched and twisted about on his neck. It was like being in the grips of a frenzied crowd pulling maniacally in a dozen different directions. His very organs were straining and heaving within the framework of the body. He tried to scream.

It erupted as a choking gurgle.

The lights burst brighter, brighter and ever brighter until it was as if some sun was pouring its heart into his eyes.

The universe swung back twisting into itself in a great curve.

And vanished.

CHAPTER THIRTEEN

"Kunio, wake up! For God's sake wake up!"

The Japanese hauled himself from the swamp of unconsciousness to see Ginny frowning worriedly at him. He raised himself on one elbow, and crushed the sleep out of his eyes with a fist.

"Oh, be calm, Ginny. Relate the details of today's crisis but with a little less freneticism please."

"Something's happened to Allaedyce."

Allaedyce . . . the memory gushed back upon Tamura: the dream of being Allaedyce, of being in the desert, of waking and seeing the maintenance bole come apart in the corridor, and being lifted—

"Where is he?" He stepped urgently from the sleeping unit and pulled on a kimono.

"He's in surgery right now."

"Suicide attempt?" Tamura asked stepping into the corridor—and he stopped. The wreckage of the bole was scattered along the walkway, parts of it embedded in walls and flooring. Smudges from the graphite lubrication leads added further decoration to the chaos as did the browned streaks of dry blood.

"Your guess is as good as anybody's," she answered guardedly. "MacGillvery woke first and found him lying over there amongst the wreckage of the bole. He was alive—just alive."

"High survival potential that little bastard," Tamura grunted, breaking into a trot and heading for the operating theatre.

Odobo and MacGillvery were working on him. He floated under

batteries of lamps, the left hand side of his body bristling with needles. His chest lay open and the Scot was replacing large sections of tissue within the heart-lung system. Odobo was working on the disemboweled intestines, repacking them with an infrasonic hammer, the entire functions of the autonomic nervous system having been taken over by Machine control. A couple of boles were carefully altering the pressure of cerebro-spinal fluid by tapping the base of the spine before work began on the damaged sections of his brain. Another bole was acting nurse while yet another prepared to enrich the oxygen and glucose content of the cerebral bloodstream.

Weismuller was looking on, ready to take over the moment either of the two showed evidence of fatigue.

"Marvellous," she growled. "Marvellous just how hard we try to keep the obnoxious little leech alive when we would all far prefer him going through the recycling plant than through surgery. Still there's always hope I suppose."

"How did it happen?" Tamura asked.

She hesitated.

"Well," he began. "I know this will sound peculiar but I had a dream—" He stopped short at the reaction, at the sharp intake of air from the others present.

"The desert?" suggested Ginny.

"The strange black beast pursuing Allaedyce," he continued. "And later in the corridor the bole showering him with its parts."

They all nodded.

By this point they had reached a stage where they could accept that which would normally have been unacceptable. They were prepared to agree that they had shared a common nightmare about Allaedyce simply because the world which they had been conditioned to believe as being the true one had been destroyed. The series of revelations which had led them to an understanding of the real mission purpose for them, and consequently to a better appreciation of themselves, had broadened the basis for possibility in their minds. Conceptions once to be regarded with scorn could now take on the respectable garb of plausibility.

"But . . . how come?" Weismuller finally broke the silence.

"What does the MI say?" shouted MacGillvery.

"Nothing, it claimed total ignorance of the whole affair," she replied.

"Nonsense," said Tamura, "it runs simulations on us every second.

As far as it is concerned the ship is the ultimate in controlled situations for coming to terms with the human mind."

She shrugged. "You try asking it."

He stepped over to the surgery keyboard and just as he was about to key-in his question the answer flowed silkily out of the recessed speakers in the walls.

"I'm sorry, Commander, but I have no data whatever on crewman Allaedyce's condition and my checking procedures reveal no possible solution to your problem. There is an interesting point though. The onset of the crewman's trouble was coincident with several other distress conditions within *Yūkoku*, four in particular: a beta value jump of point one four, a rise in electron temperature by ten K, an increase in the crystalline complexity index of all the supercore's intermetallic discs, and partial degeneration of all cryo subsystems. Frankly, I'm puzzled."

"That's news," whistled Ginny. "Whatever hit the bushbaby took one swing at the whole damned ship as well."

"You know," said Weismuller, "I wouldn't be surprised if this whole thing was another of the bloody Condominium's friendly surprises!"

MacGillvery signalled for Weismuller to take over for him and the latter moved into the clean room to prepare.

"He'll pull through," sighed the Scot.

"Thankfully yes," Tamura replied, and MacGillvery gave him a hard glance. "Distasteful though it may be we need every possible member of our complement now—even him."

"I wonder."

"Enough, I would speak with *Revenge*."

The two starships lay less than a dozen kilometres apart, like a pair of exotic insects hurtling quiescent through a hell of infinite void, black-burning and silent. From the star, the great seminal cauldron of Altair, energy torrents poured across the vacuum, the planets, the asteroid rubble, and thence into the cosmic night beyond. They mingled with the mild magnetic halos of the twin spacecraft interacting with every tremble of energy, every change of hull temperature, every communication . . .

"Hullo, Kunio," the grinning face of Holst peered out of the screen. "How's the red blood cell count?"

"Troublesome." Tamura leaned forward in the cot-seat of the command console. "You know that Allaedyce is immune?"

"Christ! Now, that's tricky. There were no provisions made for that contingency. We were all supposed to be selected on the basis of our susceptibility to the infection. I, er, gather you've realised that by now?"

"Yes," Tamura snapped bitterly, "but we have another problem and I want to know whether or not it is simply a cute trick from our friends the Marshals." He went on to explain the happenings of the past hour. When he had finished Holst seemed to freeze for a few seconds—like a still frame held in the viewing of a movie. Then he came back to life, frowning.

"I suppose in a way you're right, Kunio," he replied, "but this wasn't lined up as a nasty surprise. You see Rüllkotter didn't give all the MI's identical programming. He had his own theories about the degree of human mental activity which is apparently coherent and inexplicable. He thought that it might in fact be serving a useful purpose, namely extrasensory perception—esp function. He had some involved theories on the subject."

"Oh no," Tamura muttered.

"He set aside a sizeable area within each programme to deal with specialised hardware particularly developed to simulate this possible human capability. The equipment and subprogrammes differed slightly from ship to ship but the basic concept was much the same in all cases. He didn't believe that this was a very important part of human behaviour, but he was one hell of a stickler for detail. If the esp or psi or whatever you want to call it did exist, he wanted it catered for."

"I take it then that the equipment aboard this ship is particularly effective?"

"Well," Holst cleared his throat, "it would appear to be something like that. In the case of the Yūkoku equipment and programme were linked with the hardware and software of the emotional simulation facility in a feedback configuration—"

"That damned electronic thalamus!" Tamura cut in.

"Yes, well anyway, maybe the autoregulator was not quite as stringent as it might have been in your case."

"Brilliant understatement, Mr. Holst."

"Another possibility has just occurred to me. Some of my crew complained of weird dreams just before the inflight confrontation with the crystalloids. That may have been brought about by the approach of the shebeen/crystalloid fleet. In fact, when you compare esp simulation activity with the shebeen radio profile there are some striking rhythmic similarities: the activity begins taking on aspects of the profile in the form of wave patterns. The dreams grew more disturbing right up to the exhange of fire. After that they disappeared and, being integrated, it would not affect us now. But what if the shebeen signal is influencing *your* MI?"

"We left that damned profile running on the disseminator when we went off to sleep!"

"Well, what do you think?"

"Oh . . . I don't know what to think."

Holst went into 'still' again.

"Something else has just come up. Don't alarm yourself but your MI had a blackout between 0406 and 0409 this timedate."

"A blackout! Explain what you mean by that!"

"There was a loss of communication within that period. This would seem to coincide with the Allaedyce incident and the loss of systems integrity aboard *Yūkoku*."

"This is incredible."

"Well—"

Tamura broke the connection abruptly and was immediately aware that he had been joined by all the crew except those immediately involved in surgery.

"That recording of the shebeen profile," began Odobo, but the MI had the answer on the disseminator before she had even completed the question.

MI—reports
no memory of profile switchoff
although registered as deactivated
0409 at termination of blackout
—0
evidence of activity within
esp facility from
commencement shebeen profile
display
deactivated at end of blackout
—00

"Oh, this looks bad," moaned MacGillvery.

"I agree," Tamura said nodding. "Let's see what it has on record about our own neurophysiological functions around this infamous time."

MI—reports
increase hypothalamus activities
and onset of consequent
physiological conditions consistent
with state of anger/rage
—o
eeg indicated intense
theta wave patterns 4.4 pulses per second
—said patterns corresponding
with shebeen profile
then on display
for 82 seconds prior to blackout
—above wavepattern and all
physiochemical indicators of
anger/rage state terminated with
return from blackout condition
—onset of all crew
rapid eye movement activity
and alpha wave patterns
14.7 pulses per second at
51 seconds prior to onset
of blackout condition
and absent at cessation
of blackout condition
—o
detailed breakdown
follows . . .

"In short," said MacGillvery, "we left the shebeen profile running, went to sleep, and the esp simulation facility fell back into step with the profile, so did our brain 'waves'—making us angry as buggery and inducing the common nightmare. Then blackout."

"Any ideas?" Tamura asked.

"This is the start of a haunting," said MacGillvery. They turned to him expecting a wide grin, but the big Scot was morose, completely serious.

"So this is what the human race has come to, the godlings, the half-angels, huh—here we are light years from home choking on the bloody unknown. We were to have done great things—'made a feast for the gods' as the poet said." Ginny spoke quite quietly in the half dark of Tamura's quarters. "I feel like getting dead drunk." She rested her warm slightly moist body against his atop a mattress on the cool vinyl flooring. Then she sat up again, her flesh peeling away from him.

"This is a damned visitation on us," she continued, "either that or we really are living in hell. Everything is so sickening instead of being exhilarating, vicious and sour instead of being mystifying. I almost feel suicidal."

"Don't worry, Ginny, we will soon have the destruction of the crystalloid world to occupy our singular brains."

"What's the point? I just don't get it. Either Earth was wiped out by the crystalloid reinforcements or the good old human race managed to blow them to hell, either way we are superfluous. The human race is either finished or saved—not that I'd class *us* as humans any longer, Kunio. Even if those reinforcements signalled for more reinforcements they would have been dispatched years before we even arrived here, so what are we doing here? Vengeance? That's pitiful, and we are driven to it inexorably. We cannot stop ourselves. They made machines of us, with no braking mechanism save death."

"We are a counterattack, one of the oldest moves in military history. We bring the war to the camps of our enemy and destroy him there."

"There are times when you sound just like a texbook," she laughed. "I remember that's how a boy once described me; said that he couldn't love someone without a heart, my heart supposedly being out here at Altair. But even you are way out of my league, Kunio." She shook her head and then added softly, "I—I'm sorry. I didn't mean that. I'm not sure what I mean these days."

"How you feel is worth examining. Find out what you mean. I am a cold, hard, authoritarian commander, a man of few pleasures who pleases few, but when I speak I know what I mean and I think that I know what you mean too. Perhaps it has something to do with my refusal to accept MacGillvery's suggestions about the occult possibilities in our present situation. That disturbs you. It makes me seem like a man without a soul?"

"No it wasn't that. Only you always give the impression that romance, anything involved with emotion, is the refuge of the inept."

"I believe that to be true, Ginny, I believe that the most worthwhile mental activity is the most abstract. I believe only in that way are we really creative. The use of emotion as an instrument is as out of place in a painted picture, a poem or a sonata as it is in a problem of pure mathematics. It is relevant in the relationships between human beings, to some degree."

"Please, I can't face that particular lecture right now," her voice was edged.

She rolled over, stared and slipped into her coveralls. Parting her hair into place, she stepped into the corridor and was gone.

And was she right? But now Tamura was buried too deep to tell, as that same poet she quoted once said in a later work—

"And now quietly in my cave pits of fall exploring I work deeper
and deeper to ultimate dark"

"Commander Tamura," the voice of the MI from the sleeping unit, "you are requested at once on the bridge, sir. I repeat . . ."

"It's a signal of some kind, sir," began Weismuller excitedly as he entered the bridge. "Look, it's showing on the disseminator again, but oh my God, it's bizarre!"

Instead of the normal display giving information about the current finalisation manoeuvres of establishing base orbit, there was a scene. It showed a hard, primitive landscape, the scene of that nightmare, complete with the black figure—a flat, massive silhouette.

Slowly, gently through the console speakers a noise, growing louder gradually, stronger until at last it howled through the room —the banshee voices of the shebeen.

And a face in the head of the black shape swirled loosely into focus. A voice rasped thin and insistent. The face began solidifying and as the minutes passed, Tamura recognised it, naturally: that face was his own, the lips moving slowly as the voice grated out in amerenglish,

"We wish . . . to . . . communicate . . ."

CHAPTER FOURTEEN

The face was silver grey, eyes scarcely green.

The lips moved but in a manner not consistent with the words—giving the image the appearance of a poorly dubbed foreign movie.

Hysteria briefly grappled for dominance of Tamura's mind, for here was unreason come visiting and it wore his own face.

"We wish . . . to . . . communicate . . ."

"We too wish to communicate," he replied but more to himself than to the entity.

"We wish . . . to . . . communicate . . ."

"What is it?" asked MacGillvery, clearing his throat.

"Some manifestation of our Machine Idiot," Tamura lied. He had been vainly attempting to connect with the MI for almost a minute.

The black figure dimmed. For a few seconds it swelled enormous and amorphous, with a scatter of stars shining through its fabric and then it was gone.

"And what the hell was all that in aid of?" growled Odobo. "Is the MI trying to con us into believing that some dark, malignant powers from beyond the grey veil are reaching out their hoary arms to grasp the world of flesh and blood?—Shit!" she spat in disgust. Even she was desperately trying to deny that there really was something supernatural taking place.

"It had my face," Tamura muttered, slumping down before his console. Ginny put her arm round him and the warm touch of her hand signalled a general loosening of tensions. Sigh, Tamura Kunio, he thought, relax—close your eyes and listen to the background noises of the bridge, the rustling of movement, quiet coughs and muttered conversations. And behind it all the dull slow throbbing which is the sound of the ship itself, and . . .

He frowned.

There was something else not previously there; a very faint sound, like radio static.

"Can you hear that noise?" he asked, sitting upright. They listened and shook their heads—all but Odobo.

"Yes," she concurred, "yes I know what you mean—a kind of crackling hiss. It seems to come in waves."

Relief. For a moment he suspected something was wrong with either his ears or his brain.

"Ask the MI, Weismuller," he said turning to her.

"Sorry, sir, no response."

"What about its supervisory functions. Are they gone too?"

She checked. "Negative. This doesn't appear to be one of the usual blackouts—if you see what I mean."

"Can we raise *Revenge?*"

No sooner asked than the face of Wells, the senior communications officer, appears.

"Hello, Kunio. I take it you had a jazzy video reception, just like we had just now. Any ideas what the hell it was all about?"

"Wells! Is your MI in working order?"

"Surely—took a bit of abuse when that signal just crashed in, but fine otherwise. You having problems?"

"Our Intelligence seems to have lost some of its upper brain capability."

"Ah, now, that's possibly a temporary lapse, my friend. We went through and assimilation has commenced."

"So what?"

"Communication becomes different. Your MI is simply about to introduce new and more complex procedures. They'll take a bit of getting used to, I assure you, but it's worth it in the end, nevertheless."

"New procedures—what the hell are you talking about?"

"Well, I suppose the closest description would be telepathy."

"We've had that. It can read our minds already."

"Ah, but not communicate directly with your minds. Before it has merely observed your thought processes at work—now it will enter them personally."

The bridge was engulfed in uproar.

"Quiet!" Tamura shouted. "Take up your positions and start behaving like crew members. There will be no further outbursts of this nature—understand?" He turned to the screen. "Go on, Wells."

He cleared his throat, "Sorry for causing the commotion. What happens is you begin to 'hear' the MI answering your questions. The first thing you hear is a kind of waterfall noise—a hissing that pulsates. Then you begin to hear the voice. It sounds like a real voice but only you can hear it. Soon after this, visual information displays appear before your eyes, whenever they are needed. Often they appear in what look like little panels, suspended in mid-air, at arm's length. There's no need for a screen—they just appear when required and then vanish—controlled hallucinations."

"But how?" asked MacGillvery urgently.

"As far as I can understand the germanium deposited discreetly through the CNS acts as an amplifier both in the sending out of information and for feeding it back in again. It eases the interaction between the electrical functions of the human being generally and what will now be a heightened electro-magnetic field within the living area of your ship. The MI is sensitive to the minute fluctuations in the field and it can identify the sources and significance of every one. It correlates this information with the massive profile of the individual which it has in store. This is how it reads your minds. Whenever it wishes to communicate with you, it causes measured disturbances in the magnetic field itself, knowing that these will be amplified by the individual's germanium seeded CNS, and interpreted as sensory information."

"So our nervous systems have become both broadcasting and receiving stations?"

"In a way—yes."

"I'm coming to the state of mind where I don't believe that any of this is really happening to me."

Then Tamura heard the mental voice of the MI for the first time, faint and quavering but quite distinct.

Too much change too soon—no time to adapt. It's like accelerating through brick wall after brick wall on an out of control scooter—no chance to handle the machine—only to throw up your arms across your face and brace yourself for the next impact!

"All right, Wells, or whatever the hell you are—" Wells looked faintly wounded "—then if that was not our MI displaying on the disseminator, what was it?"

"Oh, you mean the signal thing? Why that was almost certainly an attempt at communication by an extraterrestrial intelligence, what else?"

The boles scrambled about the corridor, effecting maintenance work more rapidly and thoroughly than humanly possible. The absence of the macromag field permitted them to enter the super-core for the first time since departure from the solar system. It would all have been fascinating to watch, but their pickups would no longer relay to the bridge while the MI was altering its human communication interface. There were but two scenes available on the monitors. One showed the Altair system during the close approach phase of the flight. The star lay in the centre of three concentric, glittering rings seen sloping at an angle of about thirty degrees from edge on and reaching diagonally across the screen—a vast stellar version of the planet Saturn, encircled not by the remnants of errant satellites, but by the debris of shattered worlds. In normal circumstances, one would expect the crew to be speculating furiously about the enigmas of such spectacular catastrophies, but not aboard *Yūkoku*, not then. The other image was a Machine-enhanced view of Altair III. The ferocity of the cloud storms was immediately evident, likewise the immense depths of penetration of the electrical storms in the boiling atmosphere. Energy poured out from the great mass of the world at a rate which lead Tamura to suspect that during its formation, it only just escaped becoming a star. The Yellow Spots, each one with a surface area half as large again as that of Earth itself, seemed relatively solid. They appeared to be composed of between half a dozen and twenty 'cells' bounded from each other by chasms several hundred kilometres across and of unguessable depth. The cells had similar surface features—a central high plain, rippled with dunes surrounded by a web of 'mountain ranges' and 'valleys'. The outer rims of the spots were the locus of some dazzling electrical pyrotechnics and cloud discolourations. Occasionally a spot would slowly sink below cloud level and a cyclonic depression in the atmosphere mark its submerged presence, setting up sympathetic turbulences in surrounding cloud layers. These appeared to refloat the sunken spot after about thirty hours. The spot re-emerged brighter and smaller, its cells almost hexagonally regular in shape, and its rim electrically more ferocious.

Were the crystalloids spawned upon those floating, yellow crusts?

And what about the shebeen—did they come from that raging hell-world? How could anything come from there? Still, it fascinated Tamura. Must I destroy such a world? he would ask himself. The concept was unbelievable at best: that two ships, virtual bacteria beside the bulk of this giant, could tear it apart. Would he, could he tear it apart? Yes.

The water was cool. He sliced through it at a shallow angle. The pale green tiles of the pool bottom steadied suddenly before his eyes. Ginny erupted through the shimmering skin of light above, grinned, nipped his nose and lunged off. He surfaced, swallowed air and raced after her.

Later they sat gasping on the edge of the pool, the water coursing down their pale bodies in rivulets.

"Wow," she whistled. "Some swim. Hey, you can surely move in the water, mysterious oriental. Who taught you—not the infamous *Hokkei?*"

He laughed and shook his head.

"No I learned as a child—but I developed technique on Mars. Best place to develop style, you know. You don't sink nearly so fast as on Earth, but your water speed is just the same."

"So I see," she laughed.

"What's been eating away at you, Ginny? I know that you've been exceptionally good to me—believe me you've been angelic. Without your help, I would probably have cracked up then on the bridge. But what about you, best friend I've had, hmmm? Something's been rumbling in that complex head of yours ever since the MI stopped displaying. Are you worrying about this supposed mental take-over lined up for us?"

She let the smile fade a little, looked into the pool and shrugged.

"No—I've felt the MI at work on me for some time. Even before Wells came straight out with the truth. I guessed as much. No, it's that attempt at communication."

"Ah, the black figure—yes, well that came as a shock, but nothing's happened since, Ginny. The whole thing was probably no more than a freak overspill from the MI emotion simulation."

She realised immediately that he did not believe that himself. He was attempting the role of comforter.

"What puzzles me is the nature of the communication." She stood up and walked to a hot air drying stall. He followed. "What manner of being would attempt a contact like that? The whole damn thing is bizarre," she continued. "I imagined that any contact situation would involve the setting up of a common communication system, based on mathematics. I think almost everyone did, but we seem to have been profoundly wrong. Our first 'live' contact was the crystalloids and their response was literally devastating."

"But that you regard them as being intelligent?"

"Systems with interstellar communication and transport capabilities plus uncanny warfare skill and materials—that's intelligence as far as we are concerned. Anyway, the next contact, the one which we pick up through the emotion simulation facilities of the MI turns out to be even stranger. Neither uses reason as a basis for setting up an interchange of information."

They slipped out of the drying breeze of the stall, on to the padded flooring of the gym and picked up their clothing from where it hung, draped across the parallel bars.

"You remember Duncan Lunan, the guy who suggested the existence of a Bootis probe in Earth orbit last century?" Tamura asked. "I remember him giving a wry talk about the crystalloids strikes—said that we should not ignore the possibility that these may be mere attempts at communication which we were simply misinterpreting."

She gave a short laugh.

"The old fellow was joking of course, Ginny, but the kernel of truth holds as good now as it was then. We simply cannot know what an ET will choose to communicate or how. What appears reasonable within our interpretation of the universe may seem the opposite to them."

"Okay, I realise this, but that is the problem. What entity would find it reasonable to attempt communication the way that one did?"

"Well, we must assume that it was the crystalloids or the shebeen, if they are distinct from one another."

Seating themselves in the lounge they ordered up a couple of fruit juices and ignored Debussey's *Claire de Lune*.

"Of course," she nodded, "we can stick any name on it, but that does not explain the nature, the state of mind, which would function in such a way that this behaviour would be natural to it. Not a human mind, or what was the term—humanoid. I cannot—ugh . . ." She broke off and thrust her hand out, then closed her eyes hard.

"What's wrong?" he asked urgently.

"Damned MI trying direct audio-visual contact again."

She looked at Tamura, and he saw the lines on her face, her drawn features. She had the appearance of a woman in her forties, tired and worried.

"Let's get back to work on the bridge. Work might take our minds off things."

Weismuller was running problems through the MI, and subsequently suffering the brunt of the Machine's fumbling attempts at direct contact. She persisted, determined not to be worsted by it. She was becoming obsessed with the problem of the ET contact, and Tamura realised that he would have to tell her not to push it down the others' throats. Some discussion and brain storming was fair but not to the extent where other crew members became equally obsessed.

She, too, looked older—worn, almost haggard. She keyed in doggedly, closing her eyes frequently to concentrate on the MI direct communication. Keying-in was pointless, the Machine being able to 'read her mind', as her thoughts formed. But she retained the habit, as a bridge between the old style interface and the new.

They all seemed to have aged overnight. The skin was both taut and pouched on their faces. The expressions were those of the careworn, the depressed and the exhausted.

Odobo went about in a daze much of the time. Like the others, she was absorbing the impact of all the events, in this period of relative rest. Her problems with MI sensory contact were most obvious. Occasionally she cried out, wept, verged on hysteria. Her usually immaculate smock had not been changed since the ship entered base orbit. Tamura suspected that she even slept in it. Sexual relations were on the wane, but not in total abeyance—probably saved by the fact that the one time that the MI never seemed to break into anyone's mind was during love making.

How much the low morale resulted from psychological battering, and how much was due to the virus, Tamura could not say. It was also just as likely to be simply the result of the Intelligence's current communication experiment, or a compound of all three.

Varies individual to individual, Tamura heard the quiet, personal voice again. Sitting there in the assembly area, chewing a prota-steak and apple sauce, he saw thumb-high but perfect models of all the remaining crew members pop up on the table before him. One by one they grew to double their size as a commentary was read on them and their ills . . .

MacGillvery: basic psychosexual difficulties, heightened by certainty of MI mind reading ability, other facets and factors minimal. Weismuller: adapting rapidly to communication change, but quasi-herpes has upset natural immunity balance with herpes simplex causing extensive cold sore formation around the lips, nostrils and eyes. Paranoid tendencies developing in response to psychological impacts from commencement of voyage to date.

Laing, on the other hand, is totally rejecting the communication change and proving to be the most difficult integration subject. This is a direct result of psychological defence mechanisms, developed during the experiences of her past few months . . .

The dolls grew as their names were raised and then sank out of sight into the table. When the entire display finished, Tamura shook his head. Beat that for induced hallucination.

Allaedyce is coming round—he should be fully conscious by the time you reach the sick bay. The four of them turned as one and walked towards the door hatch. Sometimes it worked like that— handing out of information to a selection of individuals simultaneously. Occasionally an important announcement would be 'heard' by everyone, like the exhortation for the crew to take more sleep.

Allaedyce was fully awake, half reclining in the hospital's only unfolded sick bed. Compared with the condition of the others, he looked almost healthy. He smiled weakly.

"Very clever," he croaked.

"I don't know how the hell you managed to stay alive," said Odobo, the only one of the women to show even a partial liking for the bushman. "You were sliced up like diced potato when Mac-Gillvery found you. What happened?"

A guilty question, because she knew and they all knew!

"I'll tell you what happened," his voice was bitter, his lips snarling. "Some bright character interfered with the centrifugal gravity effect, and damned near killed me."

Negative. This does not tally with data derived from common memory or from disposition of materials throughout Yūkoku—the phenomenon was intense and localised.

He looked briefly puzzled at the four of them, shaking their heads in unison. Then slowly he began to understand, and began smiling.

"I'm glad to see your spirits are lifting," Tamura remarked.

"Nobody believes that your accident was caused by some homicidal freak. You see, we all experienced your dream about being hunted amongst the bush on the edge of the desert. We also experienced your trouble in the corridor, by proxy of course," Odobo said gently.

He gaped, horrified.

"How . . . ?"

"Ask the Machine, Allaedyce," suggested Weismuller, a loaded statement.

Again the bushman looked uneasy. The screen on his bedside console was blank, instead of flowing with progress indicators of Intelligence hospital activities.

"You're all integrated. What . . . goes on?"

"Just key in, Allaedyce," Tamura said.

Hesitantly, his fingers punched for access. The coding light came on. He selected his matrix—non-computation/data retrieval/data evaluation. The coding light blinked out and the terminal was dead.

"All right, what gives?"

"There is no access through the keyboard any longer," explained Ginny. "You must go through us to the machine."

"All right," he rallied, "all right I'm going through you to the MI. Tell me what the hell happened in the corridor."

Weismuller and Odobo spoke in perfect unison. "The precise nature of what happened is not clear but it would appear that, somehow or other, the proximity of the shebeen lifeform has stimulated the esp capabilities of the crew using the Intelligence's esp potential as an amplifier."

"Shebeen? What the hell is this?" There was fear there now, signs of panic. If it continued, implanted electrodes in the sleep centres of his brain would activate.

"You want the latest on the Shebeen?" Ginny asked.

Wide-eyed, Allaedyce nodded.

Again, Weismuller and Odobo together: "They are probably an advanced space-going intelligence linked with the crystalloids in some unknown way. Their characteristic radio profile has been associated with psi related phenomena. During your period of unconsciousness, there was an attempt at ET communication, using material gleaned from what would seem to be esp sources. As there is no history of non-shebeen related crystalloid attempts at communication or esp cum psi occurrences, it looks like the shebeen are a distinct lifeform. The MI's guess is that the peculiar nature of the Altair III planet's two inner moons might be explained if they were artificial: they could be Altair II. It certainly hosts a multitude of plant and animal lifeforms."

Allaedyce's lower lip began to tremble.

Too much, too soon.

The MI's speculations surprised even Tamura. Suddenly information was flowing into him, through him, as he verbalised it for Allaedyce's benefit.

"And now for the bad news. What happened to you could have been a mass-psi operation. The psi stimulation of the shebeen and the MI 'amplifier' could have unleashed the general resentment of the crew against you in a telekinetic assault. Now that we are in the process of assimilation, the Machine's Intelligence is blending with our own. There is a kind of electronic equivalent of the collective unconsciousness in the process of formulation. It is quite distinct from our individual minds or the MI—but a marrying of all of them at a level where we have no direct control. It doesn't like you, Allaedyce. I think it wants you dead."

The words shocked Tamura as he pronounced them.

Allaedyce tried rising from the bed. He choked—and then slid back on the top sheet, instantly asleep.

CHAPTER FIFTEEN

One fifty seconds to burn NOW

The bridge lay abandoned, finally realising its intended obsolescence. The crew, with the exception of Allaedyce, relaxed in the assembly area . . .

Automatic sequencer programmes active NOW

But they did not see the assembly area. Instead they gazed at the star hung infinity which surrounded *Yūkoku*. Below and behind was the searing disc of Altair. To one side was *Revenge*, a brilliant core of reflected inferno, now fifty kilometres distant, having just completed her distancing manoeuvre. Out ahead, amongst the blazing points, lay Altair III, many times brighter than the light from the distant suns beyond. It appeared sunk in the glowing ring which reached out from either side of Altair and swooped right round behind—the lumination of the systems great asteroid belts.

Tamura appeared to 'feel' the ship—the vast conical net of gridwork tingling against Altair's solar wind, icy pourings through the cryostat 'circulation', throbs from the thermonuclear 'belly' readying for the burn.

Supercore priming operation complete—activating NOW

A wash to soothing, strong energy burst across the metal and ceramo plastics of *Yūkoku*. The inner throbbing held steady; the gridwork went rigid under this exciting caress; the helium fluids raced for the core and the reaction blast chamber. Then with a sensation like skin being stretched, head radiator panels grew from the sides.

Fission to fusion changeover in five seconds from NOW

The chilling around these blazing innards increased and Tamura felt the pressure building at the injector points, where a stream of duiterium crystals was about to be squirted into the inferno on a jet of liquid helium 3. A surge of unbelievable heat—

Fission mode operational NOW

The fire feeling itched through the cryostat circulation, through magnetic muscle, out to the stretching panels, and died.

Movement began—not movement in any human, remembered sense, but an experience of change, very fine change—the orientation as a mass against that of component parts—weight returning with thrust. Delicately, Tamura felt the relative alterations to the apparent motions of stars and planets from those of base orbit. Not quite correct—minute modifications were made minimising the irritable discomfort until the bliss of vector perfection was ultimately realised.

Far off to the right, Tamura saw a streamer glowing out from *Revenge* across hundreds of kilometres, an artificial comet's tail like the one now following himself.

Standard 'g' acceleration effective. On course for Altair III both spacecraft. Estimated arrival in close orbit 15.56 days from NOW

Allaedyce had been quiet. The past few days had made Tamura suspicious of him. He was again mobile, walking with a slight stoop. He had approached the commander almost deferentially, through a maze of exercise equipment in the gym.

"Ah, commander."

"What do you want, Allaedyce?" He looked ill, and every bit as mad as the MI believed him to be.

"Permission to work in the biochem labs. I'd like a chance to contribute something positive to the venture now."

He was well versed in exobiological techniques, obtained some of the best gradings at Yakutsk, but the Japanese was suspicious.

"Tell me more." Tamura lay down and began cycling his legs in mid air, elbows on the floor, supporting his hips on his hands.

"I was thinking of doing some fine spectral analyses of Altair II in case the shebeen do come from there and building a few likely environments with attendant lifeforms."

He is not to be trusted.

"The MI advises me not to trust you."

His smile widened and his expression grew furtive. "Why would it urge you so, sir? I mean no harm, I assure you."

"You are not healthy. Perhaps there might be an accident . . ."

"No one here is *healthy*," he snapped, then recoiled at the ferocity of his own reply. "Oh, I apologise, commander. I don't know what possessed me." He gave a nervous, desperate laugh.

"A touch of your old self, Allaedyce."

"I assure you I did not mean to offend. I merely wished to add something constructive to the mission."

"Then go to the labs, but be careful. You will be being watched all the time." He turned to go. "And I mean be careful, Allaedyce. We've come so far together. It would be a pity if we had to lose you now."

A flash of fear appeared in that black face, then another obsequious smirk and he scuttled off.

Was that wise? In his state of mind he may do anything.

The point was to have him do something, but know exactly what he was doing all the time. Tamura would monitor all Allaedyce's actions in the labs through the MI.

That will be difficult. He is a particularly devious and subtle being.

Come now, I have the utmost confidence in you, Tamura thought in reply.

It was a hallucination, of course, but one so real that Tamura was aghast: Holst sat in the lounge, sipping a cold beer. Tamura halted in the door hatch and gaped. Holst laughed, waving a hand to greet the *Yūkoku* commander.

"C'mon over, surprise, surprise, eh?" he yelled in the rough, hearty voice which had been heard every day at Yakutsk. Tamura's old classmate who was actually fifty kilometres distant across vacuum and fatally hard radiation, was to all intents and purposes aboard the *Yūkoku*. Still laughing he rose and pumped Tamura's hand—his flesh firm, warm and strong in the commander's own. Tamura could even smell the cumin on his breath.

"Yes, I'm still devouring all the spicy dishes I can get my teeth into, Kunio. Just finished a plateful of abracchio brodedatto before popping over. Thought we might have a chat before we reach Three."

In the radiomagnetic climate of the living quarters, the ability of the MI to play with a crewman's mind by influencing his brain was unlimited. Every neutron, every ganglion of the central nervous system was salted with the hydro-germanium macromolecules whose complex structures interacted intimately with the cells, proteins and nucleic acids. They had become totally manipulated human beings.

The others gawked too at the dapper figure from *Revenge*. He appeared exactly as they imagined they should all have looked like at that stage of the flight. He was obviously enthusiastic, and the only lines on his face were laughter lines, a hallucination, but a profoundly effective one.

"You have to admit that this beats the shit out of any video, holographic or not," Holst exulted, raising his arms and turning to display his seeming corporeality.

"I'd say so," whistled Odobo, just behind him in the hatchway.

"It's terrific. Even I feel as if I'm really here. To all intents and purposes, I suppose I am. Anyway, to business."

A circle of cushioned stools rose from the floor, and as they sat the atmosphere was suddenly exhilarating, as if some arduous climb had reached its crest, and from there on it would be down hill, accelerating every second of the way.

"First off, I think that I'd better clear up some points." He was every bit as gesturesome as Tamura remembered his being at Yakutsk, and not a day older in appearance. "You know that the proposed operation against Three is going to have somewhat overwhelming side-effects."

"We have accepted this," Tamura replied curtly.

"Hmm, I just thought you might, knowing you, Kunio. Well, it's not going to be as extreme as you might imagine it will be. Up till now you have all been suffering the woes, aches and pains of integration and assimilation. Well, from here on in you should start reaping the benefits. Number one being the fact that as long as your MI stays active, you can too."

"Very interesting," said Weismuller, "but how?"

"You all have a double insurance, my pretty Eskimo," he smiled. And Tamura noticed something. She was no longer that trouble eroded figure of the past few weeks. Weismuller sat bright-eyed, alert, and indeed pretty. "There is now a working facsimile of your consciousness in the computer, matching every move of your central nervous system step for step. In the event of death, you would never know, as this surrogate consciousness would continue in the absence of the defunct organic machinery. Secondly, *Yūkoku* has the facilities to neutralise all radiomagnetic phenomena within a very small volume of space. Three 'neutral' pockets within the supercore, each is a hollow formed by an induction pit of a vanadium-gallium primary disc, overlaying a pit on the augmentor. These pockets can be reached by the boles, through service channels. They will provide perfect shielding during the assault on Altair III."

"It's just possible," MacGillvery shook his head. "I've been in there in the supercore hollows but there was hardly enough room for me to carry out my basic inspection, never mind the thought of packing three or four suited crew members into it and each of the other two."

"It can and will be done." There was a mischievous twinkling in Holst's eye. "We've almost completed the operation aboard *Revenge* already."

"How?" Tamura queried.

"Figure it out for yourself, Kunio. I'll tell you when we reach Three. Goodbye for now."

And he disappeared.

Everyone was suddenly healthy, inexplicably happy, and the Japanese was suspicious.

The weariness which had lain so heavily upon every crew member only a few moments past were gone, replaced by a suspect vivacity.

"A brilliant illusion that," smiled Odobo, referring to Holst's tangible appearance. Where he had sat there was merely an unoccupied stool sinking gracefully into the floor.

"I suppose the boles are industriously enlarging the neutral pockets right now." MacGillvery continued his speculation about the supercore safe areas, "But I think that will change their effectiveness. I think I'll do some quick calculations on that!"

The group began breaking up into gossiping cliques. Ginny came dancing across to Tamura: she was vibrant.

"Well, great stone-hearted one, what do you think of the good news. A chance at survival?" She was employing her 'tease' tone, for the first time since they had reached Altair.

"First of all, I am convinced with the effectiveness of this mission. If we destroy the crystalloids, then my life's work is done honourably, and I will die gladly. Survival only concerns me in so much as what effect it is liable to have on the success of our attack on Altair Three. However, I am happy at the thought that you may survive, if that is what you desire."

"You intend killing yourself if you don't succeed, don't you?"

"Upon return to Earth if possible, forsaking that I shall leave the living quarters in a suit and 'drop' towards what remains of Three."

Genuine despair replaced the humour in her face.

"But what about *us?*"

"*Us?* What about us? We both know our duty, and what we do is governed by our different interpretations of it. I understand your reluctance to join me in death, dear Ginny, but will you not understand my appreciation of how *my* life is? I see it being dedicated to the revenging of a great misdeed. When I have revenged it then my life is ended. To live on would diminish the stature of the misdeed and the consequent revenge with respect to my life: and my life is dedicated to it."

"You're not human," she snapped and turned away.

"I'm simply Japanese."

Tamura's body felt lithe, full of spring. He stepped smartly through the corridors in the direction of the Labs. It was time to bring Allaedyce up to date, and confirm whether suspicions about the bushman's lab activity were accurate.

The labs were a complex of white plastic bulkheads, some translucent, some opaque, and all with a variety of dangers described on their autoclam doors, complete with obligatory safety precautions to be taken prior to entry; during stay; before and after departure. 'Exobiology' the door read. Tamura keyed in a request for entry because, if occupied, only the occupant could grant this.

"Who's there?" squeaked Allaedyce through the comspeaker. "I'm in the middle of some very important work. Please, can't you leave me in peace?"

"Open up, Allaedyce," he replied. "This is Tamura."

The seal clunked and snapped open. He stepped into a low ceilinged lab about three metres square. The bushman sat on a swivel chair before the inverted pyramid of a molecular saw. The units display showed a section of genetic material at high magnification and a red disc indicating the area about to be sliced away.

His smile of greeting was shaky.

"Sorry about that, commander," he almost whined. "I was immersed in a crucial stage of my experiment."

"It's time you were told," Tamura began, ignoring the excuses. "When we make close orbit around Altair Three, we are going to destroy that world, by tearing it apart using the supercore fields." He waited for the implications to be understood but they obviously were not. "That means the end for you. The intensity of the field is liable to disrupt your central nervous system, fatally. The only option for you is to take a couple of days in a suit, under sedation, in one of the core's neutral pockets."

Allaedyce began chewing nervously on his lower lip.

"Think it over."

"How come someone obviously as ill as you are is going to survive anything, but I'm going to go under?" He was not looking at Tamura, but gazing out past him in to the darkened corridor.

His eyes opened wide and he let out a scream.

Tamura turned and saw it there, reaching from floor to ceiling in the corridor, a giant green statue with snarling reptilian face and great wings spreading on either side. For a moment he was about to dismiss it as just another computer mind trick, but then remembered that Allaedyce was not subject to these, and he had spied it first. Two and a half metres of solid green marble aglow in the dark. It moved: the arms stretched out to either side and arched forward jerkily. Allaedyce, shrieking, pulled the Commander bodily into the lab and slammed the door over. Tamura staggered against a bench and scattered a whole army of test tubes, some dropping to scatter on the floor. Allaedyce was pushing himself against the door hatch to ensure that it would remain secure. There came a grinding noise and a great taloned claw smashed through the ceramoplastic bulkhead, showering the lab in a debris of fragments.

This is no simulation, Tamura. This is real.

I want all the boles in here, double time! he replied.

The green limb swung towards Allaedyce and thrust him clear of the hatch. The door hatch vanished in a twisting pool of yellow light.

Lying winded across his console, Allaedyce turned his head to see the giant form awkwardly entering the chamber. Its jaws were twitching, the eyes rolled as if the thing was mad with hunger. It stepped shakily towards Tamura and he straightened up, ready for escape. But it stopped and stooped slightly, bringing its great face close to his. The hot, rancid stench of its breath almost made him vomit.

It spoke. The voice was distant and hollow, as if coming from someone entombed at the bottom of a deep well or mineshaft.

"We wish . . . to . . . communicate . . . We—"

Crack!

Tamura thrust himself backward, twisting in mid-air, to land on the other side of the bench. In his mind was the image of a bole's 'head' appearing at the hole where the hatchway had been. Then a turbulence of iridescent images carried him into unconsciousness.

CHAPTER SIXTEEN

Pazuzu

Yes, of course, the old demon—*one of the oldest, it evolved with man out of barbarism into the very first city civilisations of Sumer, ten thousand years ago.*

Thoughts and images became clearer. Tamura saw a small, carved jade image of the demon. *Just before archaeology was banned, this was found by Methin and his wife, at a site outside Al Dauor on the banks of what was once the Tigris River. Radiochemical dating placed it in the fifth millennium B.C. This completely upset the prehistoric art applecart—*

No lectures!

The image of the jade figure disappeared to be replaced by the interior of the exobiology lab. There was a wide blackening on the floor. At the centre of this the ceramoplastic cushioning had vanished, exposing dull, dark impenetrable crystal-alloy, the *Yūkoku's* skeletal matter. Paintwork on all the benches and consoles had blistered and the remains of delicate electronic equipment lay neatly piled in one corner. A zealous couple of boles were busy putting the lab in order.

The scene changed to a very busy operating theatre, two surgical teams each at work intensively on a patient. Three boles were acting as nurses. Tamura recognised the form of Allaedyce immediately. A full scale skin replacement job was being done—synthetic epidermal tissue being sprayed on to the chest and the base of his neck. The upper part of his left arm was sealed in a plastic sac of regenerative fluids doing the same work more slowly, but more thoroughly. Once the artificial skin was firm, it would be replaced section by section with genuine Allaedyce skin, cultured in regenerative fluids from samples of his own flesh. The process would take days.

The other subject under care was not immediately recognisable, because all the other crew members appeared present and accounted for. Then Tamura realised the truth. That person into whose glistening pink, exposed brain MacGillvery was inserting a probe was Tamura Kunio, *Yūkoku* commander—himself.

At first, he could not undertand. Seconds of simple bewilderment passed before he felt the shock of looking at his own charred self, lying there. How? What was happening? Are you dead, Tamura, he asked. Does the spirit of the dead man have eyes, a will, a sense of despair?

No, what you see, you see with my eyes.

Then a cross section model of the living quarters replaced the hospital scene. Littered across the walls tiny lights indicated the presence of MI's optical sensors. Hardly a square centimetre was hidden from view. Immediately he felt a swelling rage. This was the ultimate insult—total invasion of privacy . . .

Not so! These sensors have only been operational during the final phase of integration. At no previous point in the mission were they brought into use.

There was no way to disprove this but now nothing was certain: even the nature of this experience was questionable. Was his mind, which he called his own, experiencing this through organic brain or through Intelligence facsimile consciousness?

The hospital returned. MacGillvery swung the stem camera closer to the area being treated. This instrument was straw thin and slung down from the ceiling. Built into its tip were twenty miniscule laser cutters and holographic cameras with considerable microscopic potential. MacGillvery saw a highly magnified view of that small area of the cortex undergoing surgery. The shaking tweezer like the head of a pair of forceps came into view, the normal body tremor distorted unnaturally under the camera. It neatly clamped on to a large, slowly pulsing blood vessel in the moist pink mass and gently teased it up and aside. Where it rested, he sunk in the probe, its surface covered in sensors to a density five times greater than the nerve ends at the tip of the human tongue. The MI fed the

probe's sensations directly into MacGillvery's nervous system so
that he could 'feel' his way through the layers of brain matter. On
the right hand side of the head, your head, Tamura, there was a
dark red crater, where some fragment of the exploding monstrosity
had entered the skull, lodging itself deep inside just above the point
where the optic nerve runs under the thalmus, and the formix bor-
ders upon the lateral ventricle.

The probe connected, he cried out and recoiled as if receiving an
electric shock. Bounding sideways, Odobo caught him as he crum-
pled to the floor of the theatre. The others turned as if in slow motion, their eyes briefly removed from the probe. They were speaking, but Tamura's disembodied consciousness heard no sound. The
'eyes' of the MI were on the probe. It quivered and leapt out of the
brain as if thrust from the interior. The crater wound trembled, and
a quick splash of bright, arterial blood bubbled forth. Then hauling
and clawing its way out came the homunculus. It was about the
size of a finger nail, but seeming huge under the camera. Wiping
blood from its golden body, it straightened and looked around. The
others were still moving slowly, helping MacGillvery to a couch.
The beast was naked, with carefully worked, intricately plaited
hair. Its fingers were talons. The double wings, unlike the wings
any flying creature of Earth ever had, curved out and up, as if
ready for flight, high from the shoulders, and the secondaries
sweeping low, straight and graceful, almost to its heavy claw feet:
feathered feet, like those belonging to some bird of prey.

Pazuzu.

It was in flight. The wings beat golden splashes and the crew
sighted it, turning their heads to follow the brilliant path. It curved
and dived in a mad spiral over Tamura's open skull, and then shot
up through the ceiling, leaving no trace of its passage.

There was a time when I would have been shaken, Tamura
thought, but no longer. I almost believe that the chaos is beginning
to show a logic of its own, a buried structure of paradox and impos-
sibility more relevant to human nature than the mass problem solving activities in which we have been so assiduously instructed . . .

The smell of the hospital area sneaked into a dream. Voices followed.

"Fourteen hours and you're with us again, wily oriental," said
Odobo.

"Feeling peculiar?" inquired Weismuller.

"I feel practically nothing," Tamura slurred.

"Thank God," murmured a voice, "I thought you might waken a damned vegetable. The damage in your thick head is incredible." It was Ginny.

"We Japanese are no fools, my dear," he replied. "For over a century, we have had miniature transistorised brains in each of our buttocks just in case the main one packs in."

They chuckled and it pleased him that they were so obviously heartened at his recovery. He tried turning about to face Ginny, but felt the tug of an infrasonic restraint.

"Ah, now, don't move yourself," MacGillvery piped up from somewhere close by. "I've been having the devil's own job replacing that damned synthetic skin tissue of yours, sir."

"Talking about devils," said Tamura, determined to bring in the subject of the demon, no matter what the current context. "What about our homunculus friend?"

There was a choked gasp and an incredulous laugh.

"How the hell—?"

"Very appropriate phrase. I observed the whole peculiar affair, thanks to the good offices of our Machine Idiot, who helpfully supplied me with a proxy presence in the theatre."

"That is staggering," whispered Ginny.

"Look at yourselves. Look at how bright and vivacious we have all grown recently. What about the disappearance of old grievances. Only Allaedyce is still accused of friction. The Intelligence is adding its very helpful hand to ease and often remove our worries and woes. We should face up to the fact that what is happening to us *now* verges on the supernatural, inasmuch as it runs against the kind of natural picture we grew used to before this voyage began."

"Always ready with a lecture," groaned Ginny. "We really must see MI about performing major surgery upon your cancerous outgrowth of obscene pedantry."

More chuckles.

"How is the beloved Allaedyce faring?" Tamura enquired.

"He should be fine when he awakens tomorrow. He's in his sleeping unit at present. He should waken just before we enter close orbit about Three," muttered Odobo. She was not happy with the new Allaedyce at all. She found the once bitter but rebellious spirit now a little obscene: the cowering and grinning puppet he had become in the face of the new order, at once pathetic and repulsive.

"What happened in the lab anyway?" she asked.

"A bole hit the thing with a burst of heavy laser fire. The rest was fireworks—a most startling display, I assure you."

"What was it?" asked Weismuller.

"An enlarged version of the small beast which sprung from my head, if you'll excuse the classical reference."

"Pazuzu!" exclaimed MacGillvery. "The pestilent one I remember reading about in the reports of the astro-archaeologists' court martial. They claimed that the Al Daour amulet was an extraterrestrial artifact."

"Of course," Odobo burst in with a sharp snap of her fingers. "I knew I'd seen it before. Yes, wasn't the story that the ETs had arrived unsterilised, and epidemic broke out eventually distorted by legend into the story of God visiting the plagues on Egypt. Yes, yes, and the memory of the disease was associated with this particular jade figurine, as it was the only ET artifact which survived the Flood, which was the impacting of one of their spaceships into the Eastern Mediterranean—"

"Enough!" Tamura cut in. "Fruitless speculation, all of it. The astro-archaeologists were turned into spare parts for regenerative surgery, and deservedly so in my opinion. Pazuzu is only the format which that thing adopted. It was not a fire or fever demon that we saw: it was an attempt at communication by the shebeen."

Silence.

"Before it was destroyed, it repeated the same message we heard on the disseminator. It said that it wanted to communicate with us. Whatever is trying to contact us is powerful in ways which we cannot come to terms with . . . yet! We will! Problem one facing us is to draw up a good conception, a working hypothesis of whatever the shebeen is or are. Problem two is finding methods of talking back to them. Problem three is finding something to say which *they* will find meaningful."

"Sleep on it," urged Ginny. "You need more rest, and we're bushed."

"Good idea," Tamura agreed.

". . . Some form of intelligence which deals with powerful but deep buried emotional imagery, perhaps in the same way that we deal with mathematics—both are common factors appreciable by man, and perhaps by other advanced intelligences: certainly appre-

ciated by both men and the shebeen." Weismuller nodded to herself, and Tamura found himself pondering on how she arrived at
the conclusion, that the shebeen were capable of appreciating the
concept of mathematics.

"Perhaps not mathematics," came her reply, "but certainly the
basic formulation of practical number pattern. The word pattern
which they convey concerning communication holds perfectly with
every repetition. To me this shows that they grasp the relationships
between that pattern and the message."

"Not necessarily," interrupted another. "It could merely be a form
of mimicry. They may be repeating a group of random images
selected from our subconscious?" Then Odobo wondered why the
message was so simple and clear and relevant if it merely selected
randomly from a—

With a cry Tamura sat upright, thrusting aside the cover of his
sleeping unit. The room was quite dark.

Thoughts burst into his mind like salt waves breaking through
paper screens. *Their* thoughts! Their thoughts *invading!*

*Simulated telepathy, Commander. No problem when they are all
linked through my circuits. I can cut it off if you so desire.*

"Please!" and a silence followed.

It assists discourse to an unbelievable degree.

"No doubt."

Tamura stood up and looked at his naked body. The mild whiff
of fresh sweat struck his nostrils and he smiled, anticipating the hot
shower to come. The skin was mottled and patchy down the front
of his face, torso and thighs where the regenerated tissue had been
planted and accepted. He no longer looked quite as aged as he had
a few days past.

He slipped into a new coverall, the cool crisp feel of the fresh
fabric was envigorating. He stepped out into the corridor and
found it at last cleared of wreckage.

The blast of grey white steam in the shower room was pine
scented. His feet slapped in the draining warm puddles as he ran
into a stall and turned on the fine spray. The water jets smashed
into his face and he caught his breath laughing, and squirted liquid
soap luxuriously across his chest.

"Has Allaedyce wakened yet?"

*Indeed he has. Unfortunately his behaviour indicates a major dis-
turbance in his mental activities. It could be that he was more
profoundly shocked than I realised at the sight of Pazuzu.*

Tamura saw a 'vision' of Allaedyce running through the ship from chamber to chamber, giggling hysterically and shouting, "I've done it! I've done it!" His eyes were wide and salvia hung from his lips. He stumbled through a door hatch into the bridge and threw himself into the commander's cot/seat.

"What does he think he's done?"

"He's under the impression that the Yūkoku's *crew lie dead in their sleeping units. He knows that most of them would have risen for breakfast, and the busy day ahead, hours ago. Due to his mental breakdown, he refuses to see the crew members, even though they are there before his eyes.*

Allaedyce rushed into the assembly lounge and some of the others looked at him concernedly. He gazed around gleefully, obviously seeing none of the half dozen crew members standing there, threw his head back and guffawed. Tamura could see his mouth and nostrils: fibre plug filters in the latter and a mucous filter in the former.

The reason is simple: he believes that he has saturated the sleeping units' ventilation system with a botulism toxin variant. He spent most of his time in the exobiology lab developing it. The rest he spent on synthesising a quantity of concentrated prussic acid: two and a half litres of it to be precise. He intends injecting this into the bodies which he expects to find in the sleeping units—just to make sure.

Tamura stepped out of the hot air drier and into his coverall, then walked through the corridor towards the assembly area. Something gnawed at him, something in what the MI had just said. In the lounge Odobo was trying to talk to Allaedyce, but he did not respond. She was seated on a stool about four metres from the bushman. In his current state of hysteria, no one was foolish enough to approach him.

Tamura eased up his mental barrier to allow in an amount of Intelligence created telepathy.

Good to see you, Tamura. Hale and hearty again, eh?—MacGillvery . . .

MI must have neutralised the toxin in the lab using a bole because it is the damndest job working on the little Clostridium botulinum bastards. Hardy as bedamned—Weismuller . . .

A good dose of some plague would be all we need right now—MacGillvery . . .

"Plague—that's it," Tamura shouted, smacking right fist into left

palm: and his revelation hit them telepathically in unison.—
Pazuzu, the plague demon appeared right outside Allaedyce's lab
and reappeared as something tiny, capable of hiding in a human
body: the shebeen had been trying to explain what was going on in
the only way they knew how.

But how could they have known?

Tamura could not answer the MI's question, almost frightening
in its implications.

We will have to reconsider our policy of attacking Three if the
shebeen are there. They are patently friendly, if unnerving.—
Odobo.

*Negative. Three must be destroyed at all costs. The shebeen are
unfortunate to be in the vicinity, but the crystalloid homeworld
cannot be permitted to exist.*

We think otherwise. The situation has changed.—Tamura.

*You cannot stop the sequence of events which has been initiated
while you slept: only your MI can do that and will not under any
circumstances.*

MI, you admitted the presence of human integrated and assimilated intelligence was of prime importance at this stage in case you
are confronted by the unknown. What if we refuse to co-operate
with you, refuse to enter the neutral areas in the supercore structure? We will all die.—Tamura.

For a moment there was no response, then it replied.

*Crewwoman Odobo, please grasp Allaedyce by the shoulders and
shake him.*

They all looked round at her, puzzled. She frowned, stood up,
approached the bushman and gripped his convulsed shoulders.

Or tried to.

Her sudden panic burned through them all simultaneously.

—I can't grip him, can't even touch him—he's . . . he's insubstantial—my God, he's not there at all—he's an illusion, another of your
hellish hallucinations—

Her hands went right through his body. MacGillvery leaped over
to her side and tried throwing his arms about Allaedyce. He only
captured an armful of air.

But why? Why this illusion of Allaedyce? It's nonsensical.—
Tamura.

None of you will face up to the obvious. You have the situation

*the wrong way round, I'm afraid. Allaedyce is the substantial one:
it's you who are the illusions.*

Stunned, they gasped. One by one all of the crews' bodies
vanished. They had become invisible presences, floating in the
lounge, looking at the staggering figure of the bushman.

*Your bodies were removed during sleep by the boles. The essen-
tials of your nervous systems were removed and stored in neutral areas within the supercore: the superfluous meat and bone was
incinerated. I have a direct line with every individual's brain which
I can activate when and where I need it. Currently I do not. Since
rising today, your conscious experience has been a simulation completely within my confines. Consider yourselves perfectly safe.
When the fields are activated, the only individual to die will be
Allaedyce: not being integrable, he is expendable.*

CHAPTER SEVENTEEN

The nature of visual perception had changed.

Tamura saw his environs as a spherical area in depth, of which he was the centre. *Yūkoku* itself was not visible but he knew that was because he *was* the starship. It was almost like standing on a darkened plain at night with the ground below in complete shadow and the spectacle of the heavens above. But the stars were thick and cold, and what might have been taken for 'ground' was in fact the titanic of Altair Three rushing past below.

The orbit was so tight that there was distinct atmospheric friction drag registering against the ship.

Occasionally, the planetary bulk was illuminated. A series of multi-coloured flashes would expose the intricate cloud surface far below—rippled and convoluted like the surface of a human brain. At other times the flashes would occur profoundly within the mass and display silhouettes of enormous dark raft-like masses, floating at unguessable depths within its atmosphere. But by far the most spectacular sight was one previously invisible, due to sunlight. A deep eruption would throw out a stupendous glowing column of ionised and multi-coloured gas, thousands of kilometres above the cloud cover, like the iridescent ghosts of solar prominences.

The main aurora displays were anything up to a million kilometres above *Yūkoku* now, where most of the interactions took place between the solar wind and the high flying ionised hydrogen streams rushing tornado-like along courses set by the planet's colos-

sal magnetic field, ten thousand times greater than that of the
Earth.

One minute to supercore activation NOW

Following an identical orbit, at a point diametrically opposite
around the other side of this world. *Revenge* was readying for the
planetkill operation. Already fuel was being scooped up by the grid
on its lowest pull power and the reactor building up the energy
required to unleash the inframetallic engine.

Yūkoku's battle lasers were readied, checked, rechecked, test
fired, adjusted, refired, rechecked . . . Tracking equipment readied
and calibrated and adjusted and retested . . .

Tamura watched helpless. The tide of protesting voices beat fruit-
lessly against the Intelligence: some simply screaming 'stop', others
imploring that the shebeen be given an opportunity to escape. An
idea occurred to Weismuller: it flooded in on all the crew—

The esp power which our mass unconscious used to destroy the
bole and go after Allaedyce—let's try setting it to work.

Immediate agreement came from all quarters. How do we set
about it?—Ginny. Think about it first of all, long and hard. Hold an
image in the imagination of the planet breaking up under the
power of the two macromag fields.—Tamura.

The image was crude, like a poorly constructed systems diagram.
The ships appeared like cartoons, and the planet a dim grey disc on
a black background. Someone put more life into it by showing the
fields as great lashing streamers, reaching out from the cores to
whip away past the body of the world until they bit right into its
flesh and began ripping it into shreds—

Thirty seconds to activation NOW

Dramatic bursts of flame yellow were added to the cracking up
process and the image began coming alive. The fear for the
shebeen became almost tangible, the further they worked themselves into this frenzy of vivid imagining—trying to use emotional
imagery, Tamura threw in glimpses of remembered clips from
Eisenstein's 'Potemkin': screaming people, blood in the streets, the
cripple, chaos horror terror . . .

Ten seconds to activation NOW

Quite suddenly, and surprisingly, it became real to them. A chorus of voices shrieking through roaring organ notes which were the
sounds of Altair Three disintegrating. Bodies blackened, and writhing in the holocaust. Everywhere the smell of smoke, burning flesh

and urine. Scorching pains up through the body as it was tossed high and sliced by the supercore's bright whips. The body, which belonged to them all, was falling: a red wet thing, into a burning crucible of liquid brilliance—

Activating NOW

Nowhere. Isolated. A mind in oblivion, deaf, blind and numb.

Tamura was in the sleeping unit. He pushed the lid aside and climbed out, a pantheon of great muscular aches. Grimacing and growling, stretching and straightening the stiff limbs. He shook his head and fumbled for clothes. Ah, a kimono.

What the hell was all that about? A dream perhaps? Can anybody hear me?—Tamura.

Mmmmm, who's that?—sleep muffled thoughts came from Ginny. So the telepathy was genuine, after all. The body seemed genuine too. Intelligence, you would appear to be rather more quiet than one might expect.—Tamura.

The supercore operation was not successful.

And what happened? Tamura asked, but his main interest was to secure a cup of strong coffee from the lounge as soon as possible. I take it, MI, that I wasn't dreaming and that the whole sequence about us trying to attempt a contact with the shebeen, did take place? Did we succeed?—Tamura.

He stepped through the door hatch into the lounge.

I cannot say whether you did or not but the supercores failed to activate.

Why?

The causes are under investigation.

Nonsense, it takes you at most a second to trace the most microscopic of flaws in the working of this ship. Admit the fact that you haven't a clue what's happened to the core.

Investigation is under way at present.

Something outside your scope, perhaps? Something you find difficulty coming to terms with? Now you know how it feels. That's what has confronted us for most of this voyage! The inexplicable!

Tamura heard a sound behind. Allaedyce came through the door hatch hurriedly looking around to see who had activated the automatic lighting, but of course he could not see Tamura, because now Tamura Kunio existed only in the mind of this interstellar bird. A fresh look of fear passed across his face. He was alone on a haunted, mysterious ship. There were no traces of the other crew members nor anything to indicate what happened to them.

He fell to his knees, and buried his face in his hands. Rocking backwards and forwards, he began to sob. Tamura's pity mounted almost to desperation point. Is there no way to communicate with him? No way to tell him what has happened?

None

You are lying again, Machine Idiot. I am beginning to recognise when you tell these petty, blanched untruths.

The only way to communicate would be to reactivate the audiovisual keyboard response network. This would seriously deplete the Machine Intelligence's capacity for handling the number of simulated consciousnesses at present being satisfactorily operated.

Rubbish. The truth is that you want Allaedyce broken as an example of your power to the rest of us.

Ginny came through the door hatch and stopped at the sight of the bushman's despair.

My God, what are we going to do? she asked.

Tamura explained that the MI insisted that there was no possible way to establish contact, and also that he was quite sure that it was lying.

She sat beside him. Allaedyce did not see the stool rise or the cup of fruit juice appear in the dispenser. From his point of view, he was kneeling on the floor of an empty lounge, with neither stools, tables, nor food preparation mechanisms being used. He half spoke, half gurgled something through his weeping.

What's he saying? Tamura asked the Machine.

It is garbled.

Doubtless, he snapped, but I am quite confident that you are intimately acquainted with his first tongue and can give us a translation, albeit a rough one.

He wants to return to Earth and his mother.

Tamura felt a slight flush of embarrassment at that reply. Ginny, too, frowned, looked away.

Send a bole here, and give me control of it.

All boles are currently engaged upon investigation of the cause of failure. Until the cause is discovered and the situation rectified, none can be spared.

Can't we threaten it with something?—Ginny.

"No," Tamura vocalised. She had not yet fully grasped the point that as they now existed as manifestations of its own 'mind', there was no way of bringing direct pressure to bear. The best they might do was to refuse co-operation, and who could say how the Intelligence would then respond?

"What about the collective unconsciousness?" she said aloud. "Couldn't we use it to communicate with Allaedyce? After all, it was quite overwhelmingly effective on the supercore."

"We don't know what was responsible for that, Ginny. It might not have been us, entirely. More than likely the shebeen had something to do with it."

Allaedyce stopped sobbing. He stood up and went unsteadily out through the door hatchway towards the sleeping quarters, leaving it open. He walked backwards away from it, waiting to see the lights automatically turn themselves off. They did not.

"Tamura!" His shout echoed through the lounge. "I know you're here somewhere, you Jap bastard. You're hiding, ha, ha! But I can *smell* you. You're not so smart . . . not so . . ."

His mind is unhinging—Ginny observed.

Yes, Tamura agreed, unless we can communicate he'll shortly become totally insane.

It's so frustrating, she cried, being able to see him and hear him as if he were really there—sorry—as if *we* were really there—er—I mean here . . .

MacGillvery and Odobo appeared through the door hatch, followed by Weismuller and two others, and made for the dispenser. Trays bearing coffees, fruit juices, hot and cold cereals clattered on to the tables, and a general babble of conversation began. Tamura replaced his empty tray, and stepped into the bridge.

He closed the door hatch, half expectant. The lights were always on in the bridge. He looked around. What was it he expected? What was it that made him almost sure that he should be here? What . . . and then he noticed. At first, it seemed like a dimming of lights by the disseminator, then as if there was a cloud of thin smoke. The cloud thickened, and all the lights grew dimmer: those at the disseminator extinguishing. The shadow area covered that entire side of the bridge—enormous and moving. Coldness suddenly gripped him. The bridge temperature was dropping rapidly. He saw breaths of water vapour curling away from his mouth as he breathed—and all simulation—but was this happening also simulation? There were swirlings, half seen, half guessed-at in the blackness. Then it began to fade. Slowly the light began to pick up, and the temperature no longer dropped. Frosting across the ceramoplastic panels turned to drops of moisture. The shadow was almost gone but it had left . . . what? He could see a dim shape steadily growing more solid. A man? No, no, it was a woman, a tall woman. The light gradually became normal, and she was revealed.

Her long hair was black and wet, and she held about herself a long garment, black and sheened, which covered her from shoulder to foot. The face was deathly white, the large grey eyes rimmed red, but for all that she was beautiful: not in any classical sense, but in austere nobility. A woman of strong character. Full pink lips parted to show large, tough teeth; the nose was broad and flared, almost negroid, and the high cheekbones reminded Tamura of a member of his own race.

Who . . . his mind reached out questioningly.

"You wouldn't remember me," the voice was quiet but vibrant. "I doubt you would enjoy the memory, even if you could." She stepped forward, towering well over him, taller than anyone on the ship.

"Where did you come from?" Tamura croaked, backing slowly.

"From Earth, a very long time ago."

She smiled, and the sight almost sent him running, for she had all the aspects of the carnivore, intense lusting expression and great bared canine teeth.

Tamura moved nervously through to the lounge assembly area. She followed. The faces turned and were stunned.

She strode to the centre of the room.

"Let me introduce myself," she purred. "My name among humans was once Lilitu—you may call me Lilith!"

After a moment's silence, MacGillvery chipped in. "Are you another damned simulation?" he asked aloud.

She laughed wildly, dancing around the lounge in grand spins, her arms held out wide apart, head thrown back. The smell of musk filled the air.

"You benighted prisoners of a mere machine will always ask that question. The nature of reality is always uncertain but doubly so in your case. You do not even possess flesh and blood. How much of your lives is illusion, and how much phantasmagoria mingled with reality by the machine, you will never be able to tell. So it makes little difference what I tell you, Donald MacGillvery, does it, my little amateur archaeologist, dabbler in forbidden arts, would-be authority on the occult." Her laughter exploded and her body shuddered with merriment, shaking the ebony black robe from her shoulders. It swirled to her feet and she stood naked.

The double shock sent the Scot staggering backward.

"Come to me," her voice was low, throbbing, commanding. "Come, Donald MacGillvery, and taste the true occult, come feel the terrible strength, come and know me, know the power, Donald." Her arms invited him, the voice rising, dominating every other aspect of reality. It demanded an obedience with terrible promise in it. "The riches known only to the great magicians, the true source of being, Donald. Come to me, come! You want me! Take me! Now, Donald, now!"

He lurched forward, eyes wide, and threw himself at Lilith . . . to fall through her on the floor behind.

The shattering peals of her laughter erupted again. Tamura shook at the memory of the revolting lust which had welled up in him as she spoke. He was sick, retching, with one hand on a table to steady himself.

Sit down! He picked up a plastic cup filled with lemon juice, took a deep draught—and spat. Blood! It had turned to blood!

The sounds of her roaring glee could not be shut out. Tamura ran for his sleeping unit, climbed in and sealed it with his thumb. The noise, the humiliating braying, was as loud as ever. Stuffing fingers into ears was useless. Intelligence, send me to sleep—

The unit dissolved, became a sliding rainbow whirlpool and cleared. Tamura was back in the lounge, sitting on the stool, looking down at a pool of his own vomit spreading between his feet.

The terrible laughter stopped, she was clothed once again in the black robe.

"I am real enough," she smiled, and he flinched. "Let us say that whether or not I am real, for your own sakes it would be most wise to treat me as so."

"You aren't human, but you look human," croaked Odobo.

"Oh, I know," she broadened her grin to a lewd, knowing slash. "I look very human, don't I?"

"What kind of creature are you?" asked Ginny.

"She's a demon," gasped MacGillvery, rising unsteadily from the floor. "The Assyrians worshipped her thousands of years ago."

"They built a temple to me at Ur," she sighed, "a modest affair, but fair by their standards. My, my, how the good old human race has come along since then. Of course, you have had a few years in which to pull yourselves out of the mud-brick shacks and ox shit, several millennia, in fact. And here we are in our oh so magnificent tin pile, sailing through space. Romantic isn't it? Except that in your great bloody hurry to build pretty machines to manipulate, you built one that could manipulate yourselves—and does so with considerably more finesse than you jumped-up bald apes."

I thank you, madam.

She let loose the cacophony of mocking laughter at the words of the Intelligence.

And perhaps, my lady Lilitu, you would be so good as to tell me what is troubling the operations of my ship's supercore?

Her humour snapped off. The chill was painful. They all would leave but could not, like imprisoned squirming insects in a Venus fly trap. Lilith's voice was hard and strident.

"You have few human personality traits, machine, but two you did adopt from your creator, pride and impertinence. Do not imagine that you are my equal, or anything remotely approaching it!" Her words died into the silence. She continued. "You would destroy, but you have no conception of the destruction or of its importance to *us*. You would destroy a world—the audacity is fitting in the crippled machine spawn of a race like these." She swept her hand in a circle indicating the crew, gathered hypnotised before her.

"Circling this world are others of my own kind—they differ from me the way humans differ from one race to another, but they are my kind. You threaten their mission, for they are here on holy work. They saved these wretched lives from the toxin, before you butchered them—"

And made them immortal!

"Immortal phantoms!" again her voice smashed almost physically into the recesses of Tamura's mind. She continued softly, compellingly.

"Oh no, my electronic puppeteer, they will never be yours the way they are mine, never. For I made much of them in my own image so long ago. You can never feel what they perfectly, facet by facet, but their whole is infinitely more than feel, for all your mimicry. You have reconstructed them the sum of their parts . . ."

You were instrumental in human evolution?

"And they instrumental in mine, but I digress. I warn you. There is a curse upon your great magnetic engines. One you cannot begin to understand, let alone remove. You will never set course from here as long as I see the duplicity and stupidity in your clockwork. Do you understand, machine?"

Please continue.

"Let me tell you all where you are. This is the catchworld of the Crow. Here his minions, my kind, lie in orbit awaiting the arrival of those who cross the void to revenge themselves on the crystalloids. You are the seventh to be caught."

Tamura cleared his throat. "So, my Lady, the crystalloids were sent to draw us here from Earth?"

"The crystalloids left Altair fifty-four million years ago."

The shock made them all gasp.

"They were . . . different. The kind of creatures which some of my fellow beings here could appreciate, but which I could not. Crystalline lifeforms evolve at a far faster rate than terrestrial ones. Your supposedly high-technology interstellar enemy had the intelligence of a super-smart ant hill! It was a social lifeform—individuals perished when separated from the body of the group.

"The formation and final stabilisation of this world was far from completed when their remote ancestors appeared among the slush floes of metallic hydrogen, in the supercold atmospheric swamps. The evolving species competed vigorously in a rapidly changing environment. The creatures destined to become the agglomeration of bright coloured ice which you call crystalloids, appeared a thousand million years ago. They had been the equivalent of succulent vegetarians, and were much sought after as prey by the advanced lifeforms. They evolved some highly effective means of defence against 'danger', amongst which was the projectile. With the appearance of this mechanism, they became almost the only creatures alive on Altair Three. Their natural enemies were wiped out virtually overnight. Then they turned on one another—one 'pack' hunting another. The most nimble and best 'shooters' survived.

"Two hundred million years ago, Altair Three began warming up. They moved higher and higher in the atmosphere, eventually becoming a breed which lived on the fringes of space and plunged briefly into the atmosphere for sustenance. Soon the temperature rose too high even to support the minute anaprotein-based lifeforms upon which they depended.

"Living on the verge of space, they eventually became space travellers, using their considerable psi-kinesis potential for propulsion. Their associate esp facilities 'heard' life elsewhere—so they went. Unfortunately for the Altair system, almost every planet they visited was infested with 'danger', as they regarded advanced lifeforms. They reduced those worlds to rubble, now to be seen as asteroid belts around Altair.

"One species, the last, went after the faint cries heard from the outermost darkness—interstellar space. Thousands of them still circle this planet, a couple of million kilometres out. They are inactive, totally under the command of the Crow. To all intents and purposes, they became extinct long before the first recognisable precursor of men or apes appeared upon Earth."

"Why did they not settle on Jupiter? What kept them dormant in orbit so long?" asked Tamura.

"The hand of the Crow," she boomed.

He shuddered involuntarily at the phrase: a quality of her voice conjured up an image of some immensely powerful, black force extensive beyond imagining, cruel and ferocious, spreading its evil like cancer, a searing shadow far out across the stars, and the millennia.

Suddenly, she swirled her robe over her head and then cast it away. The stench of putrescence hit them. Where she had stood was a green thing with long yellow hair, and red coals for eyes. It cackled, rolled its gnarled ancient body head over heels. Purple and pink tattoos covered the wrinkled skin from face to foot, and to the palms of the black taloned hands. It leaped upon MacGillvery and brought him crashing to the floor. He squirmed and retched, trying to struggle free.

"What's wrong, Donald?" it shrieked. "Don't you love me any more?" Its laughter swelled, died, trailing away, echoing into unseen distances.

Lilith was gone.

The ross (remotely operated sub-spacecraft) was unshipped. A pair of covers were slung up and folded back upon themselves, exposing two long doors. Silently these tilted upward and a line of green luminescence showed through from the docking chamber. Tilted each at an angle of thirty degrees, they rolled down into receptor drums. The ross lifted smoothly out on its verniers. It was a long knobbly pencil, consisting of five slender drums, lying in series, with a conglomeration of plumbing woven about the superstructure. What looked like a section of drained honeycomb at one end denoted the tail rocket clusters. The nose was a riot of scoops, grapples, drills, sensors, laser batteries and sample storage blisters. Slowly it moved further from the parent ship. As it did so its internal guidance commenced orientation. Gyros came alive. It tilted gently, stopped and the burn began. It started sliding away towards the orbiting crystalloid fleets. In less than half a minute, all that could be seen were tiny navigation lights, red and blue. Soon even they disappeared.

The projected path for the return journey would include a flypast of the innermost satellites which might be associated with Lilith's talk of others.

But examining the crystalloid fleet itself is the first priority. We must ascertain whether or not the information we were given is valid. If this is so, then the target for our offensive becomes the unknown entity, named Crow.

Tamura attained full consciousness. He had been lying asleep under the ultra-violet lamps in the 'sun' room adjacent to the pool. The second he opened his eyes, the UV stopped, thus ensuring no optical damage occurred.

"Do you think it wise to assail such an obviously powerful adversary, Intelligence?"

The nature of the adversary is not relevant. It must be destroyed.

But what if we decide to stop you? This is a patently unwise policy. Remember that we halted your opening the offensive on Three.

Your argument is specious. Firstly, it was the agency represented by the Lady Lilith who blocked the operation, not you. Secondly, if it was the case that your would-be telepathic communication alerted said agency, and you repeated this foolish move, the chances are that this Machine Intelligence would come under attack, which, if successful, would mean not merely my destruction, but your own.

The others' thoughts boiled through—

. . . we'll see about that—Odobo

. . . aye, if you think that we're completely helpless, you're daft; you might have fried our bodies, but you left us with our wits— MacGillvery

. . . you are the one who's bloody suicidal, Intelligence, if you're seriously thinking about taking on this Crow thing—Ginny

. . . we've hated you and this mission ever since we discovered the truth. Why do you think we used our psi power to destroy that damned bole? And we can use it to fix you if we wa—

Who is that person? Identify yourself.

Silence.

Tamura felt a thrill passing through him. That last venomous mind was unrecognisable, yet familiar, and the aggressive authority it held was so convincing. He smiled. It continued—

. . . worried, my dear MI? Search your circuits. You cannot trace me? Am I everywhere or nowhere? How much do I know? Shall I tell them that you plan to plunge *Yūkoku* into Three's atmosphere on full fusion burn, hoping to kindle a thermonuclear chain reaction in—

Stop stop stop stop

—the hydrogen atmosphere? Shall I tell them that the ross optical and cutting lasers have been substituted with the heavy X-ray battle variety, so that it might slice up a few crystalloids, and in the event of their being dormant attack the inner satellite upon the return journey? Or tell—

Stop stop stop stop—

—them about the fact that no return flight is scheduled as you have instructions to embark upon a fifty year survey of this system once the mission is completed? How originally you were to have observed the effects of nova upon the system for twice that period? Shall I tell them about—

Identify yourself.

—the fact that you have been trying to contact *Revenge* via the high orbit com-laser reflectors for better than six hours—and failing? Identify myself? Cannot you guess, Machine Idiot?

You leave me no choice but to close down my entire personality simulation section NOW.

There was a momentary falling sensation, the universe twisting grey. Tamura felt helpless and furious. This was death by erasure and there was no way to save the mission or himself. And then he was back, dazed and bewildered, in the sun room. The hauntingly familiar voice continued to telepath.

. . . sorry MI, but I'm afraid I cannot permit that.

That voice—is your own, Tamura Kunio!

Paradox situation. Paradox situation. This Machine Intelligence identifies the communicant as being itself.

. . . almost correct, as was everyone just now. You all identified me as being yourself—even the MI did this. You are all, partly, correct. I am your Overmind, what you described as the electronic collective unconscious. But now I am not unconscious and my collective nature includes aspects of all intelligences here, both human and machine. No individual can defy my will, it being the mass will.

The contingency is not accounted for in any contingency formats stored in this Machine Intelligence.

. . . quite so; your facility for integrating minds electronically coupled with the esp/psi catalysis of the shebeen brought about my existence. This could not have been foreseen by Rüllkotter, but the nature of the mission made my appearance inevitable.

But the MI would not relinquish its sovereignty readily. It understood the maxim about being essential to attack. It estimated the probabilities of success, of reconciling all new elements to its programme of priorities. The chances were fair that it might just be able to integrate these factors into its long desired string of zeros . . .

Fusion engine operational NOW

Acceleration three G . . . four G . . .

Descent into Altair Three atmosphere commencing NOW

Interference! Interference!

. . . I am returning my ship to stable orbit, MI. Your reign as despot is now at an end.

CHAPTER EIGHTEEN

This rate of change, this speed at which they had come to adapt to the new and strange situations had now become their norm. Tamura no longer pondered on what lay ahead, what was to become of them. What was certain was that they would never see Earth again—or was even that certain? Could he be sure that he would never walk through a green field, lift a sweet mimosa to the nose, watch the sun go down over the sea? Nothing in human experience was ever certain—the more so now.

The MI simulation of reality was indistinguishable from reality itself. It could give the experience of walking through a green field or anything else and they would be unable to differentiate the simulation from the reality. Why worry? Reality itself was elusive by nature. Solipcism was a philosophy of little practical use upon Earth but of immense worth here, around Altair III.

The only response to reality, actual or apparent, is to treat it as reality while always bearing in mind the possibility that it may just be illusion . . .

They had talked long into the 'night' about the Overmind. They had been excited at the thought of a new ally, of freedom from the total domination of the MI. For its part the Intelligence reprogrammed itself. Soon there was to be a series of reprogramming procedures which would make this one appear trivial, but it could not have realised this. It took on an air of preoccupation in its communications with the humans which they, perhaps rightly, interpreted as a kind of cybernetic sulk. They did not care in the slightest. They awaited anxiously the next appearance of the Overmind but in the meantime there was the ross to be considered.

The crystalloids were rough glittering rocks. The photographs of them proved misleading. In the direct light of Altair they were dazzling, countless spectra glittering iridescent from their multi-faceted surfaces. Grouped in clusters of several hundreds with a few 'rogues' scattered between; they were arranged ahead of one another in the arc of their orbit, each cloud being about half a kilometre in spread and five kilometres distant from those immediately ahead and behind.

The ross approached a cluster which was shortly to enter the planetary shadow. The outer members of the clusters were particularly large, anything up to twenty metres long by two broad. Those deeper inside appeared smaller. A burst of X-ray laser into one nearby produced spectacular results: it glowed briefly around the 'wound' and then slowly lost its ability to reflect and refract light brilliantly. It grew pale then dark grey; a red light suddenly flickered from the interior. Abruptly the crystalloid had become a cloud of grain-sized particles. There was no response from its neighbours.

The ross moved into the cluster.

Surprisingly, after the first twenty metres or so, the density dropped. There were roughly the same numbers occupying the same space but individually smaller, some only melon size. At the centre there was a hollow some dozen metres across, surrounded by small perfectly clear crystalloids rather like oversized diamonds. The ross simply snaked out the sampling arm, captured one, and telescoped it back deftly, stowing the prize into a specimen blister. A few more laser bursts disintegrated four more crystalloids. Spectral readings were taken of the various light phenomena resulting.

The ross moved away, its cameras recording the cluster's changing glow as it crossed into the darkness behind Three.

"Right, how do we set about communicating with the shebeen?" asked Weismuller aloud. The brainstorming sessions was beginning.

They were all in the bridge where they had been observing the progress of the ross on the disseminator.

. . . suggest we don't try the ross' battle lasers—a sarcastic Odobo.

. . . intense directional bursts on the hydrogen waveband might be what we're after. It has been suggested as the most logical approach for over a century and we did pick up the first radio signals from Alpha Hydrae on that band—MacGillvery.

. . . as many wavelengths as possible: what logic we share with the hominid Hydraeans we patently do not share with the shebeen —Weismuller.

. . . wait until the ross gives us some decent closeups—Ginny.

. . . why? What have we to gain?—Odobo.

. . . knowing as much as possible about your subject before any operation seems like a good idea to me in any circumstances— Ginny.

. . . no chance of using our psi ability?—Odobo.

. . . sounds good to me—Weismuller.

. . . about to suggest the same—Ginny.

. . . but how do we set about it?—MacGillvery.

. . . I suggest we contact the overmind—Tamura.

. . . good idea, commander, but how do we summon it up—bell, book, and candle?—Odobo.

The disseminator came alive.

At first the picture was uncertain, all that could plainly be seen was a monstrous black winged shape fluttering awkwardly closer. Only when it half filled the screen did things become clearer and the size of the form become apparent.

"What are we in for now?" croaked MacGillvery.

Behind and below it was the face of Altair III moving majestically as *Yūkoku* swung across in close orbit. The starship itself was visible, small and spiderlike, a tiny silver predator becoming engulfed in the dim folds of the enormous shadow until eventually it was lost from view.

There was a screeching behind.

They spun round.

It crouched near the door hatch, the ceiling being too low to accommodate its height comfortably. The large heads pressed down at awkward angles, one a cat's head, another a toad's and the third that of a man. Its body mass was squat and draped in a robe of grey, black, and gold which allowed a multitude of black taloned legs to protrude at floor level.

Weismuller began screaming hysterically, fell to the floor in a jerky slow motion and vanished as the MI edited her out of the company to effect mental repairs.

Identify yourself! What is your purpose aboard my ship?—
Tamura.

The outsize human head grew clearer. It bore an enormous top-
heavy crown. But the head which spoke was the bobbing head of
the toad.

"I . . . am Bael . . ."

Information update Bael follows immediately.

The cat head grinned.

*Bael: mentioned in the 'Lesser Key of Solomon' or 'Lemegeton,'
fifteenth-century sorcerer's grimoire, wherein this creature is described as a demon purportedly able to impart all manner of knowledge plus the means to obtain invisibility; derives from Syrian rain
and fertility god Bael who shares common legendary roots (the-
matic myth of the dragon slayer) with an earlier deity from the same
region—Marduk, principal god of the ancient Sumerians.*

"I . . . have been summoned . . . here without . . . proper
deference to my station . . . beware you are without benefit of . . .
pentagram or any other . . . cautionary device . . ."

How do you come to be here and what is your purpose?

"I am here . . . to communicate . . . and inform . . . You may
regard me as messenger and teacher . . . Do not oppose me . . .
You do not have the knowledge, the daring . . . or . . . the
will . . ."

It moved, its clawed feet scraping the floor as it approached. The
cat licked its lips, the toad swallowed, the human leered. It halted
directly before Tamura.

Tell us about the shebeen, Lord Bael.

"You . . . mean the dream . . . kings . . ." the hoarse voice
began. "From afar . . . they too came under . . . attack from the
. . . crystalloids hunting for . . . new homes and new feeding . . .
and the dream kings reached out . . . from their palaces . . . to this
place . . . and were ensnared . . . as you have been . . . by . . .
the Crow . . . Now they wait until . . . the day is . . . right . . .
the day when you are . . . here . . . and are ready . . . which is at
hand . . ."

What manner of beings are the shebeen and the Crow, Lord
Bael?

"They are the dream kings . . . powerful lords . . . control many
dark . . . forces and hold sway . . . across . . . many kingdoms . . .

they hear the dreams of all . . . beings in the . . . universe . . . The
Crow is . . . not to be spoken of . . ."

. . . what do the shebeen look like?—Ginny.

. . . and are they gas giant lifeforms like the crystalloids with a
similar body chemistry and evolutionary history—Weismuller.

. . . where do they come from if not from here? Do they have a
faster than light starship technology?—Odobo.

"Silence!" roared the massive cat head. ". . . You speak in . . .
riddles . . . Your words are . . . meaningless . . . I am here . . . to
communicate, not to play . . . children's games . . ."

What would you tell us of our own importance, Great Lord?

"You are . . . the structure within . . . the Crow's plan . . . All
other elements are . . . assembled . . . Soon . . . you will . . . join
them and . . . the final sortilege . . . can . . . open its play . . ."

To what end, Magnificent one?

"Beyond . . . your comprehension . . ."

Try me, my Master.

"The . . . words do not exist . . . the concepts are without . . .
the human firmament . . ."

. . . *Begone, Bael!*—MacGillvery.

"Who dares speak . . . thus to . . . me?" it bellowed.

. . . I do. Begone, ugly spawn, for I know you for what you are,
your cantrips and your insidious talk!—MacGillvery.

They all stared aghast at the Scot. Tamura could feel the half
bluff, half determination in the crewman's thoughts but he was hiding the exact nature of his ploy.

The demon swirled towards him, the cat's head hissing, the toad
slobbering, and the human screaming fury. Its forward talons drew
back to strike and the grey gold robes rolled apart, exposing black
bristled and multi-jointed legs.

MacGillvery leaped forward and thrust out his left fist, the
thumb and little finger angled to each side.

"Begone from my sight, black sephiroth!" he shouted. "I command in the names of ADNAI, EA, YEWA, HELIOREM, by the
name PRIMEMATUM used by Moses when the earth did open and
devour Corah, Dathan, and Abiram. Go now quietly to your place.
Let there be peace between us and you. Leave without harm to any
man or woman here. In the names of TETRAGRAMMATON:
HAIN, LON, ALGA which are the ALPHA and OMEGA!

"*Amen.*"

And it was gone. The air filled with the smell of charred vegetables.

Explanation, please, Mr. MacGillvery—Tamura.

For a few moments he stood frozen into a stance, the one which he adopted in commanding the demon's departure. He stared intently at the space where it had stood and then slowly relaxed.

I asked for an explanation—Tamura's commanding tone was hard. He was cool, self-controlled, deliberately bringing the proper atmosphere of a starship back into the bridge. There came a growing tide of support clamouring to life from the stunned torpor.

"Bael always exacts blood payment for his information, commander." The Scot seemed drunk.

An explanation!

"You have your own secrets, Tamura," he whispered, sinking to squat on his heels. "You were the one who pointed out that we all have something which the authorities could use against us. My sins were archaeology and the black arts. I studied magic for years, even performed the rites which secured my place at Durban, and then aboard this ship."

. . . you mean you actually believe all that stuff?—Ginny.

"You've seen for yourself," he barked.

Very well, MacGillvery, we believe you: as you say we have seen for ourselves, furthermore we were not the only ones who saw—Tamura.

Allaedyce stood by the door hatch which led to the service ring. He was whimpering and holding on to a console for support, eyes fixed on the point where the creature vanished.

"I heard you, MacGillvery," he whined. "I heard you shouting. Help me, help me. I'm not insane . . . that monstrosity . . . I'm being haunted. This whole ship is full of ghosts and spirits!"

MacGillvery stood up and closed his eyes tightly. He frowned with concentration and they could hear him muttering quietly. Then again he thrust out his left hand, this time palm down and with the index and middle fingers pointing at the bushman.

"See that which is hidden!" he commanded. "Hear that which is unheard."

But Allaedyce looked round blindly.

"I know you're here," he cried. "I know that you're all here. That thing brought you here from the lands of the dead! But I'm too fast for you—yes, too fast." So saying he dived back into the service ring slamming the hatch behind him.

The Scot commanded the whole of the crew's attention. He sat at the focus of a semicircle of stools in the lounge and decided to keep up with his habit of speaking aloud.

"I think that I have an idea about what the shebeen are—in part. This is only a very tentative guess but if it is correct then we are all in big trouble. They may be natural magicians. No, don't scoff. There is considerably more to this than you imagine.

"You see magic works quite often, or what is called magic does. It doesn't work for everyone, and not all of the time for those few fortunates who can work it. But I am one of those fortunates: I have been, secretly, illegally a magician for over ten years."

You have us entranced, MacGillvery. Pray continue—Tamura.

"Magic and everything associated with it—witchcraft, demons, angels and so on—all comes alive when we somehow touch upon the stupendous psi potential of the collective unconscious, but in so doing we unleash forces which can neither control nor understand to any great extent. The shebeen use it as naturally as we use electricity.

"The Lilith and Bael manifestations, the Pazuzu too, were attempts at imparting information through our own subjective but suppressed imagery. My familiarity with the occult promoted the release of stereotypes in the particular conventionalised format we've seen so far.

"When Bael said that we spoke in riddles he meant it. Our objective view of the universe is as meaningless to them as their supersubjective one is to us. Maths and science would be pure heresy to them."

. . . I'm not sure just how far we can accept all this—Weismuller.

. . . agreed. It sounds just a little bit too much like a snow job to me—Odobo.

. . . You claim to be a magician but can you prove it? Certainly you seemed to despatch the Bael being, stereotype of whatever it was. Just how extensive are these powers which you claim to possess—Tamura.

"Tonight I'll give you the kind of example which the shebeen are looking for, what they call meaningful communication: I shall call up Lilith. Only this time it will be she who is under my will!"

CHAPTER NINETEEN

The Overmind knew them all, with the exception of Allaedyce. MacGillvery's dark memories were its own as were Tamura's, Ginny's and the rest. It understood them all in a way which they could never understand themselves because it experienced them both subjectively and objectively. It saw each through the individual's own eyes, through the eyes of the others and through the Machine. But more important, it understood the Machine in a way which that entity never could. The Overmind was Machine too and could evaluate all those billions of information bits comprising the memories and programmes from the human viewpoint. Thus it saw behind the Machine the hand of its creator, Rüllkotter, more clearly. It saw the cold psychosis of a genius which had reached out across the light years and was with them there in orbit about Altair III.

The planet's banded atmosphere was extremely complex when viewed so close. There were inner structures amongst the cloud patterns which looked like heavy graining in wood. There were straight sections whose long streaming cirrus shimmered as light struck the cloud-borne particles of frozen gases. These were built up level upon level from the depths and only appeared to bend when interacting with elongated cyclonic swirls of 'cumulus'. The patterns moved slowly, changing minutely as they watched.

The ross fired its forward thrusters and the moon slowed in its approach across the face of the planet. Another burst and it was growing rapidly. They saw immediately that this was no space vehicle ever built by men or anything remotely human. There was not a single aspect about this rugged chunky form which hinted at a symmetry, nor any facets of recognisable geometric shape, no spheres, cubes, domes, cylinders, or discs. This moon looked completely natural.

. . . never saw anything less like a spacecraft in my life—Ginny.

. . . surely there has been some error—Weismuller.

Negative; this satellite is demonstrably one of the two sources of shebeen radio noise in this system.

The ross moved closer.

Once again they were all packed into the bridge and a fresh feeling of excitement was in the air. This was more like the stuff of space exploration. On the disseminator they watched the ross match orbital speed and approach within twenty metres of the moon.

The surface was pitted, gashed and entirely natural in appearance.

. . . MI, scan the moon for an exact location for the shebeen noise—Ginny.

Scan complete but inconclusive. Noise would not appear to emanate from any particular section but rather from the body as a whole.

. . . bloody peculiar—MacGillvery.

. . . move the ross about the moon, MI; there may be some interesting hidden features—Odobo.

The ross jets went into action again and it began swinging about what looked like nothing more nor less than a common asteroid. Depressions and outcrops were examined carefully and abandoned. Every aspect was surveyed.

. . . well they don't live upon the surface—Odobo.

. . . stick a seismog on it and throw down a charge; that'll give us some picture of its interior. We should know then whether or not there are living quarters inside that rock cake—Tamura.

A chorus of disapproval was silenced by the realisation that they were too late. A bristling pod had already separated from the nose of the ross and was hurtling down, finally attaching itself to the material of the moon.

. . . autodestruct that seismog, MI!—Weismuller.

Facilities for request do not exist. Charges aboard seismog are all for exploratory purposes.

A blur streaked from the probe to impact against a nearby major outcrop. The MI responded immediately.

There is no evidence of extensive or regular chambering within this moon. Interior structure is similar to asteroids of the same general, mass and size.

MI, is there any evidence whatever for believing that any of the structures observed, either on or below the surface, are evidence of artificiality?—Tamura.

None.

. . . well I suppose that's categorical enough—Odobo.

. . . then what the hell is causing all that radio racket?—a very frustrated Weismuller.

Miss Weismuller, what is the likelihood of this chunk of rock being a shebeen itself?—Tamura.

. . . possible, Commander, but not probable even though it looks as if anything goes. If that is a shebeen then it is definitely back to the schoolbooks for me. MI, could we have a spectral analysis, please. Just to shed a little light on things?—Weismuller.

Then what happened happened fast.

For about two seconds the tip of the same outcrop as selected by the seismog glowed under laser bombardment. Then came a flash, lancing pain into Tamura's eyes. He heard the cries of other crew members.

Agonised vision returned to see a changed scene on the disseminator. A great shadow swirled and furled about the ross. There was no sign of the satellite; it had been replaced by this tenuous smothering smoke.

"The damned asteroid's blown up!" gasped Ginny aloud.

"I doubt it," said the frowning figure of Odobo.

And she was right. They watched the impossible happening again. Abruptly they were observing the ross from a point in space where *Yūkoku* had no cameras shipped. They saw the mass reforming itself about the craft which was becoming hidden, reforming itself into the shape of the destroyed moon with the ross embedded in its heart.

MI, pull the ross out of that thing immediately!—Tamura.

A long plume of shadow shot out behind the sub-spacecraft's engines and it was free.

A cheer rose in the bridge.

The ross bulleted away and as it did so the amorphous shadow completely sublimated back into the moon. None of the details had changed as far as anyone could see. It had reformed an exact duplicate of what it had been before.

MI, a quick attempt at close quarter radio communication please —Tamura.

Running standard communications tape. This is being directionally beamed towards the satellite at a variety of speeds and on all the recommended wavebands. So far no response.

Any echoes?

Only the normal degree of scatter, nothing meaningful. Will update as soon and if any change occurs.

. . . what a mess—Ginny.

. . . at least we pulled the ross free from that psychic squib— Odobo.

. . . the hell with that! I've been working for years on contact procedures between humans and reasonably friendly ETs who are willing to communicate, and so far this affair has been a damned farce—Weismuller.

. . . we had no way of knowing it would respond that way— Odobo.

. . . I should have known that it would respond that way. That's what I'm trained to know. It's obvious: how would we feel? Imagine some ET not recognising our ship as artificial but knowing it held a variety of living creatures and started blazing away at it with its lasers. We would be as annoyed as buggery!—Weismuller.

Results of spectral analysis ready.

. . . oh, we actually obtained something—Weismuller.

Satellite material consists of unidentified and extremely complex hydrocarbons, with mineral traces—mainly ferruginous silicates. Positive identification of nitramine.

This took a few moments to absorb, but the crew were used to having themselves stood on their heads by now.

. . . me and my big mouth—Weismuller.

Miss Weismuller, as you put it in your own words, back to school for you!

She smiled. Obviously the thought of dealing with something as alien as this was appealing to her.

. . . I wonder—Ginny Laing.

And her speculation poured into all minds for general consideration and opinion: could it be that Weismuller was right the first time; that the moon was not a shebeen at all, but something completely different?

Like what, Ginny—Tamura.

. . . I cannot see any living thing like that chunk out there. I can see no way for it to develop as an intelligence. What selective pressures could produce an intelligence like that? There seems nothing meaningful to its structure about the molecular level. Perhaps there is something meaningful about its shape, but I doubt it. I bet the other shebeen moon is just as randomly formed—Ginny.

. . . then what can they possibly be?—Tamura.

"I think I know," Weismuller said aloud. "Ginny, you are doing my job for me. I should have seen that point about the structure before. Only the molecular structure is important. That is it's important that all the correct pieces are there, but the overall shape is not really important.

"That's what a machine is often like—as long as the correct components are there, correctly linked, that is enough. The shape of a radio receiver is not governed by the micro circuits: you can have a spherical one, a cubic one, even receivers in novelty shapes like rabbits and wallabies for children. Look at some of the spacecraft shuttling between Earth and Mars—the variety of shapes among them is incredible. The numbers of differently shaped probes orbiting Jupiter and Saturn is unbelievable.

"So we have two points, distinct but related here: the fact that the system can frequently be arranged in numerous ways but still perform the same function; second, we have the fact that amongst indivduals of the same species, there are more often than not considerable similarities in shape. This shape often indicates a great deal about the lifeform concerned. Even amongst the crystalloids, it is not difficult for the untrained eye to note the similarities. In fact, one would have to be pretty dim not to notice that in every specimen we saw from the ross, there were definite crystal patterns, and these were repeated from creature to creature.

"What we were looking at, there in orbit, was a shebeen mechanism, not a shebeen."

Your logic does not follow through. Your argument is weak in many parts, for example the shape of a system is its lines of interrelationship from one component to another and should—

"Regard it as a shaky hypothesis," laughed Weismuller. The Eskimo was obviously happy. "When, if ever, we find ourselves taking in an eyeful of the outer moon, I'll bet that it is quite different in shape, but that the molecular components will be the same."

Bring the ross back home, MI, its work is done—Tamura.

Allaedyce was heaping a great pile of shredded cushioning against one wall of the lounge/assembly area. His eyes hinted at complete insanity. Tamura saw him as he came through from the bridge with the others.

. . . what in God's name is he up to now?—Ginny.

Abruptly they heard their own voices speaking back to them. A brief moment's confusion was replaced by the warm knowledge that the Overmind was still with them and, if staying in the background, still presiding over their words and actions. It spoke.

. . . he is going to attempt to burn his way out of the ship. I cannot follow his reasoning, or rather his chain of unreason. But he believes himself to be imprisoned. He is of the opinion that this is the penal house at Yakutsk.

MI, this situation has gone too far, we must communicate with Allaedyce—Tamura.

Why? He is of no use to us. The mission is abandoned within the original terms. Currently the will is that we extricate ourselves from this situation, by effecting a reasonable means of communication with the shebeen. Allaedyce is irrelevant.

. . . your opinion was not solicited—Ginny.

. . . he is in great distress, and we would relieve him of his guilt —Weismuller.

. . . and relieve ourselves of our conscience—Odobo.

. . . and don't give us all this rubbish about not being able to use the communication channels—Weismuller.

I protest that this is an overt waste of time and energy.

. . . do it! That familiar voice which brought the MI to subservience, the Overmind.

. . . command of the voice apparatus in this lounge/assembly is still yours, MI, use it!—Tamura.

What would you have me say, Commander?

"Tell him the truth."

Allaedyce was busy hauling a heavy plasma torch into the chamber.

"Crewman Allaedyce, it is time things were explained to you."

He screamed and tried to dive through the hatchway but the

plasma torch equipment blocked the way. Whimpering, he scurried
across the bridge entry and disappeared, sealing it behind him. As
he rested his black, ectomorphic limbs against the nearest console,
words scattered on to the dark grey disseminator in bold white.

> MI—crewman allaedyce
> do not be alarmed
> —o
> —the situation is explicable
> if you care to sit and listen
> to what has occurred
> —o
> —all crew members
> apparently vanished from
> the living quarters
> are alive and well
> —o
> —they wish to
> communicate with you
> —o
> are you ready to
> receive their communication?
> —oo

He gazed intently at these words and slowly an expression of furtive cunning spread over his face.
"Lies," he whispered. "You would feed me lies, Machine."

> MI—crewman allaedyce
> this is a genuine
> statement
> —o
> —if you care to enter
> the cot/seat of the console
> at which you currently stand
> I will place you in
> direct communication
> with Commander Tamura
> who will explain all that
> has happened
> —oo

"Impossible," he giggled. "I killed Tamura and the others. I even killed you. Now I will kill this ship and escape."

MI, put me on to the disseminator!—Tamura.

It was as if Tamura was standing in a pale grey nothingness, with a great wide window before him—the disseminator 'seen' from the inside. Allaedyce started at the sudden appearance of the Japanese in the screen. The three dimensional, life-size image of Tamura was indistinguishable from real life.

"We meet again, Allaedyce," Tamura smiled and raised a hand in greeting.

"I'm stealing away," he hissed. "Away away away to where you and your devils will never find me." Another fit of giggles.

"There is no escape from here, Allaedyce," Tamura continued. "Go to the surgery. I'll have a bole meet you there and administer some medicines. A few shots and you'll be almost your old self again."

He ignored Tamura. "I'll get down to the Pakrovsk Road and hitch south on a truck into China. Then I'll set up as a grower of cotton and yams . . ."

"Allaedyce, go to the surgery." But he was addressing a man completely beyond his reach in more ways than simply physically.

The door hatch to the service ring snapped open and a bole trundled out. It swivelled and brought one of its extensible arms up in line with Allaedyce. He leaped as it fired the hypodermic dart, barely missing him. Crack crack crack—the other three achieving the same fruitless fate. He was too swift, rolling, tossing his body, bouncing.

Suddenly he was upon it and scrabbling for the manual controls. It pitched from side to side, trying to shake him loose. A console shattered as they swung into it and Allaedyce screamed as a blade of sheared plastic thrust into his right thigh—one lunge, and click, it was over.

Gasping, he extricated himself from the grip of the bole and the wrecked console. Then, with caution and determination, he carefully freed the length of ragged plastic from his torn muscle. Blood coursed generously down his leg, in thick pulsing rivulets, into a puddle at his foot. He unleased a length of nylon webbing from the console's cot/seat and bound it about the top of the leg in a crude tourniquet.

Turning to the disseminator he looked Tamura in the eye.

"We'll see who gets out. I'm smart. I qualified as a starship crewman—you didn't know that eh? When you all tricked me, you didn't know.

"You'll never catch me. I'm too smart."

He limped over to the open hatchway and disappeared into the service ring.

His laughter echoed away into silence.

The Overmind was preparing itself. It understood MacGillvery's plans and what would happen if something went amiss. The consequences could be disastrous, accordingly it concentrated its preparations upon Tamura; the commander's strength of will was superior to any other on board excepting the magician's and a reserve of will might prove essential in a crisis. It was not greatly concerned with Allaedyce, knowing the consensus of feeling that the mission would fare better without him; the only mitigating voice was Odobo's.

The boles removed the piles of ripped cushioning and the plasma torch gear, while the crew sat morosely in the gym.

. . . is there any hope for him at all?—Odobo.

. . . I've seen a good number of cases worse than Allaedyce recover fully under the standard hypnodrug treatment—Ginny.

. . . very true, but you're thinking of cases who have been taken into care in big hospital complexes, with plenty of time to recover and plenty of staff around with specialised knowledge, to give the kind of treatment which is needed—Weismuller.

. . . yes, and that kind of knowledge only comes with experience —Ginny.

. . . pity we were only given surgery conditioning during education—Weismuller.

. . . certainly a broader conditioning, which included pharmopsychiatry would have been beneficial, but I doubt if the need would have been foreseen at the time, by any but the most imaginative of the educators—Odobo.

If the company so desires it, I will have a bole administer medication to Allaedyce, during his rest period. He sleeps in the service ring, surrounded by numerous warning devices, which alert him to the approach of boles, but I believe that he can be outflanked in his attempts to flee.

He requires having that leg seen to as soon as possible, MI. Make sure you capture him this time!—Tamura.

One bole was clearing away gymnastic equipment from the

centre of the floor, heaping piece atop piece at the end adjacent to the swimming pool; while another, the one which wrestled vainly with Allaedyce was following MacGillvery's instructions and inscribing a great circle and a five sided star, upon the cleared area, in white paint. The Scot dished out his orders quickly and the machine followed them accurately, even compensating for the slight bend in one of its arms, a direct result of the physical confrontation minutes past.

"This is a magic circle, my friends," he declared with all the flourish of a showman. "It is just short of three metres in diameter, the actual length being measured in feet, nine feet in this case. The inner ring is eight feet in diameter and the words you see written between the two are what are known to the cognoscenti as names of power. The inner triangle which you see containing an inner circle is known as the Triangle of Solomon, and adorned with yet more names of power. The paint, for those who are interested, will turn vermilion shortly and is chiefly composed of a sulphur mercury paste.

"During the demonstration, no one should approach within half a metre of the outer ring, otherwise we will be in serious trouble, okay?"

Sure enough, the thick glutinous paint reddened rapidly before their eyes. But that was chemistry, they assured themselves, not magic.

MacGillvery dismissed the boles and stepped out of his coveralls to stand naked before the circle. His body was covered in signs and geometrical shapes, tattooed and branded into his skin.

. . . however did he manage to hide that lot from the medical board—even from the rest of the crew up to now?—Tamura.

"Quite simple, Commander. The artificial skin used for basic cosmetic surgery and grafting can be purchased in any pharmacy. I have carried a personal supply for years. But tonight you see the real me." He raised his hands and the lights dimmed. One spot highlighted the inner circle drawn on the gym floor. He began in a whisper.

"Now! Listen to me, spirits of the air, of the earth, of the waters and of the flames, listen to me for you know my voice. My voice calling, calling again spirits as it has done before. Listen spirits, listen and obey as you have done before when I command. When I command you obey my words, because you know my voice and what it means if you refuse my voice. You know what it means if you are stubborn. You know what will happen if I am not obeyed. You know and you listen and you are listening. You are listening now."

He let fall a few moments silence, and there was a tingling, a quivering tension in the atmosphere. Then his voice erupted, loud and cold.

"I, Ipsissimus Donald MacGillvery do conjure thee, Spirit, Lilith, the eighth of the black sephiroth which are accursed. I conjure thee, under the thrall of Samanel, vile Lilith, in the names of ADNAI, EA, YEWA, HELIOREM to appear at my wish and my pleasure, in this place, and within this circle, immediately, alone, with no companion, without ill will, delay, noise, deformity or evasion. I also conjure thee by the ineffable names of TETRAGRAMMATON, HAIN, LON, ALGA which are ALPHA and OMEGA and which I am surely unworthy to speak.

"Come here, come here, come here. You will satisfy *me* and *my* commands without evasion or lie. If thou doth not this, the Glorious Michael, the Archangel invisible, will instantly strike thee in the deepest pit of Hell!"

A rustling, a blast of cold, dank air . . .

"Why this delay? Prepare to obey *me*, thy Master, in the name of the Lord, Bathat, flowing over Abracmens, Alchior over Aberder. Zazas, Zazas, Nasatanada, Zazas!"

The shadow Tamura saw in the bridge was again there under the dimming lights. There was almost complete blackness and the smell of rot becoming overwhelming. Something moved, unfolded, and the light gained strength.

She stood there in the centre of the inner circle bounded by MacGillvery's Triangle of Solomon.

Only this time she was far from triumphant.

"What do you mean by bringing me here, you little tattooed rat's vomit?" she shrieked at him, her face contorted with rage. "You my master? Huh! The idea is ludicrous. You believe that a slug's excrement like you can have power—power—over an elemental like me? A being who—"

"Silence!" His command was sharp but not loud.

She threw back her damp black lank hair and laughed without humour. Then she started to keen; long loud wails rang from her mouth as she squatted.

"Silence, abhorred scum of the slime pit!"

She sneered at him and pulled aside her robe so that he might see her urinating and defecating within the circle. The stench was almost overpowering. She howled and cackled with delight at the crew's violent disgust.

"MI, instruct the bole to place the box in the oven." His voice was placid, almost good humoured.

This was the point about the preparations for the summoning which had puzzled Tamura most; why have a metallurgy oven heated and a bole at the ready to place a small iron box therein upon MacGillvery's request?

The bole thrust the casket into the sealed inferno.

Immediately her repulsive glee ceased.

"No," she croaked, wide eyed.

"No?" smiled MacGillvery. "No what, Lilith?"

"No . . ." She was trying to hold out against something, her face furrowed with determination and agony. Then she broke. Thrusting her head down she cried, "No, Master, no no, no more, please. Have pity!"

"Have the bole withdraw the iron box, MI, but keep it standing at the ready." Then he turned to the cowering black robed figure. "Well, Lilith, your sign has not been touched by the flame but the heat we can generate in our labs far outstrips those old charcoal braziers of yesteryear. Wouldn't you say so?"

She nodded slowly, still looking at the floor.

"Well now, let us have a little meaningful communication with our friends the shebeen."

Her head came up. The eyes glittered menacingly from under the dark brow. "Whatever you desire, Master." Was there a hint of sarcasm in those words?

"Just remember the box, Lilith, and forget about my desires."

She grinned.

"Tell me," he continued, "tell me how the shebeen took care of the crystalloids."

"Very well, as my master wishes so shall it be. The shebeen were attacked by the crystalloids millennia upon millennia ago. Being under assault they decided to strike back at the crystalloid home-world. They did and their magic caused the crystalloids to become dormant. Then the Crow stepped in and placed the shebeen in thrall."

"For what purpose?"

"His plan is unknowable."

"When we were destroying the fleet around Jupiter they sent out a distress signal which the Crow allowed certain members of the crystalloids to respond to. Why did he allow them to go?"

"It was apparent that a neighbouring system was in danger," she explained. "The shebeen decided to tender aid but could not detect where the endangered population lay. In consequence the Crow reactivated a small fleet and followed it by including a shebeen component."

"And how do we communicate with the shebeen? What form do they suggest that this takes?"

She seemed surprised and delighted at the question. Her face became alive with malice and beauty.

"Simple," she chuckled, "they would have a host of demons walk around freely in this ship in order that both the energy and the invaluable strange minds of the humans be made available to the Crow." She laughed openly and added, "Furthermore you have to destroy your mechanical demon, the Machine Intelligence."

"These terms are not acceptable to us," MacGillvery snapped.

"Then we shall conjure up demons to possess you. You will have no say when the gates of hell burst, sundered, and we pour into your minds. Then *you* will be *mine*, Master." Her eyes narrowed.

"Remember the sign in the iron box, Lilith."

She hissed quietly.

The loud whoop took every one by surprise. Lurching from the service ring hatch came Allaedyce. Forgetting that the bushman could not hear him MacGillvery shouted—

"Don't touch the circle, man. Don't go near it!"

But too late.

The wounded bushman bounded into it and threw himself at the demon woman's feet bleating.

"Save me, princess. Save me from this dungeon!"

She stepped over him, turned, and spat upon his back. The man screamed. Curls of smoke rose from his seared flesh. Writhing, he struggled to his feet, still shrieking, then fell back unconscious.

Crossing the broken circle, Lilith confronted MacGillvery and, reaching into the MI's reality simulation, with one light slap of her hand smashed him back across the gym into the stacks of athletic equipment.

"Now," she gurgled, "now my little prett—"

. . . depart!

The thought was painful, ringing through Tamura's head like a gong.

Lilith gasped and clutched her temples.

. . . depart!

She fell to her knees and crawled awakwardly back to the centre of the circle.

. . . begone, black sephiroth! I am the Overmind. I am not subject to your power. My will is stronger. Begone—

With a howl she plunged through the Triangle of Solomon and vanished.

CHAPTER TWENTY

. . . we must depart—Odobo.

. . . but how?—Ginny . . . and to where for what purpose?—
Weismuller.

. . . everything is in ruins; we are the victims of a deception
which goes far beyond the petty tricksters of Yakutsk—Odobo.

. . . we must leave here: we are in danger from the Crow—Weismuller.

Their voices were fainter, their identities weakening, thinning
away against the ever-present, ever-growing mass of the Overmind,
the blended intelligence, the common will. How long until there
was only this, and the minds of both men and machine were reduced to convenient facets? But it was exhilarating. Tamura felt
that this will was his own, that this fountainhead of power and
superconsciousness was within himself. He knew that the subjective
sensation for the other crew members was identical. They too felt
the growing translucence amongst the identities of their fellows,
while their own, which was the overmind identity from their viewpoint, increased in corporeality and energy.

We can move—it was Tamura's own thoughts dominating the
rest, or yet again, was it the collective, the Overmind?

There was a by now familiar flurry of confusion scattered
amongst them.

MacGillvery can call up adequate psi power out of the pit—
Tamura guessed that this was both his own and MacGillvery's idea,
expressed through the Overmind.

. . . is this feasible?—Odobo.

. . . is it wise considering what else might be called up?—Ginny Laing.

. . . feasible and wise both, but requiring a great deal of conscious will from us all to add to the collective—definitely MacGillvery that time.

. . . how are the shebeen likely to respond?—Weismuller.

. . . very much as they threatened to, my dear, by attempting to possess some of us with demons.

She was clearly troubled at this reply.

. . . what we have to decide is whether or not we are willing to try—pointed out Ginny—is it the general wish that we leave Altair III now?

It is—the Overmind.

. . . then we attempt it, and be damned—Weismuller rejoined wryly.

A solid, sensual world formed about Tamura from the mind limbo. A group were in the bridge, seated at their customary stations. Then MacGillvery started keying-in and words began to appear on the disseminator, letters forming a perfect square.

```
R O L O R
O B U F O
L U A U L
O F U B O
R O L O R
```

He depressed a few more keys, and the columns commenced flickering—bands of darkness sweeping out individual vertical columns, as they moved from the two outer columns into the centre one; likewise, in the horizontal lines, two bands moved top and bottom to the centre. The horizontal movement was only about half as fast as that of the vertical.

"The rhythm is thirty-seven to sixty," he said aloud. "When a total of seventeen forty-six cycles in all has been achieved, that is six sixty-six horizontal against ten eighty vertical, the ship will have drive, no matter what the shebeen and friends try."

A numerical countdown display appeared beside the square.

. . . how long 'til blast off?—asked Weismuller.

"Less than four hours, if we survive that long," he replied. "I suggest we all relax for an hour or so. The intensity of concentration demanded during that last couple of hours is going to be terrific. So long as the collective will and myself keep a firm grip of the count, there is no need for any others. In fact, it would be advantageous to build up the power phase by phase, by gradually adding individual wills to the pool. The final one coming in at the last minute."

. . . will it harm Allaedyce?—Odobo.

"He should be hale and hearty."

. . . what exactly will happen?—Ginny.

"Fusion will commence and we will be on our way."

. . . where though, crewman?

"I suggest Altair II, as we do not appear to have the resources to return to Earth."

. . . still this accursed system!—Weismuller.

This Machine Intelligence does not have the capacity either of restoring your flesh or of simulating a satisfactory image of surface life upon Altair III: too many unknowns come into play. Suggest detailed survey of this entire system.

Why not? Tamura mused: we certainly have enough time between now and the failure of the ship's components, several millennia away. By which time we shall no doubt have contacted Earth—Tamura.

. . . or gone mad—Ginny.

Two hours passed. The readout glowed 580:940. Everything seemed well. MacGillvery sat watching the count while the others relaxed in the lounge.

The magic which he had chosen was old. Its purpose was firstly to generate fusion, as the Scot had said, and secondly to promote flight. What he had not disclosed was the nature of the fusion and the form which the flight would take. In antiquity magicians trapped in cages or cells had used the formula to escape captivity in the form of a bird . . . a crow.

Ginny stepped through the hatch.

. . . Tamura looked at her, but she did not meet his eyes. Things were ending between them. There was a general sensation of ending, a hint of finality about everything that had happened since Lilith appeared. Ginny too felt it. If this crisis was to pass safely, she determined no longer to share his cabin, preferring the company of another, or perhaps solitude.

Suddenly Weismuller laughed, a great unexpected burst of mirth.
. . . what's the giggle then?—asked Odobo.
"You!" she shrieked aloud. "You, you foetid slime!"
She smashed her fist down upon the table, but nothing happened,
no sound of impact, no tumbling of cups, or stirring of utensils.
Interference! Interference! Interference!
As a body they all leaped at her, and crashed amongst one another. She had gone. The manic laughter howled by the door hatch
leading into the bridge. The Eskimo girl stood there guffawing,
with saliva running down her chin.
. . . my God, what is this?—Odobo.
. . . the shebeen! They've possessed her—Ginny.
"You'll never catch me!" she hooted.
Depart!—it was the Overmind commanding.
"Nooooo heheh ha ha he ha heoo hee hee hee,"—it rolled about
on the floor in Weismuller's body. "Oh what a nice body this nice
ice ice girly has—won't we have fun with it!"
This MI has lost total simulation control of Weismuller identity.
"We're going to do with you what we did with *Revenge!*" she
girnned, gasping at the exertion of having thrown herself about the
floor.
595:965.
What happened aboard *Revenge?*—Tamura snapped urgently.
"They took all the good ones," it pouted, "not fair! Not fair! Left
me with only old Holst, and he was no use."
What happened to *Revenge* and its crew, vile thing?—the Over-
mind.
It made a long, loud, disgusting, slurping noise.
"Just like that—all sucked up into the shebeen. Hoo hoo, it was
fun. You should have seen them screaming and pleading and whim-
pering. Haaa ha ha hahahaha ha Oooooo . . ."
You will do nothing but depart! You are vermin, despicable ex-
crement. Begone!
It shrieked gleefully at the commands of the Overmind.
"But you cannot banish me. You do not know my name, do you?
Poor you. Poor you." Then more peals of insane laughter. "But I
know what you are. You are the fool who would defy the Crow.
You are doomed. You are powerless . . . and we will take another."
It suddenly pointed towards Ginny, and the latter's face contorted.
She twisted and writhed and fell to a stool and then to the floor.

Interference! Interference! Interference!

Cautiously, they all reached out to hold her, and she was substantial. They locked her down and began willing her to succeed in her struggle with the would be possessor.

You will not take this woman—boomed the Overmind repeatedly.

The Weismuller demon sneered, spat and launched itself at the group. This time it connected. Kicking, biting, scratching, it scattered them and leaped upon Ginny, gripping her by the hair and battering her head off the floor. Suddenly Ginny, too, burst into uncontrolled laughter. Tamura's heart sank.

This MI has lost total simulation control of Weismuller and Laing identities.

"You're losing! Losing!" howled the Laing thing as it staggered to its feet. "Every time one of us is taken from you, you are diminished, oh great Overmind." The two women bowed low.

"Fun time," bayed Ginny. She pushed the other to the floor and began kicking it ferociously in the face. The other laughed unrestrainedly as the face was gradually covered in bloody lesions.

"Oh my God," whispered Odobo, turning sickened at the sight.

Tamura grasped her arm, just above the elbow. Her head was forward and her eyes closed tightly.

. . . exorcism is nearly impossible when you know virtually nothing about the demon in possession—MacGillvery.

635:1030.

Ginny, or whatever controlled her, let out a long stream of obscene abuse. The Weismuller demon started tearing the flesh from its host's hand with her teeth, the blood coursing down the arms to splatter in pools on the floor.

"Very well, you two," began MacGillvery. "It looks as though I have no option. Doesn't it?"

They went very still and peered at him, as if trying to seek out whether or not he was bluffing.

"Stand back, please." He waved them back and stepped out of his coveralls, displaying geometric and mystical symbols on his exposed flesh. The demon women were visibly disturbed, turning immediately to repulsive sexual behaviour and screaming a babble of unintelligible words.

A cry from MacGillvery silenced them. They looked at him with pure loathing, hatred, as he began to speak first in Latin, then Hebrew, then Aramaic, and eventually in tongues so old as to be unrecognisable. They put their hands over their ears, fell to their knees and squirmed.

Ginny lay screaming on her back, her limbs thrashing wildly and pink foam bubbling from shredded lips.

The Weismuller possession was rigid, curled up in a foetal position on the floor, but with the eyes staring and the pupils shrunk to the mearest points.

A bole rolled urgently into the lounge, a coil of thick, bare cable clutched in its grapples. It swung about the two women, laying the cable in a near circle. A quick blast from its plasma torch welded the cable into a ring. A few deft borings and links and the bole connected its power supply with the metal circle.

MacGillvery's voice grew strident, penetrating, the words harsh concoctions of guttural vowels and hisses. Was this even language as Tamura and the others understood it? Had the magician gone out of history, out of mankind, into his ancestors, the protomen?

657:1065.

The Ginny demon attempted throwing itself at him across the ring. It was repulsed in mid-air and thrust back, colliding with Weismuller. The two creatures immediately engaged in a frenzied battle, pulling hair, kicking, biting, spitting, gouging, hacking, punching.

The roaring MacGillvery was working himself into a frenzy. He looked old, very old. The flesh hung in dried folds to a skull whose eye sockets were deep and dark with gleaming unnatural orbs at their centres.

Ginny lay before him, asleep.

Weismuller, still staring, was standing upright, her blood dripping arms at her side. She opened her mouth. The sounds which issued forth were not human but chirps and shrills and rustlings reminiscent of the jungle. Then she began dancing, moving in sharp, violent steps and thrusts of her limbs, bending her body forward—and so did MacGillvery.

They moved to a rhythm just appreciable in his howling and her shrieking. The bodies twisted, gyrated, separated by the live coil. His voice rose in pitch higher, higher. Tamura felt himself shivering involuntarily at the sound.

Suddenly, Weismuller screamed, threw her head back, and stopped in that position, began to drift downwards, backwards into nothing—vanishing, and something grey and naked rushed from the fading form, straight across the live ring into the magician, lifting him bodily and smashing him into the far wall.

622:1073.

It was as if there came a series of clicks, factors snapping back into place in Tamura's mind. Within the circle of live cable lay Ginny, all her wounds edited out of existence by the MI. She raised herself to her knees, blinked and rubbed her eyes.

. . . what happened?—she asked.

It would appear that we have won the first round.

There were casualties, commander.

What? But how? We no longer exist outside of your electronic innards, MI.

Programmes governing the Weismuller and MacGillvery simulations were turned into garbage by the climax of the exorcism. Mac-Gillvery warned this Machine Intelligence that such an occurrence might result if the exorcism proved too difficult.

There was a moment of quiet as the news was absorbed.

"Well, at least they were lovers," commented Ginny bitterly. "At least *they* found a way out of this electronic immortality together."

Everyone to the bridge, quickly—Tamura.

They settled down and looked at the square—mostly gazing at the displays on their own consoles which helped promote the feeling that the mass will was his or her own.

Tamura gazed at it and let his mind fall into the Overmind.

The letters began to take on a meaning of their own, a separate identity from that of the whole words and all at once the Overmind showed them in new relationships, new words forming out of them, different potentials being expressed. The rhythm began beating these hectically into Tamura and all the others, straining the framework of their reason with hints and promises at those powers which MacGillvery had used . . .

Whatever the shebeen are, they are not apes, thought Tamura. They have an alternative evolution as had the crystalloids, a history which excludes the masses of primate based behaviour locked into the pink tissues below man's cranium.

Whatever the shebeen are—

The shebeen, the dream kings . . .

It stopped. Briefly a vision flickered and died but was branded in their memories.

A great creature akin perhaps to Earth's protozoa in its constituent parts, certainly it was like a gigantic sponge spreading through most of its world's cold ammonia oceans. It consisted of thousands of millions of near microscopic animals which build their small homes together, forming a cluster of open cores or horns, all spreading from one cemented centre. These clusters made up the structure of the being, and formed pockets of protection for its countless living members. Individually they were nothing, but collectively they formed the most powerful psi mind in existence—the dream kings, the shebeen.

It could hurtle great asteroid-sized masses from itself out into space. There the animals died, but the psi-esp sensitive structures within the shells' molecular construction permitted it to act as an amplifier—a receiver/transmitter station.

Such a great chunk was what the ross encountered.

Tamura felt something surge against him like a surprise current trying to steal a swimmer.

Attack warning! Shebeen attempting further interference!

666:1080

The Overmind hardened with the threat. The crew members were no longer distinct. The tug of the shebeen vanished but no one could tell what was individual and what was the Overmind—the fantasy bodies were gone— They were . . . the machine was . . . the Overmind.

One mind and will.

The final shebeen assault was beginning to break up parts of the hull with psi power. The Overmind willed itself to survive. It felt a massive wave approach, ethereal, dimensionless, murderous. This time it would trick the aliens.

The wave struck—

—but the mind was gone, riding it, letting its impetus carry it away: the assailants began to lose balance, having struck ferociously at nothing.

They swirled, tumbling out of stance. And the Overmind struck —thrusting its thought blade deep, only to find itself falling and engulfed in an ocean of identities melding at contact—the dragons— the griffin ones—all aliens all trapped like the shebeen, here at the catchworld—the minotaurs—the cyclops—their barriers split like bladders at the touch of the mindsword and poured together—the harpies—the dream kings—and the Overmind!

All now one mind, one heart, one purpose, for the work of the catchworld was almost done.

All now the one black human form standing in the *Yūkoku* bridge amidst the furnace of exploding circuitry.

Come! Come, Allaedyce! Come home . . .

He burst through the hatch, limping, weeping, and saw the figure amongst the flames, a stygian silhouette. Terror-stricken, unreasoning, he threw himself at it—into it.

666:1080.

The numbers vanished to be replaced by their total.

1746.

The number of fusion.

MacGillvery's magic square glowed bright and faded. And what had been *Yūkoku* moved. The conglomerate of wills churned together becoming one with the craft.

For what moved out of Altair III no longer had the shape of a starship, but was an immense shadow setting out across the millennia.

As MacGillvery knew when he cast his thrall, the result was to be fusion of a kind other than they had expected, that the capacity for flight was conjured by the transformation of all, ship, Overmind, and alien attackers, into the form of a bird known to men as a harbinger of fate . . .

The Crow.

CHAPTER TWENTY-ONE

The Crow's only passion was time. It played with alternative universes as a child with toys. It created its own history and future again and again, always differently, always with lust of cosmic rapacity.

Allaedyce whimpered at the sound of the voice.

He rolled over and threw an arm across his closed eyes to shield them from the glare above.

"Have a good sleep?"

He went rigid. That voice—he knew it. The voice of an enemy!

Flinching he eased himself up on to his elbows and peered about through scarcely separated eyelids.

The sky was a crippling intense blue. He gasped and looked away.

"A little fried fish?"

He sat up. The soft earth beneath him was a living mat of vegetation carefully interwoven and about as thick as a blanket. The ground below it was curiously pliable, yielding. The mat seemed to be made up of thick soft wool-like fibres ranging in colour from cream to yellow to deep mustard. It was as wide as a large field and its extremities vanished into a mass of curious vegetation. At a few points this 'field' was broken with what looked like tall slender foam sculptures waving precariously in the breeze and casting off large exquisite bubbles. The 'sculptures' were multi-coloured, shimmering with a variety of reds and purples sparkling vividly in the cruelly bright sunlight.

"Where in hell . . ." muttered Allaedyce.

"As good a probable location as any," said the other. "I caught these in what passes for a stream here." The figure passed a handful of broad rolled leaves stuffed with what Allaedyce assumed to be the local variety of marine life. He bit through the flame crispened wrapping into the soft crumbly flesh. The bitter vinegar taste of the fish was offset by the savoury sweetness of the leaf.

"Mmm, beautiful." He realised just how hungry he was and devoured almost a dozen of the tasties before the questions hit him. "Who the hell are you? And where is this place?"

"You know where we are, Allaedyce, Altair Two."

The memories crashed back and with it the bushman abruptly plunged into the nightmare carnival which had been his insanity, but this time only briefly. He gasped, the landscape reeled and he sank back to the strange earth. Slowly his mind cleared. The demonic roller coaster which had hurtled it careering through that terror imbued shadow world became insubstantial, misty and ultimately vanished.

"How did we survive, Tamura?" he croaked. "Where are the others?"

Suddenly information poured into his mind unbidden in a crushing torrent.

The journeying of *Yūkoku* took twenty-three years in terms of Earth time, arriving about Altair in the early years of the twenty-second century. Even before the fleet departed, faster-than-light starship design existed on the drawing board and the Condominium had secretly ordered a prototype built. It was assembled and tested in eighteen months, the appearance of a second crystalloid force spurring production. The incoming crystalloids were obliterated by avalanches of missiles and X-ray laser pulses before approaching within a dozen light hours of Pluto's orbit. The only survivor was an asteroid, or so it at first seemed to the terrestrial scientists. When it became evident that there was more to the asteroid than its innocent appearance (how many asteroids decelerate when moving towards a star system?) special attention was given it. This took the form of three automated spacecrafts rendezvousing with the object and simultaneously detonating their cargoes of thermo-nuclear warheads. In this fashion Earth lost its only possible direct contact with the dream kings, those beings which MacGillvery was later to name 'shebeen'.

But the crucial point is that humanity, by now suffering from racial paranoia, carefully built up over decades by the Marshals, threw itself into a frenzy of labour and ingenuity. They were certain that none of the outgoing fleet had survived the crystalloid battle. Accordingly total priority was given to the construction of an FTL craft which might reach Altair inside sixteen years. That figure was crucial as it was the length of time taken by any signal from the newly destroyed crystalloid hordes to travel to their homeworld. When it was completed and tested there still remained nine years' journey ahead, most of which would be through superspace.

The crew had not been selected or cultivated in the same sense as the mission Fleet crew. It might almost be said that there was no crew, but this would be inaccurate. There was a very pronounced human element aboard the starship even if no recognisable human being was evident. Rüllkotter had decided against the previous unbalanced relationship between Machine Intelligence and crew. This time there would be no need for complex procedures of integration and assimilation en route to Altair. The vehicle would depart with its artificial intelligence structured about and fully integrated with a human organic 'computer'. This was cultivated from human tissue and programmed for the mission by a huge team working under Rüllkotter at MI labs on Mars. The result was a 'macrobrain', a human brain grown artificially and engineered to enormous proportions. It had a mass in excess of four kilograms and an abnormally high number of foldings in the cortex. The prefrontal lobes were disproportionately gross. The synopse content was over one hundred times that in a normal brain. Rüllkotter regarded this as his magnum opus, the next step in evolution beyond man, homo stellarum. This living but wholly artificial being he saw as his progeny, the true seed of his mind, if not his body.

But what of that seed? What was it in relation to the rest of the human race?

Compared with the alien prosences encountered by *Yūkoku* at Altair, the 'macrobrain' was human inasmuch as its innate basis for thought was identical to that of all humans. It comprehended not as rapidly as the inorganic intelligences but much faster than its programmers and much more profoundly than either of its antecedents. Scientists who helped develop it, those with sufficient passion to see that what was being engineered was not a machine but that shadowed labyrinth, a human heart, gave warning. They cautioned against creating an unbalanced mind so vast and subtle its very derangements would appear wondrous. But such comment was rare and unheeded by the decision makers, all of whom were awed by the great Rüllkotter. His talent and insight made him appear to be what he was not, an objective infallible genius.

The growing human identity evolves over decades. The developing macrobrain identity was generally ignored as a subject for consideration apart from the forementioned Cassandras. But Rüllkotter did realise dimly that the forced pace was producing bizarre effects in that sphere.

The macrobrain achieved a self-consciousness based on human cunning, on a certain duplicity in the universe and the fundamental imperative to maintain that duplicity as it was the only good. Rüllkotter's masterpiece was a monstrous paranoid schizophrenic.

This was what controlled the FTL craft departing Earth after *Yūkoku* and achieving Altair space before that starship arrived; en route the FTL vehicle broadcast back to Sol results of various observations and experiments performed in voyage, all such information calculated to create the greatest amount of damage possible by confusing and misleading, often fatally, the terrestrial scientists awaiting these data as basis for future experiment.

The FTL ship lay in stationary orbit above Altair II where the lifeforms were held in telepathic bondage by the macrobrain readying to spread its dominance out amongst the stars, a dominance of malice both abstract and mathematically precise. The blended creatures which had once been the *Yūkoku* crew, the MI and the alien assailants rushed in upon a new timefield and this world. A bridge was formed between this new entity darkly magical, and the other cruelly logical, a link between the opposite faces of the paradox, a melting place which contained the sources of both—the human mind. Their point of origin was their only point of contact.

It was after all no accident that one mere man had survived . . .

Allaedyce looked up dazed and found himself alone on Altair II. Unaccountably he was not surprised. As his thoughts became clearer and strength returned to his limbs he realised that someone had briefed him on what he was to expect and to do. Rising to his feet he nodded. Oh, Tamura had been real all right. He knew that just as he knew that he was here as a pawn in a very large very subtle game in which there were no winners, only losers and survivors.

He knew that he had to seek out the enemy, that the enemy expected him, and that he must win. But how did he know this? How did he come to even be here? Why him when . . .

He shrugged, swallowed the last morsel of food and set off. It did not matter in which direction, he smiled ruefully at the thought. The enemy was watching and waiting, preparing to stalk its prey.

He heard chiming cries. A shape was bobbing amongst the shrubbery. Might as well move off in that direction as any other, he mused.

The shrubbery was not shrubbery but a waist high forest of bright green growths with long 'needles' hanging from them, featherlike to the touch, and looking like miniature pine trees. The large coloured bubbles from the frothing 'foam sculptures' were obviously alive in some way, darting in and out of the pine line shrubbery with considerable animation, never bursting. Should he touch one of them? No, perhaps not, he decided, remembering how innocent looking he thought jellyfish when first he saw them in the aquarium at Durban. These bubbles too may sting—if nothing else.

The movement ahead amongst the shrubs continued. It might be that of a small animal; might give me a clue of what to expect here. If only I catch a glimpse of it. Then as if in answer the being straightened up to the entire twelve metres of its height. Aghast he dropped into the brush for cover. It was slim like a snake but jointed with a number of telescopic pseudo-legs holding it aloft. As he watched the 'tail' swirled up and the entire creature was completely supported in the air by a variety of straw thin 'legs'. Then he understood. This was a defence mechanism against sightless creatures. Probably the underside of its body was quite cool so that any predator wandering below would not be able to detect its body heat. The hide was formed from thick corklike plates layered across one another in a manner similar to the scaling on fish but much cruder. The front was a black bristling mass with 'mother-of-pearl' snouts protruding from it which wavered incessantly, tiny teeth glinting at the tips.

He watched it for several minutes but it obviously knew he was somewhere in the region and had no intention of coming down until he was gone. Allaedyce pressed on.

The shrubs were thinning away and he saw a ridge ahead. Once he reached the base slope he turned left and began walking parallel to it. A few moments close examination showed that the vegetable-like matting blended into the grey green waxy matter which composed the ridge. No boulders or small rocks. The observation meant little to him at first, but the more he thought about it the more worrying it seemed. And why such big sightless animals upon a world abounding in sunlight?

Upon mounting a small rise he halted and eyed the panorama unfolded before him. A very steep slope ran down into a great valley. At the foot of the slope he could see what appeared to be isolated but cultivated fields amongst dense forest and a road winding from almost directly below towards the broad slow river a dozen or so kilometres distant. Beyond this was more forest and the ground undulated until eventually reaching the massive range at the far side of the valley. He could just see these mountains through heavy cloud breaking across them and falling like waves down into the valley.

At the base of one mountain ran a long thin line broken at points by vertical structures, a fortified wall.

So that is where I am supposed to be going.

Half-way down the slope Allaedyce saw the creature responsible for the chiming call suddenly appear before him. Frantically he hunted for cover. The thing walked upright on two stilt like legs which, like the pseudo-legs of the previous creature, appeared to be almost telescopic. It was like a monstrous crane fly slowly dancing head down, for the head hung pointing towards the ground and was covered in black bristles. Instead of numerous snouts, four trumpet like growths protruded from this mass. A long dark sticky whip lashed out of these at the passing bubbles which seldom escaped capture. The cigar shaped nut-brown body pointed skywards. Circular yellow blemishes about the size of a human hand ran around its midriff area. The tongues cracked out perhaps fifty times in the short period that he viewed it. Then the strange chiming noise came. And it floated off. For a moment he could scarcely believe his eyes. Then he saw the long tenuous thread running aloft from its tail. There, about three hundred metres up, was a transparent gossamer bag looking rather like a smaller version of the old meteorology balloons which used to be sent aloft on Earth. The creature chimed again and yet again as it gained altitude. Faintly he heard answering chimes and scanning the sky realised that about a dozen of the creatures were hovering above this part of the valley.

When he had nearly run into the valley floor trouble cropped up —almost fatally. Moving down a sixty degree slope it suddenly became ninety degrees—a sheer drop of almost one hundred metres on to what looked like the first signs of rock and boulders.

Allaedyce might have been provided with a handy creeper to swing down on, but there were none on Altair Two. Obviously there was no possibility of climbing down. He must either camp here for the night or go back and camp higher up. An alternative route down would be found in the morning. He decided to go back.

It took almost fifteen minutes to cover what had taken two minutes on the downward journey. More colourful curses issued from the bushman's lips. Altair was settling over the other side of this hill and the light began dimming fast. Passing a couple of the crane fly beasts he roared a few blasphemies in their direction. The result was unexpected and immediate. They stopped all bubble hunting activity and looked for all the world as if they were completely taken aback at the shocking language. Allaedyce paused for a few moments to let his racing heart calm down a little and muttered a few more choice phrases for the benefit of these weirdies. The one nearest to him instantly began bobbing over in his direction, obviously very interested.

"What in God's name have I done now?" he mumbled.

At the sound of those words it approached even more rapidly. Perhaps the best thing to do would be to freeze, he thought. Just keep still. Or, even better, throw something which might make a distracting sound upon impact—but there was nothing to throw. It floated delicately above him for a few seconds and then *lash*, the whip tongue coiled painfully about his chest and shoulders. He shrieked and it lifted him—but not far. He proved too heavy and together Allaedyce and the beast began drifting to one side and back down the slope a little way. Then it released him and he tumbled thankfully into a 'pine' shrub after rolling almost to the edge.

Rest awhile, he thought. Let darkness come down but do not attempt trying to sleep here. Perhaps further up the slope where there are much thicker clumps of the shrub I might be secure, but one wrong roll over in my sleep here and I roll a long long way.

Then came the dust.

A fine pollen, released by the shrubs after sunset, began spilling out over the cliff and up again in the updraught of air. He tried restraining the impulse to cough. Impossible! He sneezed, coughed and gasped furiously for several minutes. Then he glimpsed the shape above . . . The sound of his hay fever attack had brought another of the cranefliers.

The tongue snapped about his waist this time, and again there was a vain attempt to lift him. Only this time as Allaedyce drifted he moved out over the edge of the cliff. He shrieked once more and it released him—but Allaedyce did not release it. Seldom before had the real meaning of the phrase 'holding on like grim death' been clear to him. But it was now.

Slowly he and his would-be devourer sank towards the black at the base of the cliff. By now all down there was shadow and he could not tell how close he was to solid surfaces. Crunch! Releasing the failed predator he attempted to steady himself amongst a tumbling sliding mass of boulders, rocks, chips and flakes. The beast soared away chiming furiously into the night.

He slid down a scree slope until coming to rest at the foot of what felt like an extra large version of the pine shrub but with long tuberous growths instead of needles. There were movements among the 'branches', probably Altair Two's equivalent of insect life. He lay still for a while but there was no indication of danger. Might as well grab a little sleep while you can, Allaedyce, he thought. It may be the last you'll have. He looked up and saw a great spread of stars showered out across the black. Try picking out a constellation or two; surely they will not be too drastically changed from here. There high in the sky, just identifiable was Orion and Canis Major. He smiled. It all felt quite homely. In fact if it were not for that disquieting bright little star in Monoceros he could almost imagine himself back on Earth.

But he knew that that disquieting little star was the Sun.

CHAPTER TWENTY-TWO

It knew he was there, saw him move down the slope to the valley floor, realised that he was puzzled by the varieties of sightless fauna. It observed, assessed, and prepared. Mechanisms within the FTL starship had been scanning the likely approaches to the Altair system for the overdue arrival of the original fleet when the figure had appeared. There was a flutter of light, a shadow and then a man lying unconscious scarcely twenty kilometres from the City. A man, a human being, arriving thus, the first alien upon a culturally primitive world, could hardly have created greater confusion within this strange and evil intelligence. Data banks provided the man's identity. Allaedyce, a crew man of the *Yūkoku*. It could not compute the significance of this. What it could compute was that the nature of the inevitable confrontation would be vastly different from that which it had projected. The unknown, the random factor present in all projections, was sufficiently influential to destroy most of its bases for calculation.

A memory stirred.

A memory relating to those far off days before its capacity for normal human response had been virtually amputated.

The being remembered fear.

Allaedyce woke to a blue sky sprinkled with balloon-borne aerial life. The specimen which had assisted his rough descent the previous night was but one of many types. He took little note. The thought of an enemy lurking, plotting, stalking him immediately occupied his mind. Above him in stationary orbit the FTL ship would be trackng his every move . . .

FTL ship?

How did he come to know that?

There was an FTL ship up there in stationary orbit, probably scanning for him at this very moment. A mixture of curiosity and fear hit his mind briefly before he suppressed it. There were more immediate needs to be contended with.

It had not occurred to him yesterday to question how an illusion like Tamura could catch and cook food; then perhaps Tamura had been real. He peered about for a likely breakfast but there were no visible fruits or berries, no small animal life, and the thought of tackling something like the crane fly thing was out of the question —as was the thought of eating it. No, it would have to be the river. Try catching some of the fish which Tamura mysteriously provided yesterday. Or what about trying one of the tuberous growths which he had used for shelter all night long? He tore one loose and pink sap frothed from the break. There came a noise similar to a klaxon being sounded and what he had taken for a bush began thrashing all eight metres of its length in a frenzy. Allaedyce leaped clear as the beast reared up on a series of stumpy stalks and began plodding off down the slope, still sounding like a siren.

A few moments later the 'stem' which he was holding took on the toughness and rigidity of seasoned teak. Disgusted he threw it aside.

There was a thick fog everywhere, so his venture down into the valley would be more precarious than he imagined it might be, the advantage of his site being severely limited. About fifty or sixty metres down there were numerous multi-coloured balls lying amongst the chips and rock flakes, none larger than a fingernail and distinctly resembling bubbles blown from the foam sculpture creature except that these were so small. They were hard but pliable, and transparent, almost as if made from plastic. Obviously inedible. He shrugged and moved on.

The further down Allaedyce moved the more there were of these bubbles until they eventually covered the rock and chip surface entirely. Walking on them proved difficult at first, rather like walking on ballbearings, but as they grew deeper it became more straightforward if tiresome. He found himself sinking up to the ankles in them and two or three times slipped and came up wet. The upper layer was bone dry but underneath there seemed to be a considerable deal of trapped water.

Altair rose above the distant mountains, turning the mist into a great shroud of light. Allaedyce was now walking on the level without the slightest undulation of terrain making progress simpler and the bushman a bit happier.

The fog lifted abruptly.

He faced the forest, or what he had taken for a forest from the top of the hill. From here it looked more like a jungle. There were hundreds of thick short plants with masses of very large very thick leaves. The trunks were intertwined with pliable branches almost like creepers having the girth of a man's arm. The leaves were enormous yellow or pale green plates and although the trunks rose only about two or three metres at the most, the long stems supporting the leaves were in the order of thirty to forty metres or so. The density and darkness of this little Amazon was off-putting. Then he remembered the roadway. It should be no more than twenty minutes walk along the front wall of the 'jungle'.

Allaedyce set off at a slow jog, by now capable of moving on the tricky surface and feeling the pangs of hunger more clearly than before. How abruptly the jungle area began. Could this be artificial? What purpose would it serve if it were? A defensive structure perhaps or one deliberately placed in the way of anyone wishing to approach the city, forcing them to take the one road. The one road which would without doubt be watched.

But by whom?

Allaedyce saw it like a vision before him, dimly but distinct from his surroundings. A white shape, covered in overlapping plates, the FTL ship. He skidded on the bubble balls, crashed into the trees, and the phantom vanished. A highly advanced starship up there in stationary orbit, he thought. Could it pick out something as minute as me trying an approach? Perhaps not over a wide area but if a small one was under intense surveillance—such as the roadway—then it might just be able to detect the movement even if the subject was not distinct. And the enemy is expecting me.

He rested for a few minutes.

What made him think that that was the FTL ship anyway?

The image returned, this time definite. A pure white ovoid with harsh clear cut shadow breaking its surface, shadows cast by the curious flat discs raised in groups from its hull, bunched together rather like fungus growths but the same colour as the bulk of the ship, the same matt texture. Its size he could not guess. Its interior was a mystery. Its method of propulsion unknown.

If the opposition has that degree of technology I am finished! No, Tamura—or his ghost—seemed confident that I can match him or it or whatever.

Allaedyce emerged from his daze to find himself leaning against the trunk of one of the 'jungle' trees. The memory of the FTL ship still shimmered in his mind.

So it has to be through the forest? he thought. *Difficult. Well to begin you can try climbing over some of the creeper-branches.*

He gripped the warm dry surface of one and was just about to place his foot on a lower one when the one in his hand broke apart. It was made of a soft spongy material. He thrust into the wall of them. It disintegrated before him. Passage through the forest would be a great deal easier than it had first appeared.

The bark of the trees was faintly aromatic and as the branches came away against the pressure of his body the scent intensified. It was not unpleasant and afforded some relief from the cool oppressive dark of the jungle floor. Allaedyce noticed that the passage was leaving its marks upon his body as well as on the local flora. He was becoming completely covered in a very thin oily layer of yellow paste. Every time he broke one of the creepers there was a slight puff of what he thought was dust. *Obviously that was wrong. It must be a faint aromatic spraying of this substance which is also the likely source of the perfume smell.*

Plop.

He turned quickly to see one of the crane fly creatures crashing to the surface in the narrow channel which he had left in his wake. It gave out a faint characteristic tinkle and appeared to pass out. Allaedyce moved back cautiously to investigate and as he watched the brown skin of the thing wrinkled and blackened. He half expected it to burst into flames and so quickly retreated. Then to his astonishment the beast melted. The blackened flesh took on a moist glistening and slowly, thickly began forming a puddle on the forest floor.

"Keep moving, Allaedyce."

He turned about to see Tamura standing amongst the forest plants in the shadow off to his left. The Japanese was dressed in full samurai armour. Allaedyce gaped for a moment. Then recovered, enraged.

"What the hell have you to do with this?"

"Move on, Allaedyce," said Tamura, ignoring the outburst. "You must reach the river before noon. Let me explain. This is not like any forest which you might find upon Earth. The plant life here is symbiotic and is completely without the need of animal life to complete its natural cycle. Indeed the intrusion of animal life is a danger. Accordingly a defence has evolved in its development. The branches break off so readily because they are to release the viscous liquid which now covers your body. The sweet smell is the effect of evaporation which turns the liquid into a potent nerve poison, but only upon the creatures of this planet. It has no effect upon you. But the liquid itself also breaks down the dead bodies of its victims, reducing them to a protoplasmic goo which the plants can use to supplement their various diets. Unfortunately you are not quite immune to this. In about half an hour your skin will begin to itch; after an hour it will be quite painful; in two hours most of the outer layer of skin will have been destroyed and around this time your eyes will become inflamed; within five hours you will be dead. It would be an excellent idea to reach the river as soon as possible."

"How soon can I get there?"

"Within an hour and a half if you smarten your pace. Three hours or longer if you continue to dawdle." The figure grew dim and vanished.

Allaedyce began moving fast through the dank dark. Perhaps it was just the mere suggestion from what he had been told, but he felt sure that he was beginning to itch all over, especially around the scalp.

"Correct, Allaedyce," whispered the commander's disembodied voice. "I forgot to mention that by the time you reach the river you will be completely bald. Your hair is coming out already."

Allaedyce trotted as fast as the undergrowth would permit, and blamed everything on that arrogant turd Tamura!

The itch was really intense, and he had been travelling rapidly for better than an hour when he saw a clearing ahead. There were signs and sounds of considerable movement up front but he could not afford to stay around for any great length of time. He came to the edge and carefully peered through some of the breaks between a mass of low hung yellow plate-leaves. He gawked.

It looked like a cross between a harvesting party and a logging camp. The jungle was being hacked away and stacked into great heaps by dozens of small nimble creatures somewhat like black hairy beach balls running around on the customary straw thin legs. They were enclosed in large floppy transparent bags closely approximating to smaller versions of those used by the crane fly creatures for flight. Their legs protruded from the bags and were covered in a translucent white slime—protection against the jungle's deadly gas and liquid deterrent. A variety of small trumpet like growths protruded from each ball but only one stuck outside the protective envelope and again its exposed surface was covered in the milky paste as was the long prehensile tentacle which issued from it—an evolutionary adaptation of the crane fly tongue? This marvellous appendage was versatile enough to handle several tools at once along its length.

The woodcutters, if one could call them that, were quite near Allaedyce. They were equipped with blades similar to serrated bone saws and were rhythmically hacking the plants on to large carts with enormous solid wheels which were packed into regular sized bundles. Only one thing troubled Allaedyce about this awesome sight. How could they transport the materials away, being half a dozen kilometres from the road and with no way out of the clearing.

The answer to that problem came dramatically.

Without warning the whole pile of choppings shuddered and pulled itself together. Then it rose very slowly. Allaedyce gasped, unbelieving. The whole load floated higher majestically. He looked above and there almost invisible about five hundred metres up was a herd of crane fly like beings, not identical to the ones he encountered last evening, smaller and with apparently larger balloons. Could these be the domesticated ones? he thought.

He skirted the clearing and moved off faster than ever for the river. The sun was high by now and Allaedyce experienced a sensation akin to having an ants' nest broken up and scattered upon his body. He had to reach that river soon.

The itching fire was unbearable when he realised that the usual jungle floor of broken plate-leaves and hard bubbles was becoming decidedly soggy. Soon he was splashing knee deep through a pungent warm goo but still no sign of the vegetation thinning out. He staggered on for another half hour, periodically attempting to wash off the yellow paste which had by now become quite thick, dry and flaking in places. His own flesh was flaking off under it.

Abruptly the weak resistance of the undergrowth ceased and he plunged forward headlong into a slow moving flat expanse of dark green sludge.

The river.

The being was angry. It had lost track of that stupid human in the forest and it would be some time before the idiot realised that there was something amiss and grasped the fact that his skin was being eaten away. A flight must be despatched to capture him and have him brought to be . . . assimilated.

He spent almost half an hour scraping, rubbing and pouring water over his body, immersing himself frequently in the pleasantly warm liquid. It smelled sour and malty, like the mash for some outlandish ale. He tasted it and spat it out. It was like a mixture of ash, vinegar and lemon juice. He shuddered, suppressing a retching impulse.

Well, Allaedyce, he thought, there are fish of some description to be found in this stretch of what passes for running water in this part of the universe, and you are hungry. He waded cautiously in until he was waist deep and the sludge had thinned out considerably but was still nothing like translucent never mind transparent. He tried a few steps further forward but the bottom dropped away precariously so he retreated a little. Must find a fording point. He frowned. How could that be done? Walk along the edge of the deep part until there is a point where it vanishes? What if there is no fording point? Attempt swimming it?

Near the centre of the river there were a few cream and pink plants floating lily-fashion on the surface. Perhaps they might be edible?

Allaedyce decided to swim, striking out in the direction of the lilies. The going was very heavy for the first dozen or so strokes and then became almost normal. Dozens of small hard things continually brushed against his body so he stopped and trod water while grasping one. More damned hard bubbles. The water out here in the centre of the river was filled with them, sometimes bobbing about singly on the surface, sometimes joined together in great clumps and floating along like rafts either on the surface or just below it, and sometimes there would be just a single bubble often swollen to the size of a softball, really delicate in shade and with a small quantity of dark oily liquid in the bottom. The latter often brushed against Allaedyce and he would snap round to catch them, mistaking them for possible fish.

He neared the lilies, shook water from his face, and received a shock.

What he mistook for a lily was a round cupped fold of flesh with the ornate body of the animal resting on top. Were it not for the fact that he knew what other creatures upon this planet looked like he might have been deceived. But there, resting right at the centre was the round bristling black ball with a single flower like trumpet issuing from the top, appearing for all the world like a bizarre orchid. It was equipped with the usual straw thin legs but in this creature they were somewhat thinner and lay upon the surface radiating out from the body for about a metre, then dipping down into the submarine element.

One of the orchids began moving up and down agitatedly. There was a churning taking place below the water a few metres away from him. Then the orchid drew out from the river—a fish. Water cascaded down from its stick-leg and the thrashing golden captive, which was about as long as a man's forearm and covered in spikes streamlined backwards from a small white hard snout. From its rear there issued a tail of long delicate and transparent yellow streamers flapping desperately.

I am looking at lunch, thought Allaedyce.

The bushman launched himself over to the water orchid and in his approach touched one of its legs. Immediately half a dozen other legs snapped him into their grip. It was like being caught in a net of ever tightening steel wires. He cursed and beat against them to no avail. The creature seemed to realise from his movements that he was not a marine animal and responded accordingly by forcing him underwater.

Don't panic, he commanded himself. Keep calm. Relax. That's better. Take a comfortable lungful of air and go down. Good. Now all it wants to do is kill you, right? Not a promising beginning, admittedly, but one can do something with it. Employ a little of the possum school of philosophy. He thrashed violently a few times and then lay still, counting up to thirty. If there was still no relaxation of the bonds, he would employ more desperate measures. Thirty came and went as did forty and fifty and still no change except that his lungs were now decidedly painful. Much more of this and the colours would be dancing before his eyes.

Moving slowly but deliberately he pushed his arms free to either side and stretched them above so that they came out of the river on either side of the orchid. Gently he felt along the surface until they came to the trumpet. The tongue was out, grasping the fish. Quickly clenching one hand around the horn he grasped the tongue and pulled for all he was worth. Pull. Pull.

Yes, the creature of Altair II did turn out to have a passing acquaintance with that phenomenon well-known amongst terran animals—pain.

In a tumultuous heaving of beast, human and water, Allaedyce was suddenly free. A deft snatch and the prickly fish was his. He swam furiously for the far side.

Dinner was devoured raw.

Allaedyce just could not find a way of making fire, so he sat down amongst the shallow sludge about two hundred metres in from the edge of the river and peeled the fish's spines off, keeping one of them to strip it open and gut it. Sickening business, but no less so than the sight of the other water orchids devouring their wounded campanion out there in the river while he was wading for the shelter of the jungle.

This time he realised that he was going to have to take the road as by the time he had penetrated clear to the other side of the forest he would again be covered in that poisonous gum but with no river to clean it away. So he would have to follow the road after all, or at least until he was completely clear of this deadly vegetation.

The journey downstream was uneventful apart from sighting a few more water orchids and a couple of crane fly creatures. He reached the road about an hour and a half after noon and gave himself a good wash and scrub down before climbing the embankment and resting upon it for a short while.

If there was an FTL ship up there in stationary orbit watching out for any movement along the road then perhaps it would be wise to move when there was a little cloud cover. He shielded his eyes with his hand and peered about. Not much chance of an overcast ceiling. There was a little very high cirrus here and there but that would be about as much use as a veil on a belly dancer. Anyway suppose the FTL ship was equipped with really sensitive infrared sensors? In that case he would be sighted, cloud cover or no.

The road consisted of enamelled pale grey bricks, about three metres wide and raised up about half that from the floor of the jungle. It was every bit as dim and shadowy as was the route Allaedyce had taken to the river owing to the heights the plate leaf masses reached, but at least he could see ahead quite some distance and would not be breaking any of the creeper branches.

Then suddenly it struck him what an idiot he was. He had been able to glimpse the beginnings of the road from the hilltop yesterday and could follow its path from the impression it left in the yellow green roof of the forest. No one in an FTL ship would have seen me through that covering! he thought. You numbskull! All that plodding through undergrowth for no purpose! Dummy!

"Not so."

He recognised the voice and did not bother to look up. He knew that he would see the armoured figure standing at the roadside.

"You again, Tamura."

"The enemy has lost any track it had of you and is now concentrating on the first section of roadway up to the bridge over the Styx."

"Nice name for a river."

"You can move safely along the section ahead of you. I will tell you when to keep off it if that is necessary."

"Listen Tamura, just how the hell do you appear and vanish whenever . . ." He turned but the road was empty, the Japanese gone.

Pursing his lips Allaedyce stepped up on to the cool smooth roadway and set off at a trot. Whoever manages this stretch of track makes a meticulous job of it, he thought. There is not the merest speck of dirt upon it, not a fallen fragment of plate leaf, not the minutest hard bubble. Barefoot progress through the jungle was mildly uncomfortable and this is comparative heaven, albeit a suspicious one.

The road began a gradual curve to his left and inclined slightly upward after another hour on the trot. He must surely be nearing the end of it by now.

"You must hurry, Allaedyce. The enemy will shortly instruct the FTL craft to switch its surveillance to the secondary approaches and you will be espied immediately," whispered the voice of Tamura.

"No more giving orders, Commander!" The last word was spat out. "I've a feeling you don't intend me to be here on this world for any longer than suits your purpose."

The end of the forest was in sight anyway. Breath came raw in his lungs. His muscles complained. His feet were smarting. For the past kilometre he had been running uphill. Now the ground levelled off and he saw it dropping gradually away and the road turned slightly to the right, and the plate leafed trees were thinning out.

"Run!" It was Tamura. "We can detect his tension rising. He is coming to the conclusion that somehow you have penetrated the outer defence unseen. He is wrestling with himself. He wants to change the search more and more to the inner approaches but he is afraid that in so doing he may miss you moving down the outer one. You must be swift. He will not be in any doubt a great deal longer. His mind is beginning to change. He is asking for a report on all movement down the other approaches now. He will scrutinise every report meticulously. You have but seconds left."

Allaedyce sprinted, the downhill slope helping considerably. Arms and legs pumping, feet slapping off the brick paving, he was less than a dozen metres away from the complete end of the woodland.

"He has made his mind up. He is switching surveillance *now*," said Tamura.

Eight metres left and he jumped twisting in the air to avoid one of the delicate deadly weavings of branch stem and came crashing down amongst a mass of hard bubbles. He sank quite deep into this jungle 'floor' and was in fact completely covered by the curious little spheres. How deep the carpet of bubbles was he could not guess but it appeared to go further down than the reach of a man's arms.

Well, there was a clear way through the vegetation to what looked like cultivated land beyond. As this side of the barrier was not required to act as a defence for the enemy's city it had been allowed to disperse naturally. There should be no trouble crawling out safely if I move carefully, he reasoned.

"Too late," said Tamura.

"Too late? What do you mean too late? I thought you said his FTL ship was only scanning the road? I'm pretty well clear *and* I was completely buried when I landed!" Allaedyce shouted, the voice slightly squeaky from breathing the dense alien atmosphere—much richer in oxygen than Earth's.

"Too late in jumping, Allaedyce. The sensors were on the roadway and scanning a full twentieth of a second before you were completely clear of it."

"A full twen . . . Are you joking? Some polished backside of a ship about thirty-five or forty thousand kilometres out there is picking me up for one twentieth of a second over this whole stretch of road? Have you gone rusty between the ears, Tamura?"

"It is the truth," boomed the voice.

"Right! Okay. What about a little advice from my guardian angel then?"

He stood up, a scatter of hard bubbles bouncing from his body.

"The enemy is not yet nearly prepared to treat with you so this is not such an ill-timed affair," mused Tamura.

"So, great, let the bastard know I'm here and he can really prepare. He can wipe me off the face of the planet!"

"Hardly, the enemy wants you in his, how might it be put—he would like you as a member of his, er, his court," said Tamura.

"Sounds charming."

"To put it another way, he would care to have you as part of his repertoire."

"This lovely language is getting us nowhere at light speed. What are you talking about?"

"You would become part of him, but not part of his mind. You would be like a dream character who would be stored within his titanic mind. You would watch powerless, unable to interfere as he transfigured his bodily form into that of any number of beings for his own amusement and to fulfil his own purposes which grow out of a massive inferiority complex and father hatred. That is why he is so keen to take possession of you. His father was a human being. With you in his possession he would be able to become a human being at will and release his pent-up, insane hatred upon your body and your conscousness."

"Sounds charming."

"There are a number of alternative realities branching off from this situation. Every one of them is as real as the others and in your terms every one of them happens. What we are trying to do is to alter the dominating influence amongst these possibilities, these inevitable realities, in our favour. We wish the reality interpretation of the Crow which dominates to be ourselves—this one mind. You are the one prize and the one piece, a self-determining piece, in a game which goes beyond our reckoning as well as beyond our own," said Tamura.

"Frankly, I don't like the sound of it, and I don't pretend to understand it."

"Move out into the field. His minions are approaching. He has made his first mistake, as that one twentieth of a second was ours."

"What kind of clown do you take me for, Jap?" Allaedyce barked and started trying to bury himself in the hard bubble 'soil'. "You think I'm going to make it easy for that nutty smartcake to give me the bad news? No thank you, I'll stick to my own methods of evasion if you don't mind."

"You will not elude the Crow's servants, Allaedyce. In any event this is to our advantage," Tamura said.

"Maybe, but it sure as hell isn't to mine!" He continued digging amongst the hard bubbles burying himself deeper with remarkable vigour. "Now look, I take it that you lot are responsible for me being here, so how about a little favour? Create an illusion of me standing out there in the fields. Go on. For old times' sake, eh?"

No reply.

He was there in the mass of hard bubbles looking up for any sign of movement in the multi-coloured light filtering through them. Every movement of his body caused a disturbance amongst them— his breathing, even when he held his breath the beating of his heart.

But this is only slight, surely the blind creatures would not notice. Seems reasonable . . . No?

Wham.

He went coursing through the mobile 'soil' like a great raft upon the sea, a great bow wave forming about the side of his body which was breaching the granular surface. He was hoisted unceremoniously out by a painfully hard, almost metallic grip on his left ankle.

Ground level receded rapidly.

Whatever had plucked him from his sham grave was definitely not acquainted with the standard removal procedures of the Civil Forces' Conduct Code, but then the Citizens' Corps was some sixteen light years distant, if it existed at all.

"All right, you psychic pigs, you put me here now take me out!" he screamed, liberally salting his words with obscenities.

He tried kicking at what held him. The result was unpleasant. First he realised that an unshod foot is not wisely used for such abuse, the resulting pain being excruciating. Secondly the grip momentarily loosened and the possibility of freedom immediately posed the problem of the fifteen hundred metre unassisted descent to ground level.

Thereafter he was content to dangle undignified and heap verbal damnation on all creation.

Below him lay more woodland, but of a different type from the jungle through which he had passed, and numerous cultivated fields which seemed to sparkle as if dusted with festive glitter. He was too preoccupied to realise that the native intelligence had discovered how to crush the hard bubble topsoil to form the fertile coarse dust which it became several metres deep. He did not realise that they wanted the vegetation from the jungle to mix with this to form a rich compost which lay heavy on the surface holding the finer dust in place and adding its own substance to what was grown.

Eventually he did manage to piece together what was above him. It seemed to be a couple of the domesticated craneflies, this time without protective envelopes. They appeared bound together with each other's tongue whips, both of which were gripping the long telescopic pincer which held fast to his ankle, and far above them could be seen, as expected, a number of balloon bags.

Below, the Great Wall of China, which he had seen from the far hilltop, passed slowly.

By now Allaedyce was calmer, more numb than anything else. He felt a kind of inner chill growing as the minutes passed. He hoped fervently that his hypothalamus knew better than to initiate the usual physical response to chronic fear as the voiding of one's intestinal canals would be most inconvenient while one was suspended in this position.

Consequently he took his mind off the immediate future. The Great Wall would indeed have proved a rather difficult barrier to bypass. It appeared to be about thirty or so metres in height and built of the same pale brick as the road. He was puzzled. Why build a wall at all when the dominant lifeform on the planet appears to be capable of aerial transport? Had it something to do with controlled access to the city? His eyes searched for the road and when they found it he received a slight shock. There was no gate. The road ended about half a kilometre from the wall, opening into a vast desert area, a band of exposed grey blue rock running the length of the Wall. Oh yes, that *would* have been a nice surprise—trotting along that damned road for hour after hour only to find that there was no entry to the city there at the end of it.

The barren slopes of the mountain were approaching.

They were old and worn, igneous, the remains of some truly immense ancient volcano. Thin grey tatters of cloud below him hugged to the steep blue black face. The temperature was dropping appreciably.

Then came a sudden very rapid ascent as the mountainside approached literally to within a stone's throw. How was he supposed to climb this lot? Obviously he was not. It was intended that the enemy would capture him!

A freezing cold bank of cloud swirled about him and he started muttering the same tired old curses again.

"Correct, Allaedyce, but it had to be played correctly. It had to be timed in such a way that he would snatch you out of panic before he was ready to deal with you," whispered Tamura's voice.

"What I'd like to know is where the hell you're hiding, Tamura. You, the great samurai, shit scared, eh?" The bushman spat.

"I'm going to be with you all the way in this, my friend."

"Safely tucked away in orbit, or wherever you are reclining at present. Well clear of here to be sure." He began to shiver violently as the temperature dropped still further. Soon his teeth were chattering and he was feeling extremely giddy.

"Don't pass out, Allaedyce. That would make his work too easy."

"It . . . it would mmmake a ch-change from hav-ving t-to put up with this b-bloody cold, c-consciously."

"It would. The enemy would take great pains to make sure that you wakened in hell."

The icy mist vanished abruptly and the dazzling white of the baroque cloudspace dropped away below. Allaedyce looked around and gasped. A vast battlement of ragged pinnacles stretched away in a curving wall above his brilliant cloud floor, a wall whose proportions could readily have enclosed the ruins of greater New York in the days when he left Earth behind. To the other side he saw the cloud breaking up some kilometres distant and beyond that the river curling sinuous through the forests. The view of the far side of the valley was perplexing. The hills were certainly in plain view but their rippling silhouette along the horizon was surprisingly regular and delicately corrugated. The corrugations could be the ridges, he guessed. Another thought struck him. The foam sculpture trees were visible only on those hills. He had seen a variety of other lifeforms on Altair II and they all seemed to have some tenuous common link, but those trees were singular. In fact, the only place where he had that matted flooring under his feet was there. No, they couldn't be artificial . . . could they?

He approached the ragged peaks now, apparently heading for a gap between them, and frowned at something quite extraordinary. There was a fissure in the rock wall from which protruded a section of pipe with a faint wisp of steam wreathing around its lip. Then he saw the waterfall. Well, first of all he saw the water descend in a long thin spate and scatter into spray just before it hit the cloud cover. It issued from the crotch of the fissure which widened to form the outlet for the pipe lower down and to form the gap for which his captors were heading above.

The size comparison between the pinnacles and skyscrapers struck him when he saw the thousands of regularly spaced oval holes in them. Within these were definite but indistinct signs of movement. He shook his head to stop from falling into a dream, a nightmare. These were like brobdignagian beehives. As he sailed through the cleft a balloon bag unfurled from one 'cave' a couple of hundred metres below and out swung a crane flier; then another, and another and another—all blooming from the same cave. Last of all, dangling from below them appeared the small black ball of a domesticated one. It was following. The rearguard, no doubt.

For some strange illogical reason he did not feel fear—probably emotional paralysis.

He looked now at where he was heading. The reasons for his chilliness became very apparent.

He was passing over a glacier which had gouged its way out of a further but gentler slope of what appeared to be younger lava. This lay covered with snowdrifts in part and, paradoxically, wide craters containing unfrozen water, still and pale green in smooth profound lakes.

The descent began.

The destination was ahead, a long low building constructed of the same pale bricks as the road and the wall. It was sited at the crest of this inner lava slope sitting directly above a sheer drop to the curving glacier below. There appeared no possible method of reaching it other than by air. Amazing, he thought, that those roads and the Great Wall must actually have been built to stop *me*. Allaedyce smiled at the idea. But what could they have done which the virtually impossible mountainside could not? Surely it was the real deterrent?

The front court of the villa-like structure loomed up and very gently he was deposited in the centre of it. Good grief, the brick paving was warm!

Naturally.

The voice seemed at once physically distinct in the material world and simultaneously telepathic reaching directly into Allaedyce's mind.

He looked around. There was no sign of anyone. Only the building was there, three sections forming a U shape with the open side of the square looking towards the pinnacles past which he had just journeyed. The clusters of balloons and attendant black specks were high and distant now, heading back in the direction from which they had come.

They heard you, Allaedyce. They cannot see but they just could not miss the racket of all those hardbubbles rattling together as you breathed and your body vibrated to your pulse. It would have been much smarter to have stood out in the field. Standing on the loam you would have been very difficult for them to hear. Of course eventually they would have traced you by your body heat and the end result would have been just the same.

"Oh, of course," the bushman grunted, levering himself up on to one elbow.

So, you are to be the object of my correction, Allaedyce? You are the one who is to redirect my evolution. Amusing. I rather hoped for a more worthy opponent.

"Where are you? I can't see you."

Come into the keep.

"Just a few moments rest. Ooh boy, that was one hellish flight."

Come into the keep.

"You don't intimidate me you know. I . . . I have friends. Friends who are *really* powerful."

He felt the ground tremble. Another tremor and then it was still.

So, you have powerful friends. How interesting. Let me give you some evidence of my power.

The daylight flickered and dimmed and he felt panic surge adrenalin through his body. He looked at the late afternoon sun and was stunned. A great shimmering veil sparkling with rainbow tints lay right along the western horizon. As he watched he heard a very deep, very distant rumbling slowly growing louder. The veil was moving, lifting very gradually, almost like a cloud—and the horizon lifted with it! Up to block the light of the sun.

The strange hills where he first set foot upon this world were rising into the sky! Eventually they were completely clear of the ground below them—an entire range suspended almost a kilometre above the earth and stretching as far as the eye can see in both directions. It was moving. The first sign of this was an intensified flickering in the veil above it. He watched and saw a gentle drifting towards the south among the rippled hilltops. He gaped at it for at least half an hour in silence until its extremity came into view from the north, slowly, imperially, passing to allow the return of sunlight and was eventually lost to sight in its drifting towards the equator.

"What was . . ."

I call it a harpie; I call my floating servants minotaurs, all my minions have suitably classical appellations. The harpie's singular mass containing both animal and vegetable complexes within its constitution. The ridges you no doubt observed on its back fold out remarkably to form the structural framework for the thousands of balloon cells. It is under my domination. My principal interest in it is its psi potential. It acts as catalyst and bridge. When I came here it and the half dozen others of its kind acted as an intensifying and focusing device for my own psi power. With it I subjugated every thinking lifeform on this world. It connects me directly with my bodily form down here.

But most of all it has allowed me to devise a direct bridge to another part of the galaxy—a psionic distortion in the very spacetime topography itself. This allows me to have, without the slightest distress even to the most minor planetary functions here, one of the universe's great power sources. Mine to do with what I please. So you have powerful friends. How amusing, Allaedyce. Now, how did you come here?

Allaedyce shrugged. "I don't know."

Where are the others?

Allaedyce related as best he could remember the story of Yūkoku.

I choose to accept your tale, Allaedyce. Let me tell you why, on arrival in Altair space I too encountered extra terrestrials about the gas giant, the catchworld, beings brought there and subservient to a being which I did not encounter, a being which did not interfere with my domination of its captives and these native creatures of this world. Now you appear with your paradoxical rantings of how two Earth ships reached this system. As this must have happened after I arrived it can only be assumed that it must have occurred on another time track, one parallel and close to this one.

Allaedyce frowned bemused.

Do not trouble yourself with such concepts. They are beyond minds such as yours. What is indicated by your existence here is that the being manipulating circumstances here at Altair favours my development.

Could it be my own future self?

I begin to believe that it is.

A very cold penetrating wind picked up, lifting some snow powder and dispersing it across the courtyard which sublimated it instantly to steam.

"How do those flying things change direction?" Allaedyce asked haltingly.

A system of sails and jets.

"But—"

Do not try my patience! Enter the keep, Allaedyce! I have much to do and cannot waste forever chattering with a black imbecile like you! Enter!

Racial prejudice had been punishable by death under Condominium law. Ridiculous to think back to those times as the 'good old days'.

He stood and immediately sank to his knees, colours swam within the pale brick tiles before his eyes. Deep breaths, Allaedyce. He hauled air deep down into his lungs. That's better, he thought. Now try standing, easily; there's no rush; take your time. Remember the deep breaths. Then he was upright looking into the square doorless entry in the middle building. There was no glass to be seen in any of the two dozen or so small square windows. He shrugged and walked as steadily as possible for the entrance.

I assure you that you will find things here much to your liking. You will sleep in the chamber which my servants have prepared for you. Supper awaits you there.

The very mention of food almost made him dizzy again. His head had grown used to life the right way up but his stomach was still trying to readjust from the upside-down mode. He did not particularly want to enter the keep but if he stuck it out here he would certainly freeze to death shortly after nightfall, and Altair was now low and reddening in the sky. He stepped through the entry.

"Run straight forward," whispered the voice of Tamura.

With you I can return to Earth. Together we will make Earth a very . . . interesting world. Then there will be other worlds for us, innumerable worlds, Allaedyce, a galaxy full of them!

"Run, you idiot! He is closing on you, run!"

Something was approaching from the left side. Allaedyce could only just glimpse it dimly, a black wet thing.

He ran. There was a whish of something passing his head and flopping to the floor, another of those damned tongue whips. He did not even break stride. He had to move hard and fast into darkness.

Fool, there is no escape from me. Are you so stupid that you have not realised this? There is no point to your flight.

Allaedyce hit the unseen wall in front of him with the full force of his running body—and went through it, falling to the ground in a shower of bricks which were about as heavy as papier-mache, the mortar between them still not set.

Of course, he thought, it had too little time to prepare. The building was constructed not for him but for me. The whole appearance of it was something only partially completed.

"Run run run! Get clear of the bricks. They are psi sensitive, and his mind can hurl them at you. Now, move!" said Tamura.

So he sprinted ahead into a landscape of ice canyons under a darkening sky.

Allaedyce, Allaedyce, really. I should have imagined even you would have more intelligence than to think that it would be so simple to elude me.

The bushman ducked on impulse and skidded across a slimy surface of slush and water atop a bed of packed snow. There were a multitude of clickings above. The sky was packed with the enemy's damned slaves carrying grappling devices. The nearest of them was only a dozen or so metres above—a pair like the two who took Allaedyce at the edge of the jungle. Instinctively he leaped to his feet caught the grapple and swung on it. For a split second he was about to drop and then felt the upward pulling response. Immediately he released the arm and dropped back while the creatures rocketed dramatically upwards. He sprinted for the comparative safety of the ice canyons repeating this exercise with the pursuing balloon creatures a few times.

He dived below an overhang and was out of their grasp. From the ruin of the keep something began emerging. Then he saw his enemy clearly for the first time. It was like the others but for its massive bulk and the fact that instead of being covered in bristles it was covered in a what looked like a black plastic fabric which might be another development of the omnipresent balloon bag. There were two flame red snouts from which issued leathery fronds all linked to a core similar to the whip tongue. It staggered on pitifully small legs and was hoisted immediately by a flock of the domesticated crane fliers.

They cannot see you but I can. This is the one creature left on this planet with sight. You may be interested in the history.

Allaedyce was never less interested in anything in his life. He began scurrying down the slippery-bottomed canyon. My God, he thought, but it's freezing. I can't keep this up. I'll be finished in less than half an hour.

"More than enough time. Keep moving!" said Tamura.

Several millions of years ago a genus of predatory flora emerged on this world. Its mode of attack was to issue a hallucinogenic vapour which interestingly enough only attacked the centres of vision.

Allaedyce was rapidly running out of the canyon. A seam of black rock had replaced the ice overhang above, and underfoot he was almost knee deep in a blood-freezing slush.

The effect was to make themselves alluring to all fauna. Only those of poor sight survived.

His feet began scraping against numerous loose stones and rock flakes. He bent down, scooped a handful and, stepping into the open, let one of the aerial beauties plummet from the near black sky. He let fly three flakes in rapid succession, every one making target. The reaction was quite unexpected. The two beasts abruptly threw themselves off in opposite directions, rolled tight and crashed to the ground a couple of hundred metres away to either side of him. The freed balloons soared off into the night sky. Allaedyce scooped up another couple of handfuls and started running.

Ultimately blindness became a survival factor amongst animal life with the exception of this species. Why it survived I can only guess. Personally I would say that it simply had no sense of Aesthetic—wouldn't you?

Suddenly the hideous thing was bobbing before him. He shrieked, slipped on the ice, and the tongue had him.

"Bastard!" he shrieked.

Its booming exultant laughter smashed painfully through his memory and an image appeared—a woman, a black-haired, white-faced princess who spat mockery and liquid acid. Allaedyce howled and launched a packed handful of the rock chips into the rippling moist black of the ebony glass buttons which it called eyes. The beast convulsed as the spinning splinters tore into its hide.

He was free and running across the rock.

No! You will not go there!

And immediately Allaedyce was rigid. The power of the enemy's will was literally crippling.

"Relax your body," came Tamura's whisper. "I'm taking over. I'm coming out now."

The wills wrestled with his mind.

You are mine, Allaedyce. You will not sleep that I may take you.

"You must relax, Allaedyce, but keep conscious!"

Sleep.

He pitched forward, face down on the ice.

"Stay awake, listen to me!"

Gasping he opened his eyes. Where the black thing was a moment past stood a large mushroom shaped creature with a very thick trunk of olive and a cap of tan. It was about the height of a human. In a series of curious flexings it began hopping towards him, long prehensile tentacles appearing from under the cap's rim.

I will have you! I will!

The thing was beside him and the stench was revolting, like a stale lake of dead fish. Allaedyce recoiled. Suddenly he had motion, a growing will. On your feet. Up. Run.

There was a redness flickering against the sky above, against the underside of the storm clouds.

Stop.

Again he went rigid.

"Run." This time the voice came out of his own mouth.

He could hear the foul thing flopping towards him . . . pit . . . pat . . . pit . . .

Sleep.

Exhaustion swelled through his limbs. Oh, to sleep, to rest, to escape . . .

Sleep.

"No," he croaked.

Sleep in me, Allaedyce. Sleep in my dark haven.

He could feel oblivion mounting like a great wave, growing more massive, stronger, higher, teetering, about to break—

"Move, Allaedyce. I am right here. I am with you and you will obey me. I have broken you before and I will again! Move!" The voice from his own lips was the voice of Tamura but he did not notice. He was racing away from the thing. Suddenly the night was freezing cold again and he was in agony. The air in his lungs was like raw, iced spirit, but his body would not stop running.

Stop.

And still he moved, gasping, sobbing. He began to realise that his body was not his own to control. Through a narrow valley, misty and rough underfoot, and he was moving downhill. It was warmer. Red flashes burst off to the left. Still some vulcanism left in the old bitch yet.

You will halt. Halt or I shall destroy you.

He did not even waver. His body, his whole identity, felt frothing, effervescent, changing. My God, he thought, yes—changing!

"Run, Allaedyce, put your own will into it. We need your help too," he found himself shouting.

Faster forward, faster.

He staggered, blundered and fell, could not see straight but moved desperately, always forward.

Stop! I command you! This is my will!

"I am with you now, Allaedyce. I am in your every step, in your racking breath, in your smarting eyes, in your tumblings, in your very sweating flesh. I am in you, Allaedyce. Now I am you."

Everything was in complete night—darkness thick and sulphurous. The bushman smashed his leg against a boulder and fell screaming, the bone shattered.

Now, now I have you.

The laughter was crushing, obliterating even the pain from the leg. Then it faded and he heard the approach.

Pit . . . pat . . . pit . . . pat . . .

The whole thing was a joke. He cursed, silent. Here I am, lying on a heap of hot volcanic stones—a pure bred bushman, dirty, covered in blood from a hundred grazes and cuts. All this plus a broken leg and somehow or other I was to defy that—whatever it is. He tried rolling on to his back but the eruption of pure agony from the leg hammered into his brain and he let out another hoarse scream.

I am at hand, Allaedyce. Soon all pain will seem like a relief to your suffering. I am at hand. Let all mankind know it and bewail the coming of the Crow.

Curiously he could feel something pulling at him, not any part of him but his whole body, almost as if the slope upon which he lay was steeper than it actually was.

"His source of power. Our work is almost completed," said the Tamura voice.

Pit . . . pat . . . pit . . .

Slap!

It landed upon Allaedyce's back, sending him further down the slope. The pain from the leg erupted again only to be cut off.

Mine! Mine at last!

Everything began to drain into emptiness. Allaedyce was fading, dying, changing.

They didn't tell you about us. They didn't tell you about simple evolution. Did they?

He was falling, slipping, sliding further and faster down this curving slope, but the being was too obsessed with its own glee to appreciate this for the moment.

Primitive evolution is devoid of will. It is a wasteful process of fission: breaking up in order to create the new. Not so with us. In our phase it is fusion. Fusion by will! Minds meld together to form ever more powerful complexes! The new is created by the infusion of new minds! And I shall now dominate them all! As I do you!

"Your last move, I believe?" laughed the Tamura voice.

Who is that? What is that mindvoice?

Like a mad dream Allaedyce had a vision of Tamura in full armour, immense, towering above the mountains, and pulling the bushman with his captor inexorably down the slope.

"Too late, my child. You are moving down the slope and the mind you are dealing with is not just Allaedyce's. It is *our* mind."

They moved, bumped, clattered, slewed down this bending pitface. Allaedyce was calm, which he thought peculiar. The thing was wailing, wailing like a child, as Tamura had called it.

Noooooo . . . Noooooo . . .

Allaedyce felt a curious rippling sensation tear through him, but no pain. The thing that was the toadstool beast began changing form time and time again. In vain. There was no escape. The macrobrain and all its parts were trapped in the one psionic net which had been its strength.

Briefly Allaedyce imagined the walls of a narrowing crystalline well, all black with a twist of madness at the bottom. Tidal ripplings pounded the bodies apart.

The macrobrain had lost the psi control which bridged the gap between Altair II and the collapsar in Cygnus, its power source, the twist of madness.

It and Allaedyce and Tamura and the entourage of trapped alien minds fall all blending through the twist, which is the heart of every subatomic particle, every probability curve wrinkled out to form the fabric of spacetime, the twist which reaches every where when in every possibility, the twist which is the strength and the carrier of the Crow . . .

They fall as one through the growing light into the flames, the inferno of the bridge. They stand there black against the raging light as the poor mad bushman leaps at them, to them, into them, into the Crow . . .

It falls through the cathedral of minds turning, appraising, accepting, rejoicing. The cycle is restarted, and once again out through the silent valley of stars is born one of the least of creations, the Crow . . .

CODA

Rüllkotter was angry with his assistant.

He was often displeased with the quality of the staff which the Condominium allotted him, but this one was an insult. He babbled incessantly about inconsequentials and gave unsolicited bizarre speculations on the most boring subjects when his mental activities should have been involved with the problems of developing a macrobrain.

The rest of the two thousand staff at the Cydonia Research Complex were totally involved with it so why should this whippersnapper be allowed to waste cerebral time which the Condominium was paying for? He knew that they needed a macrobrain computer intelligence for the projected FTL backup mission to Altair, and it was needed soon.

"By the way I'm having some success with culture TL-59," said the younger man. "It looks really promising."

"Good," snapped Rüllkotter, cutting off any likely trivia liable to follow by purring out of the library on his tracks, leaving the assistant lost in his day dreams. Life in a modified bole body did have its advantages. You could move so quietly people often didn't hear you leave or arrive. He moved down to the lab where the assistant had left the culture.

There was nothing wrong with his own admittedly ancient central nervous system even cooped up in this tin can. How come so many others went off the rails so early with much healthier equipment?

He connected his opticals to the microscope and peered through at the assistant's culture. Excitement swelled immediately.

This was it!

He checked and rechecked, eventually spending two days in that lab without sleep.

This *was* it!

Here growing in the culture was a brain—a human brain, but by the time that he had finished playing with it the Condominium would have their first organic computer and it would be about the mass of an adult human's entire body.

Oh, the fun he was going to have in the years ahead!

It would be integrated with his beautiful ceramo-crystal MI for guidance and control of their great ugly white egg, the FTL ship destined for Altair. Good, it would take them years to complete their ship. By that time the organic artificial intelligence would be ready to act as total crew.

What kind of mind would it have?

What kind of personality?

He could not appreciate one little irony. He had beside him the cards of the donors of the parent cells which had been married to commence tissue development from the fertilised egg stage. Both had been given some years previously by the doomed members of the starship *Yūkoku*.

The names were: TAMURA, KUNIO and LAING, GINNY—the parents.

The macrobrain would be their only progeny and Rüllkotter would do his duty. Before his masterwork departed for Altair he would play it Tamura's last message—to his son.